TRE POUND

TRE POUND

By

Jordan Belcher

Felony Books, P.O. Box 1577, Belton, MO 64012

Felony Books, a division of Olive Group, LLC,

P.O. Box 1577, Belton, MO 64012

Copyright © 2014 by Jordan Belcher

Edited by: Brittany Windom

ISBN-13: 978-1-940560-05-2
Library of Congress Control Number: 2014903368

Felony Books 3rd edition March 2014

10 9 8 7 6 5 4 3 2 1

Manufactured in the United States of America

For information regarding special discounts for bulk purchases, please contact Felony Books at www.felonybooks.com.

DEDICATIONS

This book is dedicated to all those imprisoned individuals that have a plan when released.

Stick to it.

And to my uncle, Andrew "Buddy" Henson Jr. (RIP), and my comrades: Danny "D" Milton (RIP), and Kevin "Down Low" Sherrils (RIP).

Acknowledgments

First, I'd like to thank **God** for guiding me through the system safely. I seen so much, witnessed some things people on the streets will never see, and managed to stay distanced from a lot of it. It was like I was watching an eight-year-long movie. And a lot of it was pure comedy. I was truly watched over.

I thank my father, **Joseph Belcher**, who gave me and my brothers a good upbringing despite the hardships. I'm eternally grateful to my mother, **Karen Windom**, for persevering, stickin' wit' me, and encouraging my creativity. I still remember the books I used to write in elementary that you photocopied for me. Also, thanks to the rest of my family for being an important part of my life: Joey, Stephane, Kayla, Jason "90" Belcher, Kelsye Thomas, Jaylen the Don, Kendal, Ryan, Ronald Richmond, Adaina Saxton-Ross, Kamau, Rahsheda, Uncle Bruce and Aunt Faye, Omoni, Brittany Windom, Xav, Uncle Duane, Robin, KeKe, Yvette, Keila, Dre, Uncle Mark, Crystal, Uncle Rick, Auntie Neetha, Marquita, Uncle Louis, Uncle Donald, Rekeysha, Janise Lee-Wells, Rob, George, Elaine, Aaron, Ashley, Aunt Jean (RIP), and my grandmothers: Almeta Belcher (RIP) and Myrtle Windom (RIP).

Special thanks to my wife, **Colette**, for doing so much for me I don't know where to start. You have many titles in my life—best friend, publicist, CFO, loyalist, Scrabble champion, eye candy, backbone, soulmate. This book is dedicated to you, too.

Throughout my incarceration, I had a few positive influences and met a lot of brothas who kept it one hunit. So I gotta acknowledge: Amir "Ant Live" Abdullah, O.G. Fee (Abdul Grace), Antonio Washington (Shorty), Chris, Phil Washington, Darin "Boss Hogg" Lewis, Andre Fell, Dre McDonald, Dre Walker (Montino), JT, Yntell Duley, Kenderel "KD" Rogers, Avery, Montana, Sneed, Mike Flemons, Zaki "Casino" Wyle, Cannon, Willy Stewart (Cool), Roamy Black, Taylor-El, Washington-El, Woods-Bey (Burt), Ross-Bey, Anthony McElroy, Dejaun, Ant Nevels, Chevis Burch, Atiba, Askari, Meeche, Mutulu, Tim McElroy, Bryan Cooley (Breezy), Ronnie "Cali" Williams, Sipple, Tucker, Steele, A-Dub, Tyweed, K-Tone, Tez, Terrance "Menace" Johnson, German(G), Ced Newsome, Jihad, B-Nut, Joe Cole, Chuck Stinson, Blue (Howard), Goo, Art, Darryl Cowans, Icy Mike, Breedlove, Ahmad, Short Dogg, G-Loc, Munch, Chris Griswald, E-Locc, Terry Boone, Pace, Dolla, Mousy, Curt, DeMarcus Fowler, Domingo, Doc (Sidney Rolls), Reggie Townes, Jamal (C. Lockett), Darryl X, and Psycho.

To the people I'll always be able to call friends until I expire: Nicole Verge, Rita, Walter, Marlon (Skee), Janice (Mopie), Wayne Mason, Victoria (Binky), Vanessa, Tiffany, Bell, Archie, Oasis, Rahiem, Hasan, Autura, Taha, Jon-Jon, Pierre, Pearson (Jason), Brachelle, Joe Tezz, Quentin, Brian, AR-15 (Hood), Jereil Fikes, Brittany Fikes, Anne Houston, 4MUCH, Riv Locc, P da Thizz Kid, CHOP IT UP CLICC, Brodrick, Bluey, Bull, and Boy Genius.

Special shout-out to LB Graphicz for the logo and the upcoming projects!

And thanks ahead of time to all my readers!

Funk: 1.(noun) active hostility between two or more persons 2.(verb) to attempt to kill.

Funk Artist: (noun) one that has developed many enemies; a skilled murderer

CHAPTER 1

"Can you state your name for the record?"

She cleared her throat, then leaned forward into the microphone. "Dynisha Miller."

Pacing back and forth, District Attorney Paul Wheeler said, "You were one of the last people to see Derrick Weber alive. Tell me about your last encounter with him."

"I was at home braiding his hair about an hour before he was murdered."

"Were you and Mr. Derrick Weber the only two at your house that night?"

Dynisha inhaled deeply. "No. Drought Man's—I mean Derrick Weber's friend, Rowland, was there too. They always were together. Rowland was talking on his cell phone, waiting on me to finish Derrick's hair so they could go to the club."

The prosecutor was by the jury box when he mumbled, "But they never made it to the club." He turned back to the witness stand. "What happened while you were braiding Derrick's hair?"

"I got a phone call."

Wheeler stopped pacing. He peered at her. "Who called you?"

"Tre Pound," she said, pointing to the young brotha seated behind the defense table. "Him right there. Levour King."

Her answer sparked whispers from the spectators in the courtroom. When they quieted, the prosecutor walked over to Tre Pound and held a flat hand over his head.

"Is this Levour King?"

"Yes," she said confidently.

Tre Pound's dark chocolate face remained expressionless. The 21-year-old took his lawyer's advice and tried to show as little emotion as possible.

Another tip from his lawyer influenced his attire. Initially, Tre Pound had a line of Stacy Adams suits purchased. But when his lawyer warned him that flashy suits broadcast overconfidence, which jurors loathe, he settled for less. Today, he wore a plain, crisp white-collar shirt and tan slacks. A compromise was reached and he was able to keep his Stacy Adams loafers.

"Tell me, Ms. Miller: What was discussed during your phone conversation with the defendant?" Paul Wheeler was pacing again.

"I can't remember the whole conversation," said Dynisha, "but I know he asked who was all over there."

"And did you tell him?"

"Yes. And when I did, Derrick and Rowland started complaining, saying not to tell people they were over there." Dynisha used her forefinger to brush a strand of weave behind her ear. "They was cursing me out."

An approving nod came from the studious prosecutor. "And what was Levour's reaction when you told him that Derrick was present at your home?"

"At first he didn't say nothin'. Kinda like he was thinking. Then he said he'll call me back, and hung up." Dynisha caught eye contact with Tre Pound. She was trying to tell him something. It was as if she was trying to say, "I got you now, nigga!"

Tre Pound restrained himself by gritting his teeth.

"What type of a relationship did you and the defendant have?"

"It wasn't really a relationship. I just knew him from around the way. Him and my little brother were friends."

Keep it real, Tre Pound thought to himself. Dynisha used to give up the pussy for a blunt or two. Maybe thirty, forty dollars at the most. And he and her brother, Young Ray, were never friends. *Young Ray is a bum compared to me!* Tre Pound just associated with him out of pity, because he was fucking his big sister.

Everybody was.

He whispered his thoughts to his lawyer.

"So you know the defendant pretty well," Wheeler said to his witness. "Would you consider Levour King a boss, so to speak?"

13

Tre Pound knew where the prosecutor's questioning was going. Paul Wheeler was trying to establish him as a tyrant. Tre Pound's lawyer told him about the tricks this prosecutor would play.

"His family is well known," Dynisha said. "He's a King so he automatically gets respect in the streets. But he doesn't respect the game. He uses his name to do what he wanna do. Robbing and murdering."

"Has he ever stole from you?"

She paused, thinking. "Yes. He stole two of my DVDs."

The courtroom erupted in laughter. Judge Lyons banged his gavel. "Order in the court!" he bellowed, and the courtroom quieted.

"But he stole from my brother, too," she added, as if the laughs got under her skin. "He stole my brother's rims."

Wheeler had his hands behind his back. Concerned and serious, he replied, "So he's a thief. Did any of his actions show that he was capable of murder?"

She didn't hesitate to answer. "He always carried a gun. Flashing it around. One time he pulled it out and said he was gonna knock out my front grill with it."

The prosecutor walked over to the evidence table and retrieved a replica of the murder weapon—the actual one was never found.

"Ladies and gentlemen of the jury," he said, holding a real AK-47 high over his head, "this was the type of weapon used to brutally murder 29-year-old Derrick Weber. And this ..." He returned the weapon to the table, picked up a clear plastic bag that contained a .308 casing. "... this is a shell of one of seventeen bullets used to take his life. We couldn't find the murder weapon but there were shells everywhere. And this single shell you see here had the defendant's fingerprints on it."

Tre Pound groaned. He fucked up. His prints should have never been on that bullet.

Some jury members seemed impressed by the evidence, just what the D.A. expected. Paul had one more question for his witness.

"Ms. Miller, after the heinous murder of Derrick Weber, you saw Levour King a few days later. What did he say about the crime?"

"He said Derrick should've ducked." Her tone sounded as if she felt sorry for Drought Man. Then another flurry of whispers spread through the courtroom. So she raised her voice as she added, "I know he killed Drought Man! I heard he killed Rico 'nem, too!"

"Objection!" Tre Pound's defense lawyer shot up as the spectators roared with approval and disapproval at Dynisha's remark. The defense lawyer emphatically said, "The witness is testifying to hearsay!"

This time Judge Lyon's gavel had no effect. He banged, but the courtroom continued to holler. Tre Pound looked over his shoulder and saw the victim's family and friends pointing and cursing at him. Behind him, though, were his own supporters. His aunt, Janice King, was up and shouting at the self-assured witness. Even Camille, his

15

15-year-old cousin, was yelling. Her anger was directed towards the haters on the other side of the courtroom.

The judge was finally able to restore the court to order. "The courtroom will be cleared if there is another outburst!" He sustained the defense lawyer's objection and ordered Dynisha Miller's remark stricken from the record.

Paul Wheeler made his way to his seat. "I have no further questions at this time."

"Mr. Masaccio," Judge Lyons said to Tre Pound's defense lawyer, "would you like to cross-examine the witness?"

Criminal lawyer Carlo Masaccio stood. "Yes, Your Honor." He removed his suit jacket and placed it over the back of his chair. The jury watched him straighten out his vest and proceed to the witness stand. Jurors tended to be sympathetic towards female witnesses and didn't like to see them verbally attacked by lawyers. Therefore, he spoke in a soft voice. "Good morning, Ms. Miller."

"Good morning," she replied.

In an absorbing, well-spoken manner, Carlo Masaccio began his cross-examination with minor inquiries. He asked about her family and occupation, discovered that she was single, unemployed, and living alone with two small children.

Every drug dealer, every robber, and every funk artist in Kansas City, Missouri, knew that Carlo Masaccio was the lawyer to have—especially in murder cases. He had a thorough work ethic and a high success rate. His fees were high, too. Clients were paying not only for his services, but also for his reputation. The high-powered criminal lawyer. Tre Pound believed every last dollar was well spent.

The defense lawyer's questioning deepened. "Ms. Miller, how do you make money to support yourself and your children?"

"I braid hair."

"It seems like you'd have to do a lot of braiding to support a household," he said skeptically.

"I do what I can. I do women's hair, too."

Carlo Masaccio switched topics to keep her unbalanced. "Would you say that you and my client are good friends?"

"No. We just know each other."

"Have you ever braided my client's hair?"

A few chuckles came from some of the spectators and a couple members of the jury. Tre Pound's hair was low-cut, even all around. Dynisha smiled herself. "His hair ain't nearly long enough to braid."

"Yes or no please."

"No."

"So if you and my client are not good friends and you don't braid his hair, then why did he call you on the night Derrick Weber was murdered?"

Up until now, Dynisha's answers had been clear. "Uh ..."

He didn't give her a chance to finish. "Ms. Miller, have you and my client ever been intimate?"

She was hesitant.

"Answer the question, Ms. Miller," said the judge.

17

Finally, she answered, "Maybe once or twice."

The defense lawyer moved closer to her. She didn't like that at all. "And during those times," he said, "did you ever receive payment?"

"What do you mean by 'payment'?"

"Has he ever gave you money in exchange for sex?"

Dynisha fidgeted in her seat. "He might've gave me a couple dollars for rent. But that's it. That ain't a crime."

Carlo Masaccio looked puzzled. "Yes it is, Ms. Miller. It's called prostitution."

Spectators giggled. "I didn't mean it like that," she blurted out, glancing at the jury's displeased reactions. Then she shrugged. "Well, whatever."

Wheeler dropped his pen on the paperwork in front of him. He massaged his forehead. There goes his witness's credibility.

With further questioning, Carlo Masaccio revealed to the jury that Dynisha Miller solicited sex to not just his client, but to the victim, Derrick Weber aka Drought Man, his friend, Rowland Reed, and numerous others. He made the witness cluttered and upset, ruining the nice-girl image she walked in the courtroom with. The jury frowned at her snotty remarks.

Throughout the trial, employees of the Salvation Army testified that Tre Pound was completing his community service during the time of the murder. He had to do community service because of a hit-and-run, which happened because he was trying to evade someone that was shooting at him. The Salvation Army was a solid alibi. But there was still the undeniable evidence that the prosecution's case was built on: his fingerprints were found on a bullet casing.

During a recess, Carlo Masaccio received an offer from the prosecution. He relayed the message to his client.

"They're offering seven years if you plead guilty to involuntary manslaughter. With the mandatory prison sentence, you'll be out in no more than four years." Tre Pound was slow to answer so he pressed on. "It's the best offer we're going to get. The trial could go either way at this point."

Spending a few years in prison for murder would be a lovely deal for the average criminal, but not for Tre Pound. He had accumulated so much funk in the city that if he was sentenced to any prison time he was bound to run into old enemies, or his enemies' homies and family members. There was no guarantee that he'd make it out alive.

So Tre Pound told his lawyer, "Fuck that plea. If I wanted to cop-out I would've stuck witta public defender. I paid you to beat my case."

Carlo Masaccio inhaled. "Okay, Mr. King," he said, releasing. "I'll do my best to exonerate you, keep you out of prison."

The proceedings resumed with the district attorney going into detail about the crime. He explained that after Derrick and Rowland left Dynisha's house, they stopped at the car wash. Row stayed in the car while Derrick washed it. Minutes later, after the car was soapy and wet, a man ran up and machine-gunned Derrick to death, fifteen times in the chest, twice in the head. The man then fled the scene in a black sedan, according to eyewitnesses.

"That man was Levour 'Tre Pound' King!" exclaimed Wheeler.

He then went on to show the jury gruesome photographs of the victim. Some of the jurors gasped. In one photo, the only visible image was Drought Man's head. Spilled brain matter covered one of his eyes. The other was wide open. Another photo showed him from a distance, laying dead in a car wash stall next to his Lincoln Navigator, the water nozzle still in his hand.

"Derrick Weber was murdered in cold blood!"

The prosecutor was satisfied with the case he presented thus far. It was time to implement his coup. He called his next witness—his star witness—Rowland Reed.

The bailiff escorted a bald-headed clean-shaven brotha into the courtroom. He was wearing an orange jumpsuit and a fierce look. His hands and feet were shackled. He had to take baby steps to reach the witness stand.

Row had been incarcerated since the night of Drought Man's murder two years ago. He was so devastated that fateful night that he stayed with the body of his dear friend, didn't leave the scene. The police showed up and found Row in possession of marijuana, violating his parole. The district attorney offered to put in a good word at his upcoming parole hearing if he agreed to testify against Tre Pound.

"Good morning, Mr. Reed," said Wheeler.

Row didn't return the greeting.

The prosecutor continued anyway. "You were inside the Lincoln Navigator when your friend Derrick Weber was murdered. Did you get a good look at the gunman?"

No response. Row was mugging Tre Pound. His eyes never strayed.

Tre Pound knew what Row was thinking. Row wanted revenge for the death of Drought Man. He wanted to strangle Tre Pound with his shackles.

"Answer the question, Mr. Reed," the judge ordered.

Still no response.

"Maybe I worded the question wrong," Wheeler said, straightening his necktie. "On the night your friend Derrick Weber was murdered, did you see who did the killing? I know the car was soapy. But you crawled out the backseat. Did you see the defendant?"

Row remained silent.

Judge Lyons leaned near the witness stand. "Mr. Reed, if you don't answer the question you'll be held in contempt of court. I'll personally make sure it's a felony charge. So answer the question."

Row tilted his head side-to-side, stretching his neck as if he was bored.

Sweat appeared on Paul Wheeler's forehead. His star witness wasn't cooperating!

Carlo Masaccio was elated. A small smile surfaced. "I'm not one to put all my eggs in one basket," he whispered to

Tre Pound, "but this is definitely in our favor. The jury is on our side. Count on a verdict of not guilty."

But the streets had already convicted him.

CHAPTER 2

The back of the Cinemark theatre had an absence of light, the front lit only by the enormous projection screen. Previews of upcoming movies were being shown as people found their seats.

Holding hands, a married couple shuffled through the third aisle, trying to get to the open seats. Lil' Pat and Camille King moved their legs to the side so the couple could pass.

"You sure you don't want any popcorn?" Lil' Pat asked Camille.

"I'm tryna keep my appetite," she said. "We're still going to get something to eat after this, right?"

"Yeah, but I thought you might want a little snack."

Camille smiled. "You're so sweet, Lil' Pat. But I'm fine, thank you."

To her left, an older man sat comfortably. His right arm hogged the middle armrest. Lil' Pat's arm was on the other. Camille didn't mind, though. She had her arms folded in her lap.

But her boyfriend asked, "Do you want to put your arm here?" He moved his arm to his side. "I don't mind. Go ahead."

Camille wrapped her arm around Lil' Pat's and interlaced her fingers with his. She placed their locked arms on the armrest together and smiled. "We can share it," she said.

Symphony music boomed from the surrounding speakers. The movie was about to start. And when the screen faded to pitch black, Camille slipped a pedicured bare foot out of her high-heel and rubbed it against Lil Pat's calf. He stiffened, and she felt his palm begin to sweat. She continued to rub her foot against his leg and he shivered. Her date was scared.

When the screen shined a bright white, she placed her foot back in her high-heel. The opportunity for affection was gone. She squeezed his hand. "Relax," she told him.

Throughout the whole movie Lil' Pat showed no interest in Camille. Not even a simple kiss, and kisses were mandatory. She had sighed loudly when the couple in front of them started making out, but Lil' Pat didn't get the hint. The only thing he reacted to was the monster during the scary scenes. He'd either flinch or jump completely out his seat.

If it weren't for Lil' Pat's popularity at Southeast High school, Camille wouldn't be dating him. He was 17, light-skinned with wavy hair. His dimpled cheeks made his smile attractive. Being that he was a senior and Camille only a sophomore, it made their relationship the talk of the school.

Lil' Pat had money, which was why a lot of girls were practically throwing the pussy at him. Not Camille, though. She waited until he approached her to talk to him. But it was no secret where his money came from—PCP. Lil' Pat didn't sell drugs, but his older brother, Hoodey, did. Hoodey was balling out of control.

The credits began rolling.

"You ready to go?" Lil' Pat asked.

"Sure," Camille replied, standing. She felt popcorn crumbling under her heels as she made her way out of the aisle.

Lil' Pat put his hand on the small of Camille's back to escort her outside—the first contact that wasn't coerced. Camille figured he only touched her because members of their school were there and he wanted to show that she was his, and only his.

Once outside on the Plaza streets and exposed to the city lights, Lil' Pat was graced with a clear view of her. His eyes roamed over her curvacious body. Her skin, the color of creamy peanut butter, soft and smooth. Her jean skirt did justice to her sexy baby-oiled legs. It was amazing that she was only 15, a blessing that she was still growing.

"You look beautiful," he said.

This was the fourth time that he had complimented her beauty. And she loved compliments; she deserved them. A

Jordan Belcher

proud smile appeared on her face and she gave the same response she gave the other three times. "Thank you."

They reached the corner of the sidewalk and waited for an opportunity to cross the street.

Camille bumped him with her shoulder. "Why haven't you kissed me tonight?"

"You want a kiss?"

"I shouldn't have to ask you. We go together. You never show me affection."

"I kissed you before."

"You barely ever do. I'm beginning to think you scared of me."

"I just don't want to disrespect you. I don't want yo family mad at me."

She sucked her teeth. "You *are* scared of me."

He leaned down and kissed her—on the cheek.

She sighed.

As they stood there, a sparkling creme-colored Infiniti Q45 with 22-inch chrome Lexani wheels bent the corner farther down, coming toward them.

"Damn! Get down," Camille said, pulling Lil' Pat by his wrist.

"What is it?"

She yanked on his arm until they were crouching behind a green Suzuki.

"Camille, what's goin' on?"

She looked directly at him when she said, "That's my cousin's car."

"Tre Pound?"

"Yes!"

Petrified, Lil' Pat hunkered down even further. "I thought you said yo people was coo' wit' me taking you out," he said in a shaky voice.

"They are. I don't know what he's doin' down here. I know if he sees us he's gon' start some shit." She peeked through the Suzuki's windows and saw the Infiniti passing. "Where'd you say the restaurant was?"

"It's—it's about three blocks down," he stuttered.

"C'mon, let's hurry up and get there before he turns around." She pulled on his wrist again.

Lil' Pat wouldn't budge. "We should wait a little longer. Just in case."

She kept pulling on his arm. "Pat, we have to go now!"

He finally got up, and they both scurried across the street. The white families that visited the Plaza huddled together as the two teens ran down the sidewalk.

Two more blocks to go.

Lil' Pat had stolen the lead and was now tugging Camille along. He knew all about Tre Pound. Who didn't?

"Lil' Pat, slow down." Camille was having trouble keeping up. Her heels weren't made for running.

"We're almost there."

"I know, but—" Camille tripped. Her knees hit the concrete first. "Ah!" she squealed. Luckily, her hands braced her fall or else her face would've been scarred.

Her boyfriend was still running.

"Lil' Pat!" she called out.

He stopped and turned, seeing that his girl had fallen. A light jog brought him back to her. He knelt down. "Can you stand up?"

She tried to stand. "Ouch!" she cried, and stayed down. Her right knee was bleeding.

"Do you got a Band-Aid in yo purse?" he asked. But he didn't hear her smart response because he was transfixed by what he saw at the corner—the Infiniti!

He bolted in the opposite direction, leaving Camille to fend for herself.

"Lil' Pat!" she screamed, but he kept running. "Dammit!"

The Infiniti Q45 came to a screeching halt in the middle of the street. Traffic became backed up when Tre Pound promptly hopped out his vehicle. He ignored the protests and the horn-honking as he rushed over to his little cousin.

"What the fuck you doin' on the ground?"

Camille cradled her knee. "I fell."

Looking around, Tre Pound said, "Where the fuck is yo date?"

"You scared him off," she said accusingly.

"I can't believe this. See, this is the type of shit that make me fuck muthafuckas up. How is he just gon' leave you?"

"It's not his fault. If you wouldn't have came down here, he would still be here."

Tre Pound scooped her up in his arms.

She winced. "Not so rough."

"Niggas be thinking I'm playing games. Like I'm soft or something," he said to himself, carrying Camille to his car. She helped open the door and he sat her in the passenger seat. "I try to be nice but they go and disrespect my family. Wait till I catch that lil' nigga."

As Tre Pound walked around to the driver side, an enraged Nissan Altima driver leaned out of his window. "Hey jerk, can you hurry up and move your freaking car!"

Pushed over the edge, Tre Pound removed his 9mm Browning semiautomatic. He held it by the barrel in pistol-whipping position and strode towards the Altima.

The driver was frightened and hurriedly rolled up his windows and locked his doors.

Camille intervened. "Tre Pound! I'm bleeding!"

He turned to look at his little cousin. She was showing him that she had blood on her fingers. Turning back to the Altima, he pointed a stiff finger at the driver.

"Today's yo lucky day."

He kicked the man's bumper before he got back in his Infiniti. Foot to gas, he peeled off.

CHAPTER 3

Camille studied Tre Pound closely. Every

streetlight they drove under lit up his dark face. He had a lot of diamond jewelry on, thought he was too cute. Muscles in his strong jaw protruded as he clenched his teeth. "I hate you," she said. "I hope you get the electric chair."

"It ain't no electric chair in Missouri no more, just lethal injection," he responded casually. He checked his rearview mirror, a habit of his. "Pat, right? Lil' Pat? That's who you was wit'? Hoodey's little brother?"

"So what you gon' do? You gon' kill him now," she said sarcastically.

"Did I say I was gon' kill somebody? And watch yo mouth. This car could be tapped. Feds could be listenin' in."

Being the stubborn, intolerable young lady that she was, Camille spoke into the vents as if they were bugged. "Police, if yall can hear me, my cousin is a murderer, drug dealer, robber, and everything else you can—"

Tre Pound snatched her up by the arm. "Cut that shit out! You toying wit' my life. It's real out here, and if you don't take it serious you won't last long. Don't ever do that shit again." He let her arm go.

Considering how aggressively Tre Pound treated Camille, one could only imagine how he treated people who weren't related to him. At a young age he learned from his uncle, Marcus "Cutthroat" King—rest in peace— that violence was the best persuasion.

"Why did you mess up my date?" Camille pouted. She was pressing a napkin to her knee.

"I didn't mess up yo date," he said. "Yo date messed up yo date."

"You didn't have no business being down there in the first place."

"This is my city. I go where I damn well please."

"And I asked Momma could I miss school today so I could go to yo trial to support you. And then you gon' do this to me. You didn't have nothin' better to do? Nobody else to harass?"

"I just wanted to make sure you was okay. It's a lot of purse snatches and crime on the Plaza," he said, keeping his eyes on the road. "I wasn't gon' do nothin' to yo lil' punk-ass boyfriend. You think I would go out of my way to fuck up yo date just for fun?"

"I *know* you would."

He grinned. His little cousin knew him better than he thought.

"That's not funny, Tre. You don't see me running around hatin' on the hoochies you be messin' wit'."

"I'm only lookin' out for you. And anyway, you need to be dating the kind of individual that'll stand up for you. Lil' Pat ran off and left you. I could've told you he was an off-brand before you even met him. I know because his brother is lame, too. He was probably being bootsie the whole time yall was together."

Camille recalled the jitters Lil' Pat had, the scared reactions from the film. He *was* bootsie. And she had some words for him the next time she saw him. "But that's not the point," she countered. "You don't have the right to dictate who I'm wit'."

"I do have that right. I'm yo big cousin, and I know more about these lil' niggas than you do."

"You doin' all this talkin' now. But when you was in court the judge had you on quiet time."

"Check it out," he said, clicking his left blinker. He waited for the oncoming car to pass, then he turned down her street. "Sometimes you gotta play certain roles. Fuck that courtroom. But I'd be a fool to say that in court. Respect and disrespect de jure authority as you see fit. Yo daddy taught me that."

Camille wasn't listening to him. She had just peeled off the napkin, cringing at her knee injury. Her only fear was that it would leave a scar. She liked showing off her legs, but now she'd probably have to wear jeans all the time. "Don't nothin' ever go right for me," she whimpered.

***

Janice King toiled over the list of gambling profits at the dining room table. A cigarette burned in the ashtray next to her. She was a plus-size woman, yellowish complexion and serious-looking, with twists in her hair. With the help of her daughter, she always dressed in style, wearing a cocaine white Rocawear shirt that had a low-cut neckline, exposing the crease of her big bosom.

She barely noticed her nephew, carrying her bleeding daughter, come through the door.

"What happened?" she asked dryly.

"Tre Pound made me fall," Camille told her, as she was lowered onto the couch. "And he scared off another one of my boyfriends. Momma, tell him to leave me alone. He's ruining my life."

Janice took a drag off her cigarette. "Levour, leave my daughter alone."

"A'ight," Tre Pound said, and that was it.

"He don't even get in trouble?" Camille huffed. "That ain't fair. He get to do whatever he want to." She tried to kick Tre Pound but he sidestepped it.

Suddenly, cheering and applauding erupted from the basement. Someone must've hit big at one of the gambling tables. On Monday nights, outbursts were a common occurrence in the King household.

Tre Pound was on his way upstairs when Janice stopped him.

"Where you goin'?" she asked.

"I'm finna go upstairs and get Camille somethin' for her knee. Why? Wussup?"

"Here," she said, holding out the list of gambling profits. "Fax this to Shelton first."

Camille looked aghast at her mother. "Momma, I don't want this to scar up."

"Shut up, girl," Janice shot back. "You can wait. You ain't dying." She shook the paper so Tre Pound would move quickly. "Take this. Hurry up."

The fax machine dialed Shelton's number. Once connected, the sheet was sucked through and slowly eked out. Tre Pound handed the sheet back to his auntie, then went and got some peroxide and cotton swabs and came back down. Camille hissed and twitched the whole time he was tending to her knee.

"Hold still." He dabbed around the bubbling white foam.

"You did it!" she blamed him. "And I got a talent show in a couple days and we was supposed to all wear skirts. Now look at me. You always doin' somethin' and you don't never get in trouble for it." When he applied the Band-Aid, she stood and pushed him out her way, limping up the steps. "This is a stupid family!"

"Watch your damned mouth, little girl!" Janice hollered, then took another drag. "Levour, come sit down wit' me."

He joined her at the kitchen table. "Wussup, Auntie?"

"What do you think?" she asked.

"About what?"

"The trial. I hate the fact that that girl couldn't stop running her mouth."

"Dynisha? I don't think her testimony hurt me all that much. She made herself look bad. I'ma beat this murder. You know they can't hold me, Auntie," he boasted. But he wasn't so sure ... he tried not to show it, though.

"I hope so," Janice said. "When's the last time you talked to your mom and dad?"

Tre Pound lit up a cigarette of his own. He wasn't interested in the conversation anymore. "It's been a minute," he said, and took a drag from his Newport.

When he was 15 years old, his parents kicked him out of the house for following in the footsteps of "the bad side of the family." His parents moved to Cleveland, Ohio, when his father was offered a corporate job there, and they didn't even ask Tre Pound did he want to go. He wouldn't have gone anyway. Kansas City was his home. Eventually, he bought the house he grew up in, where he resides to this day.

"Last time I talked to moms was when she found out I had a murder case. She basically just called to say I told you so, said some Jesus shit and hung up. Haven't talked to pops since he kicked me out." Tre Pound shrugged. "I don't even care, to be honest."

"And that's the attitude you should have," Janice said. "They the ones in the wrong. I didn't meet your dad until after I married Cutthroat. And that's when I saw that your dad and Cutthroat were two different people. They never got along. Your dad was a working man and Cutthroat was a gangster. And when your dad saw that you wanted to be like his brother instead of him, it hurt his little pride. But you keep being you, Levour King. Or what is it them girls call you in the street now?"

He smirked and said, "Tre Pound."

"As long as you represent the family name and keep Cutthroat's spirit alive then can't nobody tell you nothin'. You got a lot of Cutthroat in you, you know that?"

A ringing sound erupted from Tre Pound's pocket. He reached inside and came out with his cell phone, flipped it open.

"Are you still comin'?" a female voice asked in a hurried tone.

"I'll be there. Keep it warm for me," he replied, and hung up. He stood. "Auntie Janice, I gotta make a run real quick. You hold it down."

"Uh-oh. Maybe you got too much of Cutthroat in you." They both laughed and hugged each other tight. "I love you, baby."

"I love you, too, Auntie."

"Be careful out there," she warned.

"The only way I know how to be."

CHAPTER 4

"This might be him," Kaliko said anxiously. Through the blinds of the upstairs bedroom window, he saw headlights pierce the darkness outside. A car was coming down the street. As it got closer, though, he saw that it wasn't the car he was looking for.

"Is it him?" asked Joy. She fiddled with her fingernails as she sat on the edge of her bed.

"Hell nah. That was a Acura, not a Infiniti." He snatched his fingers from between the blinds and turned to face his accomplice. "I thought you said he was on his way."

"He is. Nobody can pass up a chance to get this pussy. He's comin'. Hold yo horses."

"I been holdin' my horses for ..." He checked his wrist for the time, but his watch wasn't there. He forgot—Tre Pound had stolen it. "Bitch-ass nigga," he grumbled. "I been holdin' my horses for a long time. If he don't show up, I ain't givin' you one red cent."

"Yeah right. It don't matter if he come. I'm still gettin' paid. That was the deal." Speaking to herself, she muttered,

"Using my house to kill somebody. Oh, best believe I'm gettin' my money."

Kaliko returned to his stake-out. The hatred boiling in his chest kept him at the window. He had waited this long, promising Joy the negotiated price of $13,000, and he was going to continue waiting until his work was finished. He wanted Tre Pound to have a closed casket.

Becoming restless, he turned to look at Joy again. She was light-skinned, hair dyed flaming red. Legs crossed, still picking at her fingernails, she seemed indifferent about what was about to happen. Only concerned about her money. She could care less about Tre Pound, or any other nigga for that matter. And that turned him on.

She glanced up at him. "What you lookin' at?"

"Yo sexy ass," he said, stepping towards her.

"Ain't you supposed to be watchin' out for Tre Pound?"

Kaliko sat next to her and wrapped an arm around her shoulder. "He probably won't be here for at least another 15 minutes. Let's use this time wisely."

Joy stopped picking her fingernails. "You can't be serious."

"I am comin' off a lot of bread," he pointed out. "That type of money deserves a little bonus."

"First of all, $13,000 ain't shit. Nigga, I'm doin' *you* a favor." She knocked his hand off her shoulder and stood. "That's what's wrong wit' you niggas today. Always thinkin' about gettin' some pussy when you should be handlin' business. This here"—she pointed between her legs—"is for women only. I don't do men, and I'm tired of tellin' you niggas that."

A defeated expression appeared on Kaliko's chubby face. He sucked his teeth. "You remember what to do?"

"Yeah, I know what to do. It don't take a rocket scientist to—"

"Just answer the damn question!"

"I don't know what you raising yo voice for," she said frankly, and walked over to her dresser. "Just because I don't wanna give you none, you wanna get mad. Grow up."

"I didn't want none anyway. You ain't my type. I just wanted to see what you was gon' say."

"Childish," she mumbled. In the first drawer was a pair of handcuffs. She pulled them out and dangled them between two fingers. "I put these bad boys around his wrists and call yo name when I got his pants down," she explained.

"Make sure his hands are cuffed to the bed. I don't want him to be able to grab his burner. Try to get it away from him. And you gotta make sure you call my name loud enough, too, so I can hear you while I'm in the closet. Do whatever you gotta do to get him to come upstairs."

Joy said, "I'ma back away from the bed before I call yo name. If you want to, you can just come out blasting."

Kaliko could already see Tre Pound laying helpless on the bed, begging for mercy. He'd have the ups on him, springing from the closet, gun drawn, Tre Pound scared to death. He'd take his watch back. And before he pulled the trigger, he'd try and find out where the drugs Tre Pound took from him were. If not, Kaliko would still be known as the man who killed the most notorious funk artist in Kansas City.

Faintly, treble and bass could be heard outside. Rap music. Kaliko listened closely, held up his hands to hush the room.

"You hear that?" he whispered.

"Check the window, fool."

Kaliko almost tripped and fell as he sprinted to the window, bending the blinds to look out. He watched the Infiniti Q45 park alongside the curb and got goose bumps. This was the moment he'd been waiting for!

"It's him! Get yo ass downstairs!" he told Joy, as he scurried into the closet.

Joy paced down the steps, the bottom of her worn down terrycloth robe flying up like a cape.

***

JL Audio subwoofers thumped in the trunk of the Infiniti Q45, the quality sound boisterous and crisp. Tre Pound let MC Eiht's "Streiht Up Menace" ride out before he cut the car off.

"I'ma talk so bad to Joy after I fuck. Bitch should've been let me hit," he said to himself, adjusting his 9mm handgun in the loop of his belt to keep it from falling down his pants leg again. Once before, he dropped it when he was in Blockbuster and scared half the people there.

Right when he was about to knock on the front door, Joy opened it, smiling sarcastically. "It's about time you showed up. I was about to call and tell you don't even come." Her faded red robe was fastened snugly, curving over her wide hips.

"I would've been here sooner but I had to make a stop through the Plaza. Family issues. Are you gon' let me in or what?"

"I'm still thinkin' about it," she remarked, and finally stepped to the side. "Don't ever keep me waitin' again."

He entered, scanned the junky house and leaned against the back of the sofa. "Ya girlfriend ain't home?"

"She's at work. Making that money to bring home to Momma."

"She know you 'bout to give some of her pussy to Tre Pound?"

"What she don't know won't hurt her," Joy said. "You don't wanna sit down?"

Tre Pound had seen two roaches crawl between the cushions in the sofa. "I'm coo," he replied. "I heard that you, uh ..."

She already knew what he was about to say. Unfastening the robe, she presented him with healthy breasts resting in her pushup bra. She placed her thumbs within the elastic band of her panties and folded them down until her pussy

41

hairs were showing; they were dyed red, too, same as the hair on her head.

"Is this what you wanted to know?" she asked.

Tre Pound nodded. On many occasions he had spit his best game to Joy, letting her know how he could change her lesbian lifestyle if she'd simply "get wit' a real G." He figured his previous attempts finally wore her down.

"Now it's my turn to see somethin'," Joy said, sinking to her knees.

"You don't waste no time. That's noteworthy." He placed a hand behind her head.

She knocked it away. "Don't touch my hair."

"I can respect that."

The steel Joy felt when she reached for his zipper made her pause. "What is this?" she asked, poking him with her finger.

He smiled. "Big, ain't it?"

She sucked her teeth. "I know you didn't bring a gun into my house."

"Of course I did. You familiar with my pedigree. Niggas don't seem to like me."

"Get rid of it."

"No can do."

"At least get it out the way. It might accidentally go off and blow my face off."

He removed the handgun and dropped it on the couch. "Okay, go ahead and get back to what you was doin', baby."

Tre Pound was unarmed now.

Joy stood up.

He spread his arms out, confused. "What happened?"

"Follow me," she purred, proceeding to the steps.

Her walk was mean, sexy, Tre Pound thought. With a walk like that, she had to have some good pussy. So he gladly followed her ... leaving his protection behind.

Joy let her robe fall to the floor when they were inside her bedroom. Barely naked, she strutted across the carpet, slowy placing her firm bottom on the bed. "Care to join me?"

"I don't see why not." Tre Pound wasted no time. He stood in front of her and lifted his shirt, tugging his pants and boxers to the middle of his thighs. His dick was fully erect.

"Put it up," she said firmly, wearing a scowl.

"Put what up?"

Pointing with her finger, she said, "Put ya dick back in ya pants. You don't just pull ya dick out on a lady. You gotta work yo way up to that."

"My fault. I thought you was ready for it."

Joy looked over at her closet door as Tre Pound pulled his pants back up. She seemed to be envisioning something, because she started to smile.

"What's in the closet?" Tre Pound asked.

"Oh, nothin'." Joy rose to her feet, close enough to kiss him. But she was shorter than him, and to be able to kiss him she'd have to stand on her tippy toes. She looked up

into his eyes, tacitly challenging him. "Lay down on the
bed. Shoes off."

"Bossy, I see. I can dig it. But wait till this dick get up
in you. We gon' see who's in charge." He used the opposite
foot to pry off his Air Jordan Retro 4's, then crawled into
bed and lay on his back.

Joy grabbed the handcuffs off the dresser.

He sat up quickly. "What you 'bout to do wit' them?"

"Teach you how to treat a lady."

"Hold up, Joy. I don't do cuffs. I'm allergic to 'em. Now
if *you* want to put 'em on, then be my guest. Let me move
out the way." As he began scooting to the edge of the bed,
Joy leaped on top of him. "What the—?"

He let her wrestle him on his stomach, and she held
him down by pressing her breasts into his back. "Boy," she
said, kissing the nape of his neck, "tonight is going to be ..."
She kissed again. "... the greatest moment ..." She licked his
ear. "... of your life."

"That's coo', but you didn't have to jump on me like that.
Damn near kneed me in the face." He attempted to roll
over but she wouldn't budge. "Why are you on my back?"

"Because you're under arrest." She leaned up, sitting on
his rump. She pulled his arm behind his back and clanked
a cuff around one wrist.

"What did I do?"

"Crimes against humanity. I heard all about how you
like to dog girls out, and dogs like you are the reason I hate
men. So your sentence is two hours of sex with me."

44

"Can I plea bargain? I don't think I can do all that time."

She giggled, then tried to secure the other cuff to the headboard. But a shrill sound, mixed with loud beeps and honks, blared outside—Tre Pound's alarm was going off.

He spun, knocking Joy off of him. "Get out my way," he breathed, and quickly put on his shoes.

"Wait!" Joy shouted as he ran out the bedroom.

He skipped steps as he jumped downstairs and swooped up his pistol off the couch before he bolted outside.

The four kids that were crouching beside Tre Pound's Infiniti were about 12 years old. They already had one end of the car raised on the jack and were hastily removing the bolts. Amazingly, the alarm didn't scare them, but when the lookout saw the armed Tre Pound burst out the front door, he alerted his friends. "Break!"

As the kids escaped without their tools, Tre Pound pointed his 9mm Browning in their direction. He let off several thunderous shots, startling the young thieves. The slowest runner tripped, got back up and tried to catch up with his friends.

"Get back in the house!" Joy yelled at Tre Pound. She didn't even bother to put on her robe as she rushed outside and approached him. "What the hell are you doin' out here?! You could've killed those kids!"

"I wasn't tryna hit 'em. Just scare 'em. Believe me, if I wanted to kill 'em I would've popped my trunk." He cut off his alarm. It took less than 30 seconds for him to re-tighten his bolts.

45

"You didn't have to shoot. The neighbors is gon' call the police."

"No they ain't. Niggas be shootin' in this 'hood all the time."

"Just get back in the house." Joy tugged him away from his car. "You crazy. Shootin' at children."

"They wasn't children. They tried to steal my rims. That makes 'em gangstas."

"Just like you," she said, still pulling him towards her house.

Tre Pound happened to look up. The light in the upstairs bedroom window shined a bright yellow through the closed curtains. He didn't know if he was going to make it back to her room. His hormones told him to bend Joy over the couch as soon as they got through the front door.

Then something passed in front of the window, causing Tre Pound to come to a startled halt. It was the shadowy silhouette of a man, and whoever it was moved quick.

This was a setup!

"What's the problem?" Joy asked, exhausted. "Are you comin' in? If you want this, you better come on."

"You know what ...?" he began, removing Joy's grip from his arm. "I gotta roll out. I'ma have to catch up wit' you some other time."

Joy stomped behind him and started pushing him towards her front door. "No, you're going to catch up wit' me right now."

"Watch out," he told her, and maneuvered around her, pacing back to his car.

Joy looked dumbfounded.

She couldn't let him get away so she pulled on his locked door handle, knocked on his window. "Where are you going? Come back!" She pulled on the door handle again. "Why are you actin' like this?"

He started the car, then aimed his pistol at her. "Bitch, back up!"

Joy quickly jumped backwards.

He put the car in gear, and the Pirelli tires shrieked as he zoomed away.

CHAPTER 5

Right after leaving Joy's, Tre Pound drove to

his cousin Gutta's house to get the handcuffs removed. Maurice "Gutta" King was 30 years old, dark-skinned like Tre Pound, but of a stockier build. He was the one who gave Tre Pound his first gun. And when Tre Pound's parents kicked him out the house, Gutta was who he stayed with.

Gutta's mother was Bernice Hampton. His father was Marcus "Cutthroat" King. While Cutthroat was married to Janice, he had three kids with Bernice—Gutta, and two more boys, Salomon "Cash" King and Seneca King. Out of all of Cutthroat's children, people said Gutta resembled Cutthroat the most.

"I told you about fuckin' around wit' all them different bitches," Gutta said, picking at the lock with two bobby pins. He was sitting on the footstool, facing Tre Pound, who was on the couch. "It's easy to get ya'self into a jam like that. You need to settle down. Get you one down-ass chick that's willing to be there for you and ride out life wit' you."

"Like Michelle," Tre Pound quipped.

"It'll be hard to find one like her, but that's part of the process." Gutta pursed his lips. "And what you mean by 'like Michelle'?"

"I never thought you would get married; that's all I meant. You used to be on the same shit I'm on—fuckin' bitches, gettin' money the gangsta way."

"I'm still gettin' money the gangsta way. But it's easier to do that wit' one strong woman by ya side. It cuts a lot of the bullshit in half. You don't have to worry about niggas funkin' wit' you because you fucked they girl. When you hit a lick, you'll always have yo wife as a solid alibi. Now look at you. You almost got yo head tore off behind a bitch that didn't mean nothin' to you."

Further tinkering freed Tre Pound of the handcuffs. He massaged his wrist. "I appreciate that."

"Any time," Gutta said. "So give me the scoop on what's goin' down in the 'hood."

Years ago, Gutta knew about all the illegal shit that transpired in Kansas City. But now there was a new generation running things—Tre Pound's generation. Gutta still involved himself with criminal activity but he wasn't as connected to the streets as he used to be. That was where Tre Pound was needed, to fill him in. Gutta just liked to hear about what was happening in the streets because he loved the streets—or at least that was what Tre Pound thought.

They chatted for a few minutes before they were interrupted.

"Man, what's takin' yo ass so long!" Tommy shouted from the dining room table.

Then Tony added, "If we gon' do this tonight, we don't have no time to be wastin.'"

Rising from the footstool, Gutta told Tre Pound, "I gotta attend to some business. We'll rap some other time."

"Is it a'ight if I crash here?" There was a chance Tre Pound would get pulled over if he went back out tonight. Also, he wanted to see what scheme Gutta, Tommy and Tony were planning.

"Ain't nothin' wrong wit' you stayin' here. You know that. You used to live here. Make ya'self at home. Michelle moved the sheets and blankets to the hall closet. The pillows are in my room. This ain't the Marriott so you gotta get the shit ya'self."

Aside from a cigarette burn here and there, the black comforter Tre Pound picked out looked cozy. He got two of the fluffiest pillows from his cousin's room and made himself comfortable on the couch. He watched and listened as the men conspired in the dining room.

"We gotta do everything according to plan," Gutta explained. "Five minutes tops. Anything over that time limit will get us caught."

"How much money are we talkin' about?" Tony asked.

Tommy appeared aggressive as he chimed in, "If it ain't at least 20 G's a piece, me and my brother ain't gettin' involved."

"I say around $65,000 is up in the safe. That's 20 grand a piece and some change," Gutta estimated.

"Where'd you get those figures from?" Tommy inquired.

"Last month somebody walked in the jewelry store we about to rob and came out wit' close to $70,000 in cash. He didn't even touch the jewelry. And he never got caught. Probably out robbin' somethin' right now. I know this because it was in the Metropolitan Digest. I been keepin' up wit' the newspaper to see if the guy was gonna come back and hit it again, but he hasn't. So we gon' hit it." Gutta's words became more certain as he added, "And if one person can do it, then I know the three of us can."

"We should get some of that jewelry, too," Tony suggested. "Increase our take."

"I could use some ice," Tommy thought out loud, looking at his old Fossil watch.

"We'll have to work that into the plan somehow," Gutta said, puffing on a Newport. "Let's go over everything one mo' time."

Tre Pound had heard about Tommy and Tony. Supposedly, the two brothers had been robbing banks, check cashing joints, and other establishments since the late 90's. They were around Gutta's age, small in height, and looked out of shape. They were also known to use deadly force during robberies. Unfortunately for the police, Tommy and Tony had never been caught in the act.

The 52" high-definition television cast flashes of light in the dark living room. Tre Pound pretended to be watching

C-SPAN as Gutta, Tommy and Tony rose from the dining room table. They walked in front of the TV to get to the front door.

"We'll be back in a couple hours," Gutta said. "It's some Gates barbecue in the refrigerator if you get hungry."

Tre Pound propped himself up on his elbow. "I didn't know yall was leavin' tonight."

"Just hold down the fort. And if Michelle call, tell her I stepped out for a second."

Only a few minutes after they left did the phone ring. Tre Pound picked it up and told Michelle exactly what Gutta told him to tell her. She kept calling back periodically asking if Gutta had made it back yet and he kept telling her no. After several hours passed, he stopped answering, and the phone continued to ring all night. Nevertheless, Tre Pound managed to fall into a deep sleep.

CHAPTER 6

"**I need you** to move yo car so I can pull mines in the driveway."

The soft voice penetrated Tre Pound's dream. He awoke, wiping his eyes. "Huh?"

"Yo car is in my way, Tre Pound. Get up and move it; after that, you can come back in and go to sleep."

He began to recognize where he was—still at Gutta's house. Morning light shined through the windows. He sat up, staring at the simple white shoes of the woman standing over him. He looked up at her. It was Michelle. The bright white nurse's tunic she wore put a strain on his eyes.

Though Michelle was the same age as Tre Pound, she tried to act like she was much older than him because she was married to his big cousin Gutta. She was brown-skinned, naturally pretty in the face. But she was too thin, nearly anorexic. And she could be irritating at times.

"Tre Pound, I said get up."

"Where Gutta 'nem at?" he asked, as he slipped on his Air Jordans.

"I was gon' ask you the same thing," she said, looking worried as she ran a hand along her pressed hair. "He didn't say where he was going? Who did he leave wit'?"

Tre Pound didn't know how much she knew about Gutta's criminal life, so he said, "All I know is what he told me to tell you. Why didn't you call his cell?"

"I tried to, but he didn't take it wit' him. It's in the room," she informed him. "Why'd you stop answering the phone last night?"

"Because I was tired," he grunted, folding the black comforter. "I was at trial all day yesterday morning and I had a fucked up night. Plus, I'm not a goddamn secretary."

She folded her arms under her tiny breasts. "You don't seem at all concerned about yo own cousin. He could be in trouble."

"That man is 30 years old. He can take care of hisself." Tre Pound did have a little concern about his cousin's whereabouts. Gutta wasn't back yet, and he wondered if Gutta got caught. "But if he ain't home by this evening, call me and I'll try and see if I can find out where he at."

Michelle smiled. "Thank you, Tre Pound."

"Get off my nuts."

Her smile instantly turned into a grimace. "You got a rude mouth," she retorted. "And you know not to park in the driveway. Move yo car."

"Move my car? This ain't yo house. This my cousin's shit. And I used to live here way before you did, so that driveway is just as much mines as it is yours."

"But you don't live here no more. And Gutta said you gotta respect my space." She put her hands on her hips, letting him know who the boss was.

He laughed. "I'm 'bout to leave anyway. Tre block," he said, throwing up his set.

Tre Pound lived on 35th and Agnes. He stopped there to freshen up before he hit the streets. As he showered, he thought about that shady, conniving, deceitful bitch Joy and wondered who else was in the house with her last night. It could've been anybody. A lot of people wanted to see him dead.

Joy had some explaining to do ...

Feeling brand new again, he looked in the bathroom mirror with a towel wrapped around his waist. He had a chiseled abdomen and strong back muscles. "They can't fuck wit' me," he said, jabbing in front of the mirror, bobbing and weaving as if his image was the opponent. "They tried to do me in yesterday but I came up out of it. I'm Tre muthafuckin' Pound, baby!"

He brushed his hair, then his teeth. As he spit into the porcelain sink, he heard his cell phone ring. He grabbed it out of his jeans that lay over the toilet seat.

"What you got planned for today?" Shelton asked.

"Nothin' much. 'Bout to go over to Marlon's house, chill for a minute."

"Whenever you get a chance, come up to the office."

Tre Pound rinsed his mouth out with water. "A'ight. What for?"

"I'll tell you when you get here. You ain't gotta rush, though. Just come see me after you come from Marlon's. Later." Shelton hung up.

Tre Pound drove over to his homie Marlon Hayes' house, which was on 51st and Garfield. Since he could remember, Marlon's house had always been the hangout spot, even before Mrs. Hayes died and left him the property. Recently, Marlon had gotten put on house arrest and needed all the company he could get.

All the fellas were on the porch when Tre Pound pulled up.

"There he go again," Marlon said with a smile, shaking his head as Tre Pound brazenly wheeled his Infiniti Q45 over the curb and parked it on the sidewalk. "One day the police gon' drive by and tow his shit."

Stacks, who was sitting on the porch steps next to Marlon, said, "And look at him. He still got those Lexanis on his car."

"He's a savage for ridin' around the city on them rims," Moses replied, and let out a little chuckle. "He didn't have to take 'em from Young Ray; that lil' dude don't even got shit. Tre Pound was wrong for that. But that's my nigga, though."

Playa Paul stood beside Moses, leaning against the fresh wood banister. He watched along with the rest of them as Tre Pound got out his car, adorned in dazzling jewelry. TrePound wore a platinum necklace with yellow and white diamonds in the crown pendant, which hung low to his stomach. His four-karat square-shaped earrings were also diamond encrusted. He walked up and gave everybody dap. When he shook Playa Paul's hand, Playa Paul didn't let go right away, but observed his wrist. Tre Pound had on a new Audemars Piguet watch. Envy flared up in Playa Paul's eyes.

"Can I have my hand back?" Tre Pound joked, then went and sat in between Marlon and Stacks.

"Where'd you get that from?" Playa Paul asked, already planning to buy a bigger watch.

"I been had this. Just never wore it. But I can't remember if I bought it or jacked somebody for it," Tre Pound told him, honestly trying to remember.

"That's sad," Stacks commented. "You done did so much dirt that you don't even remember where you got yo jewelry from."

"That is sad," Marlon seconded, while rolling up a cigarillo. "Seriously, Tre Pound, you need to cut back on them kick-door robberies. I heard Kaliko's lookin' for you now. The niggas you funkin' wit' could try and come at me or Moses or Playa Paul or Stacks because they know we fuck wit' you. My little sister be here. I don't want them comin' over here lookin' for you."

"I robbed Kaliko about three weeks ago. If he was gon' try and do somethin', he would've did it by now. Don't worry about that pussy." Tre Pound puffed on the blunt Marlon passed to him, then passed it on to Stacks. "And

I give you niggas first dibs on all the dope and everything else I come up on so that's the price yall gotta pay."

The weed circulated amongst them until they all were high, eyes bloodshot red. Moses ended up with the last of the weed, holding the roach between two fingernails, sucking strenuously, when he caught Playa Paul staring at him out the corner of his eye.

"Somethin' on my face?" Moses asked.

Playa Paul shook his head no. "I just noticed that yo hair ain't longer than mine," he said.

"What makes you think that?" Moses stretched out one of the plaits in his hair so Playa Paul could get a good look. "You see that hangtime. I got you beat."

"No, you don't," Playa Paul stated. From underneath his royal blue KC ballcap, cornrowed braids draped down to his shoulders. "You still got some growin' to do."

"We can settle this right now," Moses said, and asked Marlon to come be the judge.

Marlon stood wiping his rimless prescription Nike glasses on the bottom of his red-striped designer shirt. He positioned them correctly on his face again and walked through the grass to the banister. Marlon had slick, wavy hair, from his Black and Indian genes. It was cut low, professionally tapered by his barber. He didn't understand what the big deal was about whose hair was longer and probably wouldn't have participated had he not been high.

He looked at Moses and Playa Paul as they both pulled on their hair.

"Quit tilting yo head," said Moses.

"My head ain't tilted. Marlon, is my head tilted?"

The veins in Marlon's eyes were glazed red and he could barely see a thing. But he knew Playa Paul would throw a fit, possibly even start a fight if his hair wasn't longer. Playa Paul was competitive like that. So Marlon said, "Uh ... Playa Paul got you, Moses."

"I told you!" Playa Paul laughed in Moses's face. "Start washin' yo shit more often, maybe you can catch up. Apply some more grease to them dry-ass split ends."

"You always tryna be better than somebody. You got low self-esteem," Moses snarled.

As Marlon went to sit back down, he saw a shining, chameleon-painted Chevy Caprice coming down his block. The '84 box-styled Caprice boasted a sunroof, 26" chrome Daytons, platinum grill, and a compression system that suspended the body high into the air. "Stacks, you called Hoodey over here?" Marlon asked. By the time the Caprice stopped in front of his house, the paint had merged into a sparkling violet.

Immediately, Stacks got up and approached Hoodey's passenger side to make a purchase. "Dip this for me," Stacks said, handing Hoodey a thin brown More Red cigarette.

Hoodey twisted the top off his small glass vanilla bottle. He dipped the cigarette into the PCP and returned it, halfway drenched. "You good?" he asked.

"I'm good." Stacks smiled, gave Hoodey dap and stalked back to the porch.

Turning in the direction of his driver side window, Hoodey was startled by how close Tre Pound was to his face. "What's yo problem?" he chuckled.

"Do I look like I'm in a comedic mood," Tre Pound spat. "Tell yo little brother I need to holla at him." His eyes bore into the side of Hoodey's face because Hoodey had turned his head in an attempt to pay Tre Pound no mind.

Hoodey grabbed a recently dipped More Red and put it to the purple burns singed in the middle crevices of his lips. He looked older than his 31 years, and his scraggly beard showed his poor grooming. He lit the cigarette with the flame of a cigar lighter and a cloud of smoke wafted from his mouth. Time and time again he broke the cardinal code of the streets: Never get high on your own supply. Be that as it may, the large profits Hoodey raked in selling "wet" enabled him to smoke the drug whenever he wanted to, yet still live prosperously.

"I know you hear me talkin' to you," Tre Pound growled.

"What did he do?"

"He ran off and left my little cousin bleedin' on the street."

"Lil' Pat hit her?" Hoodey looked surprised. Sort of proud.

"I didn't say he hit her! And if he would've, I wouldn't be standing here talkin' to you. I would've been done dragged you out this car and purpled up yo face to match them crusty lips," he threatened. Hoodey smiled. "I said he *left* her, stranded. You don't do that when you on a date wit' my lil' cousin. So you better straighten him out, or I will."

"I'll talk to him," Hoodey said, brushing off the ashes that dropped in his lap. He wasn't concerned about Tre Pound's quarrel, but tried to act supportive. "Yeah, I'll talk to him. Tell Shelton I said wussup."

When the custom-built Chevy Caprice roared off, Tre Pound walked back over to his homies. They were conversing about Stacks' drug habit.

"That's why you so skinny," Moses said. "Smokin' that wet."

"Bitches still wanna fuck me, though," Stacks replied.

"I bet you ain't got more bitches than me," Playa Paul challenged. "I can show you how many numbers I got in my phone right now. How much you wanna put on it?"

Stacks fired up the PCP-drenched cigarette and inhaled. "I got an even better bet," he said, exhaling. "I bet you I won't give a fuck by the time I finish this stick."

Marlon suddenly reached out and snatched the lit More Red from between Stacks' lips. He threw it down on the concrete walkway and crushed it beneath his sneaker.

Stacks was so shocked he couldn't speak. He heard Moses and Playa Paul burst into laughter and his temper rose, making his boney bronze face turn red. He went and picked up the crumpled cigarette to see if it could be salvaged. Seeing that there was no hope, he towered over

Marlon angrily. "Nigga, I ain't do nothin' to you! Why'd you do that?"

Marlon looked up at him just as fierce. "I told you don't smoke that shit over my house no more. You must've thought I was playin.'"

"But you didn't have to smash it like that!"

"Yall need to go ahead and fight," Tre Pound said, scooting over out the way. "Get it over wit.' Because yall been havin' problems wit' each other for too long."

"I'm 'bout to hit him in his jaw if he keep standing over me lookin' like he 'bout to do somethin,'" Marlon said.

Stacks balled his fists. He seemed to be fighting Marlon in his head, picturing Marlon's glasses flying off his face. In the past, Stacks had damaged some of Marlon's things when he got high on wet, but he'd always pay Marlon back. At this very moment, he looked like he wanted to hit Marlon so bad.

But then he turned and started walking away.

"Where you goin'? Come back and stand up for yo'self!" Moses shouted out, laughing.

Stacks jumped inside his cherry-red '88 Camaro IROC-Z, revved up his engine and screeched off.

"He'll be back," Marlon said, swatting the air with his hand as if he wasn't worried about Stacks. "He probably just goin' to catch up wit' Hoodey to get another stick."

Moses shook his head. "Why you be doin' Stacks like that?"

"Why he be doin' me like that?" Marlon countered. "See, yall wasn't here the day before yesterday when he broke my momma's china dishes right after he smoked. My momma's dead. Them dishes had sentimental value and can't be replaced. I already told yall about the time he walked in the bathroom wit' a knife while my little sister was in the shower. Thank God he ran out when she screamed. And I told Stacks yesterday not to smoke over here no more. He did it anyway."

Just as Marlon finished his sentence, his ruby red Ford Explorer turned onto the block. His 16-year-old sister, Dominique Hayes, was driving it, listening to Keyshia Cole's "Love" with the treble all the way up. No bass. She hated bass.

"And another thing," Marlon said, pointing to the Explorer's door panel. "See that big-ass dent. Stacks did that the day before yesterday, too. He was kicking the door for no reason after I told him to go home."

"He fucked yo shit up," Moses commented with his eyebrows raised, as he watched the Ford Explorer pull up to the curb. The dent made the paint gleam awkwardly, making the whole right side look ugly.

"That's gon' take a nice chunk of change to get repaired," Playa Paul said, covering his mouth to hide his smile.

Marlon fixed the cuffs on his Girbaud jeans. "He paid me for it, but still—I'm tired of dealing wit' him when he's wet. So don't feel sorry for him. Feel sorry for me."

Tre Pound's eyes were stuck on Dominique Hayes as she got out the Ford Explorer, toting an ashen backpack. She switched her hips like a diva as she walked towards the porch. Well-fit blue jeans, a white belt, and a shoulder-baring Versace shirt laced her cocoa brown body. Covering her chestnut brown eyes were yellow-gold Chanel sunglasses.

She stopped in front of the porch, one hand gripping the shoulder strap of her backpack, the other on her hip. She crossed one high-heel over the other—a sexy stance that had been practiced in the mirror many times before.

"You had my treble blastin' again." Marlon glowered at her. "Let one of my tweeters be busted and see if I don't fuck you up."

"What's wrong wit' you?" Dominique sneered. Then she looked at her brother's friends. "Yall always over here. Don't none of yall got jobs like normal people?"

"We work for the streets," Moses said, opening his arms as if to embrace the entire world.

"And you would be the one to say some stuff like that." Dominique looked down at Tre Pound. "Cash and Seneca got caught trying to steal the principal's car."

Tre Pound gave a curt shrug.

"I don't care either," she said. "They yo cousins. They the ones that got suspended."

"You should've been home an hour ago," Marlon informed her. "School *been* out. If I find out you made a detour over a nigga's house ..."

64

"Marlon, I'm focused on school, not boys. I'm late gettin' here because I had to drop Camille and Krystal off at home like I been doin' since you started lettin' me use yo car, since you got on house arrest. If you don't believe me, have Tre Pound or Moses call one of 'em to find out. Otherwise, quit accusing me of stuff." Dominique's leg brushed up against Tre Pound's thigh as she walked up the porch steps. She looked down at him, and he looked up at her. They shared a secret glance.

And then she strutted inside the house.

Standing up, Tre Pound stretched his arms out. "I'll see yall niggas later." He gave dap to his homies.

"Where you goin'?" Marlon asked. "You just got here."

"Damn, how long you want me to stay? Playa Paul and Moses is still here to keep you company. You too old to not be able to come off the porch."

Everybody laughed.

"All I asked was where you was goin'," Marlon said, smiling. "Yall go ahead and make fun of me now. I won't be on house arrest forever."

"Shelton called me earlier. I gotta see what he want. I might slide back through later."

After starting up his car, Tre Pound glanced back at the porch. Marlon flashed him the peace sign. Playa Paul and Moses were involved in a Paper-Rock-Scissors game for who knows what reason. But behind them was the wide living room window. In it was Dominique, who was peeking out through the curtains, smiling, while biting her bottom lip. Her enticing eyes told Tre Pound that there was more to come.

CHAPTER 7

At the Go Chicken Go restaurant on Troost Avenue, two Southeast High school students, J-Dub and Kareem, sat on either side of a table near the back, eating gizzards and guzzling sodas. They were on break and didn't care that the place was busy. Up front, the other employees worked diligently to fulfill orders—bagging food, ringing up prices—as more customers poured in.

"Would you fuck her?" Kareem asked, pointing to a scantily-clad woman standing in line. She had ashy knees and elbows and wore a lopsided blonde wig.

"Nah," J-Dub responded absentmindedly, tapping his straw against the table.

"I wouldn't either. She look like she just came from Jurassic Park. I'd probably let her suck my dick, though." Kareem scoped out another woman. "Okay, what about her?"

"Nah."

"What? Her ass is *too* fat. Perfect. I'd get lost in that mufucka. But I'ma give you the benefit of the doubt. She do kinda favor Miles Davis in the face." Then Kareem finally noticed that J-Dub seemed distant. "What's on yo mind, homie? You been actin' weird all day."

"I'm just thinkin' about somethin'."

"About what?" Kareem chomped on a dinner roll and sipped some Coca Cola through his straw.

"I don't feel like talkin' about it right now."

Kareem suddenly smiled, revealing his overbite. "I know what it is. Everybody was talkin' about it at school today. Lil' Pat and Camille broke up. It got somethin' to do wit' that, don't it?"

J-Dub had been dipping the same gizzard in and out of the sauce over and over. He stopped. "I might be able to get her back now that Lil' Pat's out the picture. I don't know."

"Give it up. She don't wanna mess wit' you no more. And that's good. You already fucked her."

J-Dub shook his head, knowing Kareem didn't know the meaning of true love.

No other girl mattered to J-Dub when he was in a rela-tionship with Camille King. She was everything a nigga could want. She could be silly—they used to see who could make the funniest faces. She could be dangerous—they egged houses together, and once she pulled the fire alarm at school. She was intelligent, liked to read, and would tell him about people in history he never knew existed. Her hugs were so warm. And the day he took Camille's virginity was the day he fell in love. But shortly after that day, Tre Pound found out about their sexual encounter and stomped J-Dub out severely, and warned him to leave Camille alone. Fearing for his life, J-Dub broke up with Camille. She was highly upset, called him a "scary punkass nigga" and never wanted to speak to him again.

"You must've forgot. Tre Pound beat the *sleeves* off of you for fucking wit' Camille," Kareem stressed. "You just heard what happened to Lil' Pat last night. They was sayin' he barely escaped. Tre Pound was bustin' shots at him on the Plaza! The Plaza, J-Dub. Hundreds of people everywhere. Tre Pound is a maniac! Why would you want to put yo'self in that same situation again?"

"Because I love her," J-Dub said, looking down at his food.

"Well, when Tre Pound kills you, can I have yo Chevy?"

J-Dub looked up. "Why didn't you jump in when Tre Pound started stompin' me?"

Kareem paused. "I thought it was supposed to be a one-on-one," he said, and by the scowl on J-Dub's face, he knew that was a bad answer. "He would've killed us both if I would've jumped in. Wouldn't you rather one of us get our ass beat than both of us losing our lives? Stop being selfish ..." Then he sighed. "Okay, I'll tell you what: Next time I see Tre Pound, I'ma smack him just for you."

"Here he come now."

Kareem turned and looked. Specialty food posters were covering nearly all of the big glass windows, but he could still see outside. Tre Pound was getting out his car. He walked in and stood in line.

"You know I was playin', right?" Kareem smiled sheepishly.

"I wouldn't want you to do that anyway," J-Dub said. "I had plenty of chances to get back at him. He come in here all the time. All I would have to do is grab my strap and follow him. Pull up beside him at the light and let him have it. Come back to work, act like nothin' happened."

"Why haven't you did it yet? I know for a fact you ain't scared. You shot at other niggas before."

"It's because of Camille. She's the only thing stoppin' me. She used to tell me she don't like how he is, but she loves him, and I wouldn't want to put her through that misery. What if she found out I did it? I wouldn't have a chance of having her as my girl again. She'd hate me forever. I don't think she hates me now. I hope not."

Kareem chewed a thoroughly sauced gizzard. "You don't even have to be the one to kill Tre Pound. Somebody else will. He done robbed and killed too many people. And he's funkin' wit' everybody from almost every 'hood in the city. I'm surprised he made it this long."

"He's a funk artist, that's why. He knows what he's doing. But he's bound to slip up one of these days. And if he lose his trial, it's really over for him. It gotta be a gang of niggas in the pen that's waitin' to catch him on the yard."

Tre Pound suddenly turned their way. He looked angry. Kareem gasped. "Did he hear us?"

"Ay!" Tre Pound called out to them. "Yall see this mufucka is busy. Get the fuck up and take some of these orders." Other customers started to complain too.

J-Dub got up reluctantly. "C'mon, Kareem. Our break was over anyway."

"I hate that nigga," Kareem hissed, tying his apron behind his back. "I hope somebody get at him soon ... real soon."

CHAPTER 8

Tre Pound walked into the King Financial offices, eating out of his Go Chicken Go box.

"How is your young self doing, Mr. Levour King?" smiled Vice President Kimberly Washington. She was a humble woman, gracious and cordial, and had been working for Shelton since the company's inception. She had a mocha-colored skin tone, big lustrous flowing hair, and every time Tre Pound saw her she had on a new silk button-up tucked into a knee-length skirt. To be 40 years old, she looked very attractive.

"Wussup, Kim. I'm doin' good. And you?"

"Oh, you don't worry about how I'm doin'. I'll be all right even if I'm not all right," she said. "What is that you got there? Can I try one of those?"

Tre Pound held out the box as she picked out a gizzard. "You gotta dip it in the sauce," he instructed.

Kimberly placed a plump, saucy gizzard on her tongue, nodding pleasantly as she chewed. "Shelton is in his office.

He's expecting you. So I don't want to hold you up any longer. Thanks for the quick bite."

As Tre Pound wandered to the back of the small establishment, paperwork was being shuffled around, and women typed loudly at their desks. A few girls that worked there, one around Tre Pound's age, talked him out of most of his food. He only had two gizzards and one dinner roll left when he knocked on Shelton's office door. "Come in!"

When Tre Pound entered, Shelton held up his index finger, letting him know he'd be off the phone shortly. Tre Pound sat opposite the cherrywood desk.

Shelton looked real professional today. His slacks were held up by suspenders. His cerulean necktie was striking in contrast with his pin-striped shirt. He was light-skinned like his mother, Janice, but tall like his father, Cutthroat. He was 31 years old, Cutthroat's first child.

Shelton started King Financial over two years ago. Impoverished families could come to King Financial to acquire loans when banks turned their backs. Low monthly payments and low interest rates helped inner-city residents pay back loans with ease, therefore making King Financial an esteemed company in the community and bringing families closer to freedom from debt.

But there was more to the company that the public didn't know about.

The majority of Shelton's income came from bigshot drug dealers from all over the country. Shelton laundered money for them. But he never provided that service for dealers in Kansas City because he didn't believe in doing dirt in his own backyard.

Tre Pound was licking his fingers when Shelton hung up the phone.

"You didn't save me none?" Shelton asked.

"I would've, but all them vultures you got flying around out there swooped down on me." Tre Pound tossed the box in the trash. "Why you got only women working here now?"

"They more trustworthy in business environments. Men's egos get in the way when workin' for other men, especially wit' me being fairly young. And I remember readin' somethin' Marcus Garvey wrote. He talked about how every woman he employed played fair and true. But damn near every man he placed in a position of trust abused it. However, I do got a couple men working for me. Like my lawyer. And speaking of lawyers—yours called me this morning. That's what I needed to talk to you about."

"Why didn't he just call me?"

"He said he tried to."

Tre Pound checked his phone. He had several missed calls, mostly from Michelle, a couple from Camille, but two were from his lawyer, Carlo Masaccio. "That's Michelle's fault," he said. "She made me miss his call. I spent the night over there and she was callin' all night lookin' for Gutta, so I stopped answering. Then she started callin' my phone this morning; I stopped answering that, too. I was tryin' to get some sleep."

"Where was Gutta at?"

"He left to go rob a jewelry store wit' Tommy and Tony and never came back. I didn't tell Michelle where he went, but I told her to call me if he ain't back by this evening."

Shelton sighed. "Gutta didn't have no business fuckin' wit' them two. Everybody knows the Feds been tryin' to catch Tommy and Tony. Now he probably got hisself caught up."

Tre Pound shook his head, hoping Gutta turned up soon. "So what was the lawyer talkin' about?"

The plush office chair squeaked when Shelton leaned back into it. He looked concerned. "The jury is done deliberating. You gotta be in court tomorrow morning at eight o' clock."

"Tomorrow?" Tre Pound's heart started beating faster. For some reason, he thought this day would never come. He thought the courts would just forget about him, skip over him and prosecute somebody else. He wasn't supposed to go to prison.

"How you feelin'?" Shelton asked.

Tre Pound shrugged. "I'm feelin' the same as I always do," he lied.

"Are you?"

"How am I supposed to feel? I'm ready to get this over wit'. If I get found guilty, then I get found guilty. I don't wanna go to the joint, but shit, what can I do? It's no longer in my hands."

"Whatever happens, you know you got family behind you. If they convict you, you still got the appeals process and other options. It won't be the end. We gon' make it through this together."

Slapping the top of the armrests, Tre Pound stood up. He gave Shelton dap across the desk. "This could be my last day on the street; I'ma try and enjoy it."

"I can close up early today. I got a quarter-pound of weed left at the house. We can smoke and I can woop you in some *Madden* like I used to do."

"I'ma have to pass on that," Tre Pound said, letting out a short chuckle. "I already got somethin' else in mind."

CHAPTER 9

Buttercup lay flat on her back in her nakedness. "Beat it up, Daddy!" The satin sheets wrinkled and rustled under her, as Tre Pound savagely jabbed his manhood inside her slippery pussy.

She was a sexy 19-year-old waitress/student, light-skinned, stretching only 5'4" with her legs spread eagle. Tre Pound's dark brown immense body seemed to engulf her. But she exercised regularly, was lithe and toned, and could withstand his passionate abuse.

"I can take it, Daddy! Hurt me!" she screamed.

Tre Pound grunted like a charging gorilla, fucking her relentlessly. He was only without his shirt. His boxers and Evisu jeans were pulled down just below his ass. He still had on his jewelry, socks and a pair of never-worn-before Rockport boots. As he hovered over her, working up a good sweat, his platinum chain hung from his neck and the crown pendant rested against Buttercup's chest. She flipped the pendant over to the other side because the diamonds were scratching her breasts.

The headboard banged against the wall with every thrust. Buttercup moaned loudly, experiencing a divine orgasm. Her toes curled and her entire body quivered.

Tre Pound withdrew, sat up and held his dick in his hand and began jacking off.

"Try not to get it in my hair again. Please, Daddy?" She closed her eyes and stuck her tongue out.

"I'm 'bout to bust, B," he panted right before he ejaculated. Cum squirted out the head of his rigid dick and landed on her lips and squirmy tongue. More cum shot out that fell short and spattered her breasts.

She licked her lips and rubbed his semen into her body. "That was the shit," she said, exhausted.

Sitting on the edge of the bed, Tre Pound pulled up his boxers, his jeans. He reached for his black T-shirt.

"I hate not knowing if I'm ever going to see you again," Buttercup said, sounding heartbroken.

"Hmph." He checked his pockets—all his money was there.

"You supposed to be out here wit' me, not in somebody's jail. Whatever you need me to do, I'll do it. I'll write the judge. I did that for my ex-boyfriend and it helped him. How can I help?"

Tre Pound cut his eyes at her to see if what she was saying was genuine. He couldn't tell. "Yeah, that sounds good," he said sarcastically. "But you and I both know that you could care less about what happens to me. Quit actin' like you give a fuck."

"Tre Pound, I have feelings for you. Feelings I never felt for anybody before." She moved closer to him. "You tell me you don't wanna be my man because you don't know if I'll be a devoted girlfriend. What will it take for me to convince you? I'm willing to stick by you through whatever."

"You know how many times bitches told me shit like that? Why should I believe you? You a slut. Look how we met."

Buttercup was shocked, deeply hurt. She was close to tears. Why would he bring that up? Why would he use that against her?

Tre Pound met Buttercup through Playa Paul about a month ago. Playa Paul used to brag about how he met this "bad-ass bitch" that worked at Red Lobster. "Her name's Buttercup. She look better than all yo bitches put together," he had said to Tre Pound.

One day, Playa Paul took Tre Pound to Buttercup's house to show her off. Playa Paul went straight into her bedroom and fucked her while Tre Pound waited in the living room on the couch. After Playa Paul finished sexing her down, he went to the bathroom to pee. But by the time he came out, he was stunned—Tre Pound was in the bedroom with Buttercup, digging deep into her, making her moan in a way Playa Paul never had.

Now, Buttercup felt bad about what she did. "You the only person I ever let run a train on me," she confided in Tre Pound. "I never did that before then and I haven't did it since. A slut? Is that what you think of me?"

"I just call it like I see it."

"But I haven't messed with Paul at all since I started seeing you. He called the other day asking could he come see me; I told him no. I don't want him. I want you."

"What happens if I get some time? You gon' find somebody else to replace me wit' no hesitation," Tre Pound said, making sure his jewelry was on correctly.

"No, I'm not. When I'm committed to somebody, I'm committed. I wouldn't give up on you when you need me most."

"All I am is dick to you. And all you are is a piece of pussy." He stood to leave. "You want a relationship?" he asked, and scoffed at the idea. "You must think I'm a sucka. You ain't even my type of bitch. Tre block."

***

It was getting dark outside. The streetlights began flicking on as Tre Pound drove his luxury car down Troost Avenue. He clicked on his own lights.

Leaning back comfortably in the ostrich-leather driver seat, one hand gripping the woodgrain steering wheel, he cruised silently in deep thought. He had called Marlon to tell him about his court date tomorrow, and Marlon suggested everybody get together at his house. Tre Pound had promised to be there.

But now Joy was on his mind. He needed to know who was clever enough to use her to get to him. He needed to know now. There might not be a tomorrow.

As Tre Pound neared 35th and Prospect, he saw a group of teenage hustlers milling around on the corner, in front of a tobacco store. One of them waved at him, trying to flag him down. It seemed like a friendly wave so Tre Pound pulled over.

Two of the hustlers standing on the corner turned out to be none other than his little cousins, Cash and Seneca. Cash was the oldest of the two, 16 years old, and somewhat street-wise for his age. He was tall and handsome in a rugged way. Seneca was a little bit shorter and chubbier, and not as mature; but he was only 14.

Tre Pound felt responsible for both of them, and whenever he was around, he'd instill in them the codes of the streets—and which ones could be broken.

The brothers approached the car. Cash hopped in and Seneca just leaned against the passenger side window.

"What yall doin' out here?" Tre Pound asked. "I know yall ain't out here hustling on the corner. Yall bigger than that. Yall Kings."

"We ain't sellin' nothin'," Cash said.

"We waitin' on them to get done hustling," Seneca chimed in, nodding towards the other teenagers standing on the corner. He pulled out his pistol, a 9mm similar to Tre Pound's. "Then we gon' rob 'em!" He smiled, the upper row of his teeth encased in platinum and diamonds.

"Stop flashin' that," Cash told him. Seneca tucked his gun. "And quit talkin' so loud. You don't want them to know what we 'bout to do, do you?"

Tre Pound grinned. His cousins learned from the best.

"Wussup, Tre Pound?" greeted a boy who had a wallet chain hanging from his baggy jeans. Then a few of the other teenage hustlers standing on the corner gained enough courage to speak.

"Tre Pound, yo car is tight."

"Seneca, tell Tre Pound I said wussup."

"What it is, Tre Pound? I rep the Tre too."

Tre Pound ignored them and asked his cousins, "What yall flag me down for?"

"Momma just got through tellin' us yo last court thing is tomorrow," Seneca said.

"She want us to be there," Cash added. "We just wanted to wish you luck. We behind you, cousin."

"I appreciate that support. But luck ain't got nothin' to do wit' the outcome of my trial. I don't believe in luck. I believe in the money me and Shelton spent on my lawyer. I believe in my lawyer's expertise. The hours of research, the investigations and the questioning of witnesses. I believe the jury can say fuck all of that and fuck my life up. Luck don't exist. Not in my trial."

Across the street at the gas station, Young Ray walked out carrying a two-liter Coca Cola in a plastic bag. He stuffed his change in his baggy pants. He was a skinny

18-year-old, and his belt strap was torn so his pants sagged lower than normal.

He took a look across the street and saw a group of hustlers loitering. He didn't have 20/20 vision and couldn't make out any faces, and he would've overlooked them had it not been for the creme-colored Infiniti Q45 sitting on 22-inch chrome Lexani wheels parked over there. Those were *his* rims!

Young Ray immediately rushed to his own car, a beat-up, off-white El Camino bucket. "Dynisha, look," he said to his sister anxiously, pointing over at the Infiniti. "How could you not see him?"

"See who?" Dynisha was in the passenger seat skimming through an *Essence* magazine. People told her she looked like the actress Malinda Williams and she was trying to find her to see what recent hairstyle Malinda had so she could copy it.

"You ain't even lookin'."

Dynisha smacked shut the magazine and snapped her head around towards the street. "What am I supposed to be lookin' at? I don't see—" Then she saw it. The Infiniti. The rims. Tre Pound. "Let me out this car!" she roared, yanking on the door handle. Remembering how to open it, she rolled down the window and opened the door from the outside.

"What you about to do?" Young Ray asked. He didn't think this was a good time to confront Tre Pound. All those people were over there.

"I'm 'bout to get our muthafuckin' shit back!"

As Dynisha stormed into the street, slowing up traffic, Tre Pound spotted her. He saw Young Ray following close behind. Instinctively, Tre Pound felt his waist to make sure his 9mm Browning was still there.

"Ain't that the dude me and Seneca took the rims from?" Cash asked.

"Yeah," Tre Pound responded, getting out the car. "Stay alert."

Dynisha got in his face. "You took my DVDs, lousy muthafucka!"

"Bitch, don't ever come up to me like that," Tre Pound said, holding up his hand in a stop gesture.

"You ain't gotta call my sister a bitch," Young Ray muttered.

Tre Pound looked him up and down like he was worth nothing. "Shut the fuck up, you little street punk."

"I want my shit back, Tre Pound," Dynisha demanded.

"What I take from you?"

"You got my *Martin: Season One* and my *Shrek 2*."

Those DVDs belonged to Camille now. Camille had been searching different retail stores for them and couldn't find them, so when Tre Pound found out Dynisha had them, he took them.

"That's why you testified against me?" he asked in disbelief. "Because you think I took some fuckin' DVDs from you?"

"Why you tryna say it like you didn't do it? I know you da one who took 'em."

"How you know?"

"Because you asked me did I have 'em. And you was the last person at my house when they came up missin'. And you took my brother's rims, you bastard! You can act like you didn't take my DVDs but you can't say you didn't take his rims because they on yo goddamn car!"

Tre Pound folded his arms. "I bought these from somebody."

"You's a goddamn lie!" Dynisha screamed.

"Them is mines," Young Ray interjected. "I can tell by lookin' at 'em. I was the only one in the city wit' Lexanis."

"And it don't matter who you got 'em from," Dynisha added. "They his. You knew they was his when you supposedly bought 'em."

"You don't even need wheels like these," Tre Pound said while mean-mugging Young Ray. "They didn't even look right on that raggedy-ass El Camino you got over there."

"So you admitting you knew they was his," Dynisha said, exasperated.

"I'll tell yall what," Tre Pound proposed. "Yall pay me what I paid for the rims, and pay me for the Pirelli tires I put on 'em and I'll give 'em back."

Young Ray looked appalled. "Buy my own rims back?"

"You got us fucked up!" Dynisha spat.

"I got yall fucked up? Yall got me fucked up!" Tre Pound said, suddenly getting riled up. "Yall expect me to just give these rims back for free when you, Dynisha, just got through testifying against me in court? You snitched on me, ho!"

"So what I snitched on you," she retorted, and rolled her eyes. "I don't care about them street laws or whatever. Anybody that steal from me or my brother, I'ma get back at 'em where it hurts. I'll tell on all you niggas out here if yall cross me! Every single last one of you niggas!"

Mumbling and cursing arose from the hustlers standing on the corner. "Tell on me, bitch, and I'ma kill you," one of them said.

Young Ray, feeling threatened and outnumbered, casually reached under his shirt.

Tre Pound was so busy grimacing at Dynisha that he didn't see Young Ray's hand move.

"The only reason I ain't smoked you yet is because I don't want that backlash from the police," Tre Pound informed her. "But let me get some time, bitch. I'ma have you touched! Don't think I can't have it done. You know I can, bitch."

Suddenly, Young Ray pulled out his long, shiny 454 revolver and aimed it at Tre Pound's chest. Startled, Tre Pound slowly began putting his hands up.

"I told you not to call my sister a bitch!" Young Ray hollered.

"Now give me the keys to yo—" he started, but something solid cracked him in the back of his cranium. Seneca had crept around the car and knocked him upside the head with the butt of his pistol. Young Ray fell against the car, collapsing to the asphalt.

Tre Pound was fuming now.

"Ray!" That was all Dynisha had a chance to say before Tre Pound cocked back and let his fist fly into her mouth. The blow was so powerful it shattered her front teeth and sent her stumbling several steps back into the street. Before she had a chance to fall, a speeding yellow Hummer H2 crashed into her. She rolled up on the hood and her body smashed into the windshield.

Beside the Infiniti Q45, Cash and Seneca were brutally stomping Young Ray. Tre Pound got a couple kicks in himself before he said, "That's enough! I don't want yall to catch a murder, too. It's too many witnesses out here. Yall burn out."

While hopping in and starting up his car, Tre Pound watched to see if Dynisha moved. She lay sprawled out in the middle of the street with a bloody face and a contorted arm, which looked broken. The driver of the Hummer had stopped for a moment, then kept on driving.

Was she dead?

Tre Pound hoped so. Bitch shouldn't have snitched on him. She deserved death.

Hearing police sirens in the distance, he shifted the car in gear and reversed over Young Ray's legs. He spun the car around and veered down a backstreet. Somebody else deserved to die too.

CHAPTER 10

Joy and her girlfriend, Latrice, lay curled up next to each other on the couch. They were sound asleep. Joy had on nothing but a pair of panties and Latrice slept in a wife beater and her red, polka-dotted boxers. A bottle of half-empty Grey Goose sat on the coffee table next to a dead roach. The TV was on. Latrice's snoring was louder than the commercials.

The snoring awoke Joy. Her 36DD breasts flopped down as she sat up, untangling Latrice's arms from around her. Joy used the remote to check the time on the TV. It was 11:16 p.m.

Then she heard a loud crunching sound. She thought the mice had gotten into the chips again so she stood up, put on her robe. When she turned the corner into the kitchen, she jumped, let out a high-pitched yelp. She hurried up and covered her mouth, hoping she didn't awake Latrice.

Tre Pound sat on a stool at the kitchen counter. He ate from a bag of barbecue potato chips, wearing black-and-white Nike baseball gloves. "You don't look that good when you first wake up," he commented, chewing loudly.

Joy was frightened. There was a pistol laying on the countertop. "How did you get in my house?"

"The window in the upstairs bathroom. Most people leave it unlocked or open, thinking nobody would go through the trouble to get in that way. That's how my uncle used to break in houses."

"What are you doing here? My girlfriend will kill you and me if she finds out you're here."

"You tried to set me up."

Joy looked shocked. "Set you up? How? When?"

"You know when."

"Are you talkin' about last night? Is that why you left so quick? Why would you think I would do somethin' like that?"

"I'm upset and disappointed in you right now. Keep playin' dumb and I'ma get mad." He crunched down on another chip. "It's in yo best interest to be up front wit' me."

She took a deep breath. "A'ight, Tre Pound. I'm sorry."

"Now we gettin' somewhere," he said, dusting his gloved hands of the crumbs.

"Somethin' told me not to try it. You ain't never did nothin' wrong to me. You called me some names before 'cause I wouldn't have sex wit' you—but that's still not a good enough reason to set you up. But I needed the money. And I didn't think you'd be all that mad if somebody took yo rims. Because I heard you stole 'em from somebody anyway." She paused. "Why you lookin' at me like that? I'm tryna tell you I'm sorry for tryna take yo rims."

"Rims? You mean to tell me you know them little kids I shot at? You had them try and jack me?"

"Yeah. They stay down the street. I'll show you where they live," she offered.

Tre Pound shook his head, an incredulous smile on his face. "Joy, you amaze me."

"I'm being up front wit' you, though. What more do you want? I can tell you I'm sorry a thousand times—and I'd mean it—but that still won't take back what I did, or tried to do. Don't do nothin' to me, Tre Pound. It's not worth it." She wiped a tear from her eye with her palm, then glanced around the corner at the sofa. "Now will you please go," she whispered. "I'll make it up to you somehow. I feel bad. I'll suck yo dick or somethin'. But not now. Now you gotta go."

"Who tried to kill me, Joy?"

She stiffened. "Huh?"

"I said who tried to kill me!" he barked. "You had a nigga in this house last night waitin' on me. Who the fuck was it?"

Joy started sweating. How did he find out? she wondered. She was guilty, and she knew he could see the guilt on her face.

"Baby! Joy, where you at? I'm hungry." Latrice was awake now. She yawned heavily.

"Tre Pound, I'll explain everything to you later," Joy said rapidly. "But I need you to go. *Please.*"

"Give me his name," Tre Pound demanded.

"Baby! Is that you in the kitchen?"

Joy wiped sweat from her brow, her face, panicking. "She's comin'. My girlfriend is comin'. You can't just sit there."

Tre Pound didn't move.

"Kaliko! It was Kaliko. There, I told you. Now *go.*"

Latrice was halfway to the kitchen when Joy blocked her path. "Who was you talkin' to?" Latrice questioned.

"I wasn't talkin' to nobody. I was just singin'," Joy said, wrapping her arms around her lover.

Latrice stood taller than Joy and had a natural bulky physique, broad shoulders. She was just as strong as an athletic man, if not stronger. Her big lips smooched Joy's moist forehead. "Girl, why you sweatin'?"

"It's hot in here. Ain't you hot?"

"Standing next to you, I am." Latrice tongue-kissed Joy, opened up her robe and fondled her titties.

"Well, maybe we should go upstairs and take a bubble bath together. You can wash my back. Get some of this stickiness off of me. So do an about-face and let's get to it."

"Before we do that, I need you to line up my fade," Latrice said. "I found some clippers on the job today that still work good. And I'm starving. A bitch gotta eat before she do anything. You in my way girl, move."

"You ain't gotta go in the kitchen. I'll fix you somethin' to eat and bring it up there to you. We can dine in the tub. Just go get the water ready. And while we waitin' for the food to cook and the water to cool off, I'll line you up."

"You don't understand. My stomach is touchin' my back. I need to put somethin' in it asap." Latrice tried to walk past, but Joy grabbed her arm.

"The snacks are gone. I'ma have to cook up a couple cheesy eggs for you. That's all we got left. You're gonna have to wait, though. So go get the water ready while I do my thang down here."

"I know it's somethin' here to snack on. I can smell the chips. Joy, what's wrong wit' you? It's like you don't want me to go in the kitchen. What you hidin' from me in there?" Latrice had to practically drag Joy because she wouldn't let her arm go. Joy pulled and tugged while leaning back, but Latrice overpowered her and drug her along.

"Latrice, wait. Listen to me!"

When Latrice turned the corner into the kitchen with Joy holding on, Latrice said, "Is this what you was tryna hide from me? I knew it was still some chips left."

Joy let her arm go. She looked around the kitchen in bewilderment. Tre Pound was gone. How did he get upstairs and out the window without them seeing him? Or did he get out another way? She didn't know, but her anxiety had disappeared. She breathed easily.

"You tried to keep 'em for yo'self," Latrice said, snatching the bag off the counter. She stood there stuffing barbecue chips into her mouth. "Greedy heffa. You know I'ma beat that ass for that."

Smiling, Joy said, "Can I have somethin' to myself for once?" She took the bag. "You eat everything up. These is mines."

"Okay, just give me a couple more."

"No. Take yo big butt upstairs and do what I told you to do."

Latrice laughed. "Bitch, who you talkin' to? I wear the pants in this relationship."

"Says who?"

"Says me." Latrice backed Joy up against the countertop, lifted her up with ease and set her on top of it.

Joy put her arms around her girlfriend's neck and kissed her, then smiled. "You win. You wear the pants."

"Damn right. Now I'm 'bout to go get this water ready because I want to. And you gon' stay in this kitchen and cook my food. Ain't that right?"

"Yes, baby."

"And after you get done lining up my hair, you gon' feed me in the tub. Ain't that right?"

"We gonna feed each other."

Latrice made a wry face.

"Sorry," Joy said, giggling. Then she corrected herself. "Yes, baby."

"And why are you gon' do what I say?"

"Because you wear the pants."

"And don't you forget it."

Joy was smiling brightly, swinging her legs, as Latrice strutted proudly out the kitchen. She loved Latrice with all her heart. No man could make her feel as enamored, treasured, and secure like Latrice could. They were supposed to go get married this summer, if Latrice didn't get cold feet again.

As soon as Latrice walked out the kitchen, the unexpected happened. Tre Pound appeared from around the corner and bashed her in the head with the Grey Goose bottle, shattering glass, splashing alcohol everywhere. Surprisingly, Latrice didn't fall. She stumbled against the wall, holding her bleeding noggin.

"Get away from her!" Joy jumped down and rushed to Latrice's side. "Tre Pound, why did you do that? I told you what you wanted to know! Baby, are you hurt bad?"

Latrice moaned in pain.

"We still got some unfinished business," Tre Pound said. Liquor had spilled all over his hands; he wiped them on the thighs of his jeans.

"You hit Latrice for no reason. She didn't have nothin' to do with it. Yo problem is wit' me, not her."

Latrice pushed Joy to the side and started to charge Tre Pound, but she stopped abruptly when he leveled his 9mm at her.

"This got a 13-round clip. Fourteen wit' one in the head," he told her. "See, that's why I busted that bottle over yo fat dome. Tried to knock yo stocky ass out so I wouldn't have to deal wit' you. But I ain't got a problem wit' poppin' yo ass."

"Tre Pound, why are you in my house?" Latrice growled.

"Ask yo bitch."

When Latrice snapped her head around, Joy felt compelled to explain. "I invited him over here yesterday night," she said.

"You what?!" Latrice backhanded Joy to the carpet. "I work my ass off jumpin' up and down off trash trucks, smellin' everybody's filth all day to provide for you; all night I'm loading heavy boxes on UPS trucks, taking orders from dickhead supervisors. And you here givin' my pussy away to a man?! How could you do this to me?"

"It wasn't like that!" Joy sobbed.

"Then what was it like? Tell me what it was like before I kick the shit outta you, Joy."

"I didn't—I didn't fuck him. I made him think I was to get him over here. I tried to ... set him up. For Kaliko. Kaliko was gonna pay me $13,000 to trick Tre Pound into comin' over so he could kill him. But I guess Tre Pound found out what was goin' on somehow."

"Tell her about the rims, too," Tre Pound said.

"I tried to take his rims, too. I had Scooter from down the street and his little friends do it, but they made the car alarm go off and Tre Pound came out shooting at 'em. The whole thing was stupid of me."

"You did all this behind my back?" Latrice asked. Blood

ran down her face and dripped onto her wife beater. "For money? I guess what I do for you ain't enough, huh?"

Joy was crying. "It is enough, baby. You do more than enough for me. I'm happy with what we have. I was just tryna do somethin' for you. Get some money to ease yo struggles."

"When was you gonna tell me about this? You would've had to tell me where the money came from. Where is the money?"

"Kaliko didn't even pay me. But he was supposed to pay me ... even if it didn't go as planned."

"So you end up gettin' played in the end. I'm bleeding because of you. Bringin' this drama in our lives." Latrice pulled Joy to her feet and held her close, then turned to Tre Pound. "I don't care what she did. I'm not lettin' you harm her. You already busted me up. What else do you want? You need to be out there lookin' for Kaliko."

"I ain't got time to be lookin' for him," Tre Pound said. "He gotta come to me. Joy gotta help me wit' that."

"I'll help you," Joy said emphatically. "Kaliko ain't shit. He cheated me."

"What do you want her to do?" Latrice questioned.

"She gotta get him to come over here," he said. "The same way she did me."

"But think about that, Tre Pound," Joy responded. "Kaliko will be suspicious because he just had me try and set you up. What makes you think he'll fall for the same thing? Niggas is not that stupid."

***

Kaliko applied Chap Stick to his lips as he hurried up to Joy's front door. He pounded on it. "I hear you in there, girl!"

"I'll be there in a minute," he heard Joy say.

A few seconds passed.

"Can I come in now?"

"Not Yet!" she called.

Unwilling to wait any longer, Kaliko opened the door and walked on in. Joy was in the middle of putting a plastic covering over the sofa. Her robe was open, exposing her bare breasts, and she suddenly closed it when she saw Kaliko.

"How are you just gon' walk up in my house?" she snapped. "Yo momma ain't teach you better than that? I didn't tell you to come in yet."

"I know what you tryna do," he told her. "I'm not goin' for it." Then he reached in his pocket, walking towards her.

He was going for his gun! Joy thought. Panicking, she started backing up.

"You tryna act like you don't want me as bad as I want you," he cooed, pulling out a condom.

Joy choked out a sigh of relief.

"Makin' me wait outside. Tryna make me think you ain't eager to get on this dick. I ain't dumb. I got five sisters. I know all about the games you girls play."

"Thought you didn't wanna fuck me. You said I wasn't yo type, remember?"

"I said that?"

Joy rolled her neck. "Yes."

"Tricked yo ass. Reverse psychology is a mufucka. I made you think I didn't like you so you'll like me more. I planted that seed in yo head and it grew and grew until you couldn't take it no more. Your need for me to like you forced you to call me."

"You think you so smart."

"I know I am." He attempted to open up her robe but she wouldn't let him.

"I'm still mad at you for not payin' me my money," Joy said.

"No, you not. You wouldn't have told me to come over if you was." Kaliko kissed her. She didn't kiss him back. "C'mon, Joy, you ain't gotta act like this. I already got you figured out. You miss dick. You can't hold out forever." He kissed her again. This time she moved her lips with his. "Told you so," he said.

"Have a seat on that couch," she instructed. "I'ma put on some music."

The door on the old cassette player was broken so she tuned the radio to Hot 103 Jamz and turned it up.

"Why you got this plastic thing on here?" Kaliko asked.

"So won't no stains get on it. My girlfriend Latrice is like a detective. She'll notice cum stains on her couch."

"Where she at? Workin' late again?" He kicked his feet up on the coffee table; Joy knocked them right back down.

"Yes, she is. But that don't mean you can get comfortable." She stood in front of him with her arms folded, looking down at him impatiently. "Why are you still dressed?"

"That's a good question." Kaliko started unbuttoning his shirt, shrugging his shoulders and bobbing his head to the beat. Joy laughed at his pathetic attempt to striptease. "Uh-huh. You laughin' but I know you gettin' wet," he said, flinging his shirt at her. She set it on the coffee table.

He had a .40-caliber pistol tucked in the small of his back that he laid on top of his shirt. He kept up his carnal dance until he was down to his briefs.

"Them, too," she said.

He removed his underwear and rolled an orange-colored condom over his rock-hard member. "Now when do I get to see you naked? It better be soon 'cause this plastic is stickin' to my ass cheeks."

"You don't get to see me naked."

"Well, how do you expect me to make love to you then?"

Joy fished out a red bandanna from her robe pocket. "Blindfolded," she replied.

"I knew you was a freak. I can only imagine what else you got in store for me. I'm down for anythang! You got some beads?"

"No, but I do got a couple more surprises." She tied the rag around his head and told him to lay on his back. He got into position willingly and she sat on top of him. "No peeking."

"I can't see a thing," he said. "But you squishing my nigga down there. Let me stick it in."

"Patience, Kaliko. First, you gotta get to know my body."

She brought his face to her chest and let him suck on her nipples. That was when the basement door opened and Tre Pound stuck his head out. "His gun," Joy mouthed, pointing to the clothes stacked on the coffee table. Tre Pound nodded and crept on out.

"These suckas is soft," Kaliko uttered, tonguing each breast equally. "I can tell they real. They too big and mushy to be fake. I wanna see 'em."

"Not yet," Joy said, watching Tre Pound search slowly and silently through Kaliko's clothes.

"I'm not even a tittie man. But yours could change me, Joy." Kaliko kissed and kneaded her flesh. "By law, I'm an ass man." He dipped his hands into her panties, squeezed her buttocks, then rubbed up and down her back aggressively. He proceeded to caress more of Joy's shapely figure but she made a disgusted noise and immediately hopped up off of him.

"I'm so glad that's over," Joy said. "Yuck."

"What I do?" Then came the sound of a handgun cocking back. Kaliko snatched off the red bandanna. His eyes bulged out when he saw his own gun in Tre Pound's hand.

"If you gon' set a nigga up, do it right." Tre Pound shot him.

"Ahh!" Kaliko squealed, holding his punctured rib. "Why you doin' this? You robbed me!"

"You brought this on yo'self. What I stole from you, you should've just accepted it, took it as a loss like everybody else I rob. But you wanna be a renegade."

"Tre Pound, you ain't gotta explain nothin' to him," Joy said. "Kill him and get it over wit."

"Joy, shut up!" Kaliko screamed.

"You shut up. You should've paid me my money and you wouldn't be in this predicament."

Tre Pound shot him again. Kaliko writhed in pain and doubled over onto the carpet floor. With bloody hands, he reached out to Joy to grab her, choke her, take her with him, but she backed up so fast she tripped over a cardboard box filled with old clothes. Tre Pound fired upon Kaliko five more times, and he went down for good.

"You let him get off the couch," Joy complained, as she stood back up. "You was supposed to shoot him on the plastic. That's what I put it on for. I didn't wanna have to do no scrubbing." She proceeded to the basement door. "You didn't tie nothin' over Latrice's mouth, did you?"

"Nope."

"Good. 'Cause she got asthma." Joy opened the basement door, clicked on the wall light. Latrice lay at the bottom of the steps, hands tied behind her back with an extension cord. But Joy saw something ... there was a pool

101

of blood and a wide gash across Latrice's neck! Joy spotted a butcher knife beside the body and a horrifying scream erupted from her throat.

Tre Pound shot Joy twice in the spine, killing her instantly. She tumbled down the steps and landed on top of her lover.

He clicked the light off.

CHAPTER 11

That same night, in the upstairs bedroom of the King household, the girls laughed hysterically as they watched *Martin: Season One* on DVD. Camille had convinced her mother to let Dominique Hayes and Krystal Hamilton spend the night on a school night so they could practice their dance moves for the talent show tomorrow. They had already practiced, and were having fun watching Martin portray a rowdy security guard. Krystal was almost in tears she was laughing so hard.

Down the hall, Janice was trying to sleep. With curlers in her hair, she got up and stomped to Camille's room and flung open the door. "There's no reason for yall to be screamin' so damn loud! It's after midnight!" She eyeballed the girls. "I thought yall was supposed to be practicing."

"We done, Momma," Camille mumbled.

"Well, why are yall sittin' around the TV makin' all this noise and yall gotta get up early for school? It don't make no sense."

"We'll keep it down."

"Turn the damn TV off! If I come back in here and yall ain't sleep, you girls is going home. And Camille, you know what I'ma do to you. Try me."

After Janice left, Krystal said, "I'm sorry, Camille. I didn't mean to laugh that loud." Krystal was a 15-year-old sophomore who attended Southeast, too. She was an attractive, light-complexioned slender-bodied girl. She had been friends with Camille and Dominique since 8th grade.

"It wasn't yo fault. My momma is just mean." Camille turned the TV off. "She don't like me and I don't like that bitch either."

"Don't say that." Dominique pushed Camille. "At least you still got yo momma. You should be grateful. My momma died from leukemia and my father died fighting in Iraq. All I got left is my brother."

"I'm grateful. I love my momma. I just wished she'd love me in return, that's all."

"She does," Dominique assured her.

"I can't tell."

Camille crawled into her queen-size bed and Krystal shimmied into the sleeping bag on the floor. The futon, where Dominique chose to sleep, was positioned in a couch frame. She stretched out on it and snuggled under a fur throw.

"You didn't forget about the hundred bucks, did you, Camille?" asked Krystal.

"What hundred bucks?"

"For doin' yo hair, nails. Yo toes."

"Hundred? What happened to seventy-five?"

Dominique snickered. "Her boyfriend need some extra money."

Camille thought the same thing. "My money ain't 'bout to go to yo boyfriend, Krystal. I refuse to be a nigga's ATM. And don't he got his own money? Ain't he hustling?"

"It's not about my boyfriend. I just feel like I be doin' a good job and should be paid for it," Krystal said. "I don't be givin' all my money to Moses. Just some. Yeah, he hustles, but he needs my help until he gets where he needs to be in the game."

For as long as Camille and Dominique could remember, Krystal had been a giving person. In 8th grade, she'd give her lunch money to the first boy who asked for it. One boy talked her into bringing all her Halloween candy to school. Camille and Dominique befriended Krystal to protect her. She stopped giving stuff to any and everybody, but she found it hard to say no to boyfriends.

Like Moses, her recent boyfriend. He took constant advantage of Krystal's kindheartedness. Whenever his car broke down, she'd be the one paying to get it fixed. If he needed some re-cop money, he'd suggest it and she'd make it happen. Though her friends thought she was being used, Krystal saw it as standing by her man.

"If a man only wants you for your money, then he's not a man. He's a beast," Dominique said. "And beasts do not deserve to be in relationships wit' girls like us. Leave 'em in the wild."

"Moses is not a beast. He's a man. My man," Krystal stated.

"I don't mind payin' you for yo services. You do be doin' a good job," Camille complimented; Krystal thanked her. "I'll get the money from Tre Pound tomorrow. Have him bring it up to the school."

"Won't he be at court?" Dominique mentioned.

"Oh, that's right," Camille said with her mouth wide open, ashamed that it had slipped her mind. Earlier this morning she had tried to call her cousin to apologize for saying she hoped he got the electric chair, but he didn't answer. This evening she tried him again but got the voice mail. She didn't get to tell him sorry, goodbye, good luck, or nothing. Saddened, she said, "I'll get the money from somebody, Krystal. Do you need it right away?"

"Whenever," Krystal chirped.

Dominique scratched her shoulder because the fur throw itched. "I wonder what's gonna happen to Tre Pound. Didn't they find his prints on the gun?"

"Not the gun, one of the bullets," Camille corrected. "On the shell, I think. Tre Pound said that's even worse than havin' yo prints on the gun. But he said he didn't do it and that his lawyer said he was gon' beat it."

"Do you think he did it?" Krystal asked.

"I don't know," Camille said. However, she did think he killed Drought Man. She knew her cousin was a

106

cold-blooded killer. Before the Drought Man murder, she heard her mother and Shelton talking about some stick-up kid that Tre Pound killed. But Camille wasn't about to share that information with her friends. "Whether he did it or not, he's still my cousin. And I don't wanna see him in jail. He's my favorite cousin. I love him."

"I love him, too." Dominique had often dreamed of having Tre Pound's children. Though no one knew it, she touched his dick before, and planned on letting him be her first after they got married. But her dream would never come true if Tre Pound got convicted.

"What did you just say?" Camille and Krystal asked almost simultaneously. Camille sat up.

Snapping out of her reverie, Dominique looked at both of her friends, her mind a little blurred. "I said somethin'? I didn't say nothin'."

"We both heard you, girl," Camille stated. "You said you love my cousin."

Dominique didn't know she had spoken out loud. She smiled sheepishly. "Yall can't take a joke?"

"No, but you can take an ass whoopin'," Camille retorted, and they all laughed. "But that ain't nothin' to play about, Dominique. Fa-real. You can like Tre Pound, but you can't love him. We don't mess wit' each other's family members or boyfriends. That's the rules."

"Speaking of boyfriends," Dominique said, flipping the conversation, "what's the deal wit' you and Lil' Pat?"

Camille flopped into her pillow and yanked the covers over her head. "I don't wanna talk about it."

"You gotta tell us," Krystal said, sounding excited. "Everybody already think yall broken up because you avoided him the whole day today at school. Are yall still together or not?"

"Not," Camille murmured from under the covers.

"I don't blame you," said Dominique. "I would've dumped him, too. Ain't no point in being wit' a nigga that won't stand up for you."

Krystal saw it differently. "But what guy our age will stand up to Tre Pound? Lil' Pat didn't stand a chance. He *had* to run. Look what happened to Camille's last boyfriend, J-Dub: he got beat up so bad by Tre Pound that he had to go to the hospital for stitches."

"You can't blame it all on Tre Pound, though," Dominique countered. "Lil' Pat knew what happened to J-Dub when he hooked up wit' Camille. Lil' Pat knew what he was gettin' into. You not supposed to leave yo girl's side no matter what. Tre Pound was doin' what he was supposed to do as Camille's cousin, which is to look out for her. Tre Pound might be a little overprotective but my brother is the same way. Wit' family like ours, me and Camille gotta find somebody strong. See, Krystal, you're the only child; you don't have overprotective family like we got, so you don't understand."

"I understand, I guess."

"Okay, now let's go to sleep," Camille said. She had a lot on her mind that she didn't want to discuss. She no longer had a boyfriend, and she wondered if she'd ever find one brave enough to love her. There was a burning desire between her thighs that needed to be soothed and she wouldn't let any ole body do it.

One time she had sex. Just once. And that was with her previous ex-boyfriend, J-Dub. He seemed perfect for her, and she was happy to share that experience with him, but it turned out that he'd rather break up with her than face her cousin.

Would she ever find the right man?

Camille hated Tre Pound for sabotaging her relationships. But the hate was nothing compared to the enormous love she had for him. She prayed he didn't get convicted, and before long she fell asleep worrying about him.

A while after Camille dozed off, Krystal was still up whispering into her cell phone. She had called Moses to tell him good night and ended up talking longer than expected.

Dominique lay on the futon, restless, waiting on Krystal to go to sleep so she could perform her nightly ritual. Krystal had been on the phone for over half an hour talking to her boyfriend. The lovebirds went back and forth with I-love-yous and promises that they'd be together forever and Dominique couldn't stand it anymore.

"Krystal, you better hang up before Camille's momma come in here again. You heard what she said."

"I'm being quiet."

"That don't mean nothin'. She still will send us home. We supposed to be sleep."

With a glum look, Krystal put the phone back up to her ear and said her sweet goodbyes. But it was still another five minutes before she hung up. Nestled within the sleeping bag, she soon drifted into a calm slumber.

Dominique closed her eyes. She slid her hand into her pajama bottoms, inside her black lace panties. As she thought of a strong-bodied, masculine Tre Pound, she rubbed her pussy lips gingerly. Long, manicured nails prevented her from sticking her fingers all the way in, but the rubbing was doing just fine. She moistened and she moaned in low whispers. In less than a minute she climaxed. It felt so good. She wanted more.

Unsatisfied, Dominique opened her eyes.

CHAPTER 12

Over on 51st and Garfield, the fellas hung out as they did almost every night. But being as though Tre Pound would meet his fate in the morning, tonight called for more Hennessy and more marijuana.

On the coffee table, in a hefty glass bowl, was a mountainous pile of crumpled, seedless weed. Marlon grabbed some and sprinkled it into his fourth cigarillo. As he licked the blunt from end to end, he looked over at Tre Pound, who was chugging down Hennessy straight from the bottle.

"Where you been at all day?" Marlon asked. "You show up here all after midnight. We been waitin' on you."

Tre Pound pulled the bottle from his lips. "Had to tie up some loose ends." He saw a little bit of liquor was left and downed the rest of it. Then he leaned against the back of the couch and closed his eyes.

"Uh-uhn. No you ain't," Marlon said, scooting to the edge of the armchair. He shook Tre Pound's knee. "I ain't lettin' you go to sleep. You kicked-it wit' everybody else all day and now you gon' kick-it wit' me."

"Everybody wanna see me dead or in jail," Tre Pound said, eyes still closed. "They gon' get they wish."

"Who's everybody? Because me and everybody I fuck wit' wanna see you alive and on the streets. Everybody else is some haters. And they really gon' hate it when you beat yo case tomorrow."

"What if I don't beat it and they give me football numbers? Shit, it don't matter what they give me. I ain't gon' make it. Do you know how many niggas it is in the pen that I done shot or robbed? Day one somebody gon' have me shanked in the weight room. I ain't checkin' into protective custody. I refuse to."

"You gotta be optimistic," Marlon said, taking a powerful pull on the cigarillo. He held in a cough and smoke spouted out his nose. "You should be askin' yo'self, 'What if I do beat it?' What kinda changes are you gon' make to prevent yo'self from gettin' in this situation again? Do you really need to rob people?"

"Yeah."

"Nah, you don't."

Tre Pound laughed drunkenly. Eyes shut, he could tell by the gruffness of Marlon's voice that he was frowning.

"I don't know why you do that shit, but it ain't for financial reasons," Marlon said. "You can go legit. With the successful business Shelton's running, he won't let you fall off on whatever field you choose to pursue. But one thing's for sure: if you beat yo case, you gotta get off the path that you on now."

"You sell dope," Tre Pound slurred. "You on the same path I'm on."

"I know, man. And it scares me. I don't wanna get all day in the penitentiary and leave Dominique out here all by herself. But I gotta hustle to keep a roof over her head. And I like seeing her in baguettes and up-to-date designer shit because it gives her ... an aura of self-confidence. She smiles so glowingly knowing she's the best dressed in school and can practically have anything she wants. Me, I can do without. And maybe I'm wrong for spoiling her like I do, but I can't help it. Right now I'm stackin' her college tuition. I want her to have the best."

Slowly, Tre Pound opened his eyes and peered over at Marlon, who was staring off into space evidently thinking about his sister's future. Tre Pound suddenly felt a tinge of guilt about his fling with Dominique.

Out of all of his homies, Marlon was the closest to him. They could talk to each other on a more serious level and shared similar impressions and outlooks on life. Though they disagreed on the need to be flashy with money, they both believed that life should be lived to the fullest, and that being broke was not an option. To them, a good life was a life lived according to what they thought was good, and not by what society determined.

They met each other through Stacks. Stacks' father and Tre Pound's father used to be co-workers and their families grew close. Stacks and Marlon met at Southeast High school. At a house party, Stacks introduced Marlon to Tre Pound and they became instant friends.

"Remember how we sandwiched Tara at that party a long time ago?" Tre Pound managed to say audibly.

Marlon smiled. "Yeah. That's when I first met you. What made you think of that?"

"Just popped in my head."

"Yeah, I remember seeing you dancin' wit' her from the back so I hopped on from the front like fuck it. I think she was the sexiest broad in the town at the time. She wouldn't near let me hit, though. Did you ever get to fuck?"

Tre Pound started thinking hard.

"Keep it real," Marlon said, sensing his boy was about to lie.

"Nope," Tre Pound confessed, and they both laughed. "I fingered her, though."

Moses had been sitting at the other end of the couch, talking to his girl Krystal on his cell. "You're my everything, too," he crooned. Then she told him she had to get off the phone because Camille's mother had warned them to go to sleep. To make her feel adored, he whined about having to end their engaging conversation so soon, which led to a few more minutes of lovey-doveyness.

He flipped his phone shut with a confident smile. "Some niggas don't have they bitch on lock," he said to no one in particular. "I, for one, seem not to have that problem.

nt ask? 'Cause I'm a muthafuckin' gangsta!

with marijuana, eyes bloodshot red, Marlon decide feed into Moses's arrogance. Moses was fun to listen to when high. "What are you talkin' about now?" Marlon inquired.

"My girl. Krystal Hamilton. But I got her callin' herself Krystal Walker. That's how you know you got a bitch, when she's using yo last name and you ain't gave her no ring."

"She's young, though," Tre Pound grunted, feeling drowsy. "And she's gullible. Easily influenced. I could pull up on her and snatch her away from you. Or let any nigga of my ..." He burped. "... let any nigga of my caliber come along—she's gone."

As cocksure as ever, Moses said, "I'll congratulate the nigga that takes my girl. Shake his hand and take a picture wit' him. 'Cause you won't meet a nigga wit' that much game but once in a lifetime. Yall stop laughin', I'm serious. I'ma keep it one hunit: Bitches come and go. I can get another Krystal in record time if a nigga swoops her up. But it's not gonna happen. And if it does, the whole ordeal is bound to end up on the next episode of *Masterminds*. 'Cause the whole world gon' wanna know how the nigga done it."

Moses liked to entertain his friends, and they were surely enjoying themselves. Tre Pound was holding his stomach, guffawing so intensely that he had to lean on Moses's shoulder for support. Marlon laughed through his chronic coughing, sounding like a 70-year-old chain smoker.

"And *you*," Moses went on, shrugging Tre Pound off his shoulder. "I ain't gotta worry about you takin' Krystal from me. You 'bout to be in maximum security, makin' three-way calls for everybody in B-wing."

The room fell silent—except for the low-playing music and Moses, who started to laugh but stopped when no one else was. He spoiled the ambiance, went too far and wished he could take back what he said. The forbidding look Marlon shot his way told him to apologize.

"You know I was just playin', right?" Moses said to Tre Pound. "We coo'?"

Moses stuck his hand out.

Reluctantly, Tre Pound gave him dap. "We coo," he answered gloomily. For a brief moment, the trial had escaped his thoughts. Now he couldn't help but think about what was going to happen to him tomorrow. He'd find out soon. He had to be in court in seven hours.

"Knock! Knock!" Playa Paul shouted as he walked through the front door with Stacks, and five stunningly beautiful ladies. "It better be some weed left."

By the slow dragging steps that Stacks took, Tre Pound could tell he was high on PCP. He looked at Marlon to see if he'd say anything to Stacks, but Marlon seemed focused on the ladies.

"You got some pretty nails," Marlon said to the thickest girl, gently taking her hand within his.

"Aw, girl, thank you," she replied with a smile.

Marlon frowned at the "girl" remark. As if he heard wrong, he looked at his blunt suspiciously and put it out in the ashtray.

Stacks went and whispered something in Tre Pound's ear. He told him that Playa Paul had slandered their names on the ride over. Playa Paul had told the girls that Marlon was a homosexual; that Stacks was a recovering crackhead, which they believed because of the trance he was in. Moses was the only person Playa Paul didn't lie on. But he did tell the girls about Krystal.

"He hated on us," Stacks drawled, heavy-eyed.

"What did he say about me?" Tre Pound asked.

Stacks seemed to be thinking. Then he shrugged. "I can't remember, but I know he said something foul."

Playa Paul didn't want any of them fucking any of the girls he brought over. He just wanted to display them, and be the only one to get laid tonight. He'd be able to brag about it for ages.

Tre Pound nodded and Stacks wandered off.

One of the girls—a chocolate beauty with taut calf muscles—sat next to Moses. The intoxicating scent of her perfume alone caused him to get an erection.

"Damn, you smell good." Moses was awfully close to her, sniffing her shoulders up to her neck. "What is that?"

"It's my own mix of different perfumes," she said, politely pushing him away.

"I heard about mixing fragrances. They was talkin' 'bout it on the news the other day. Said it was bad for the skin. I wouldn't want you to break out, so let me take you upstairs and scrub yo body down wit' warm sudsy water."

"Sorry. You're cute and all, but I'm not that type of girl. Aren't you the one with the girlfriend? I wouldn't want to do that to Krystal."

"You know Krystal? Damn!"

Another one of the girls made room next to Tre Pound. She crossed her legs, looking sophisticated in her librarian glasses and canary yellow sundress that tied around the nape of her neck. Taking notice of Tre Pound's somber mood, she rubbed his back soothingly.

"It's okay, baby," she said. "Paul told me about what you're going through. Just look at it this way: at least you know now."

Tre Pound was too tired to even look at her. "I just wanna get it over wit," he said, thinking Playa Paul had told the girl about his trial.

"I can relate. I was once in your shoes. If it makes you feel any better, I'm diagnosed positive too, and I'm still enjoying life."

Tre Pound didn't understand her last comment and blamed it on him being drunk. He laid his head in her lap and she stroked his low-cut hair.

It wasn't long before everybody became aware of Stacks, who stood in the corner of the living room facing the wall. He tilted his head back, staring at the ceiling.

Moses said, "What are you doing over there, Stacks? Who put you in time-out?"

Everybody laughed and giggled.

Then Stacks turned around and the girls gasped. His flaccid penis was sticking out of his open fly. Pee dripped from the slit. He had been pissing in the corner!

In a fit of violent wrath, Marlon ran over to Stacks and tackled him to the ground. Marlon was sick of him getting high, losing control and destroying his property. So as Stacks tried to squirm away, Marlon balled his fists and mercilessly hammered them down into his boy's face.

"Momma!" Stacks screamed.

"Do somethin' yall," one of the girls pleaded.

No one intervened.

"I done told you, nigga! Didn't I?!" Marlon snarled between blows. "I'm tired of ... tellin'you ... but you gon' learn ... muthafucka!" Once blood was shed, Marlon let up. And as soon as he did, Stacks scrambled to his feet and ran outside screaming for somebody, anybody to call the police.

"Help! They tryna kill me!"

That was Tre Pound's cue to leave. He stood up, almost losing his balance, and flashed his set. "Tre block. It's too much goin' on over here."

***

119

1:00 a.m. exactly.

The drive to his neighborhood seemed short. It was late, and the traffic lights remained green longer when after midnight, giving Tre Pound a straight shot home. Sober, he sometimes drove carelessly as if he owned the streets. But while under the influence he drove properly until he arrived in front of his house.

He tottered out of the creme Infiniti Q45. His body felt unusually heavy. The Hennessy had blurred his vision and made the solid three-story structure of his house appear cloudy.

"*Stayyy scheeeemin'* ... niggas tryna get at *meeeee*," he slurred, repeating the lyrics from a radio song he'd been listening to on the ride over.

Stumbling onto the sidewalk, he heard a familiar creaking sound; it was the sound his dining room window made when opened. He treaded across his lawn to the side of the house to make sure he wasn't hearing things and, shockingly, he saw what looked like two people breaking into his house! He caught sight of someone's legs disappearing into his dining room window!

As he proceeded to his front door, he pulled out his 9mm Browning semiautomatic. The clip wasn't inserted correctly and it fell in the grass. He didn't even notice it dropped as he scurried to put the key in the dead bolt lock.

He slowly turned the knob.

It didn't matter that he was drunk and got caught off guard. Whoever was in his house wouldn't get the best of him, he thought. "I'm comin' for you," he whispered.

In a kneeling position, he budged open the door enough so he could squeeze through without making much noise. His house was dark, only moonlight shining through the windows. The entrance was clear. He crept alongside the wall, in the shadows, and peered into the dining room. It was clear. *Where are they?* he asked himself.

Then he heard someone stalking up his carpeted steps.

He peeked up the staircase and caught a glimpse of someone as they bent the corner at the top of the steps. Cautiously, with his pistol pointed up, he ascended the stairs, using his free hand to balance himself against the wall. It appeared to be more steps than usual.

Once at the top step, he was able to peek around the corner and see into his bedroom. Hazily, he saw the intruder looking around the room, probably searching for his stash. But he never kept his stash where he rested his head.

"Where's yo partner?" he breathed, scanning the upstairs hallway. From his position he could see into the bathroom. Nobody appeared to be in there. And his guest bedroom door was closed. Maybe it had only been one person he saw climbing through his window.

As Tre Pound continued watching the intruder move throughout his bedroom, the intruder did something peculiar. Slowly, the intruder pulled back the covers on the king-size bed and climbed in, bundling up. After Tre Pound saw this fatal mistake, he quickly advanced towards the bedroom and fired a single shot into the bed.

"Aaaahhh!" the intruder screamed as a girl would.

Tre Pound continuously squeezed the trigger—but no bullets discharged—as the intruder fought wildly to get out from under the sheets and out of the bed. After realizing that no bullets were coming out and his clip was missing, Tre Pound violently threw the 9mm at the intruder. He then leapt straight up in the air, grabbing the SKS that was propped above his doorway.

While screaming, the intruder managed to fight off the bedsheet and see Tre Pound as he readied the huge assault rifle.

"Tre Pound, it's me! It's me—Dominique! It's me!" She waved her trembling palms at him and dropped to her knees. "Tre Pound, it's me!"

He aimed the assault rifle at her, breathing heavily through his nose. "Keep yo hands up!" he barked at her, and she raised her hands high as she sobbed uncontrollably. He looked outside his bedroom and once again scanned up and down the hallway to see if her accomplice was coming. He pointed the gun back at her. "Who else is wit' you? Tell him to come out now!"

"I came by myself. It's just me! It's me—Dominique Hayes, Marlon's little sister."

"I know who the fuck you are. Now what the fuck are you doin' here?"

"I came—I came to see you ..."

"For what?! You in on some shit to get me, too? Tryna set me up?! Bitch, it ain't that easy! Yall can't get me!" Tre Pound reeked of alcohol and Dominique could smell it.

"You're drunk, Tre Pound! I wouldn't never hurt you," she cried. "You know that! I just wanted to be near you again, knowing this could be my last day wit' you. I don't have no gun. You can search me if you think I'm lyin.'"

As tears streamed down her face, Tre Pound realized that she wasn't a threat. Young Dominique Hayes was merely a schoolgirl, he reasoned. Only 16 years old, uncorrupted.

He dropped the SKS, lowered his head and sighed. When he turned to leave, Dominique asked, "Where are you going? Can I put my hands down?"

He went into the bathroom and turned on the faucet. He cupped his hands under the running water and splashed it on his face. Dominique touched his back.

"I'm sorry for breakin' in," she said. "I was hoping you was already here, but when nobody answered the door, I decided to wait inside."

"How'd you get over here?" He splashed his face again, then flicked the water from his fingers into the porcelain sink.

Dominique handed him a bath towel. "My brother's car, the Ford Explorer. I parked it right in front of the house. You didn't see it?"

"I wasn't even paying attention. I'm fucked up right now." After he finished drying his face, he actually observed what Dominique was wearing—a loose, aquamarine pajama set. Her Sean John coat with the fur-trimmed hood was unzipped and a pair of white slippers were on her feet. "Ain't you supposed to be at my auntie's house?"

"I snuck out. Nobody knows I'm over here."

"You stupid. They could be lookin' for you as we speak, calling yo brother to tell him you missing."

"I left when everybody went to sleep. I'll be back before they wake up. They'll never know I was gone."

"Do you realize I almost shot and killed you?"

"I'm still alive."

"Go home, Dominique."

"That's not where I came from," she said with a sly smile.

"You know what I mean."

"I'm not leaving until I get what I want."

"I thought you just wanted to see me. You saw me. Now roll out."

"There's more I want." She spoke her words softly and lustfully as she took her forefinger and trailed it along his jawline. She flicked his bottom lip.

They looked at each other directly for a moment. Dominique's eyes were emblazoned with raw passion while Tre Pound's seemed impassive. He remembered when Marlon caught a teenage boy penetrating Dominique anally in her room. Marlon didn't do anything that day except throw him out, but three weeks later the boy came up missing.

So Tre Pound knew how sensitive Marlon was towards Dominique. And Tre Pound had just had a conversation with him about her—not even 30 minutes ago.

"Say somethin.'"

"Dominique, I can't do my nigga like that."

"You did it before," she recalled.

"I let you jack me off. That was it. And I wish I wouldn't've let you do it. It's not happenin' again."

"I don't want to do that this time either." She removed her coat, letting it fall to the white tiled floor. Through her pajama top, Tre Pound could see the imprint of her erect nipples. She wasn't wearing a bra underneath. "I want you to fuck me," she said, and began unbuttoning the top. "I want you to fuck me like you do the other girls in the 'hood."

"You don't know what you talkin' 'bout."

Tre Pound found himself becoming aroused, unable to resist Dominique Hayes—just like their previous encounter. But the cause of what happened before wasn't entirely her doing. He used to give her enticing glances and would lick his lips at her when Marlon wasn't looking. It led to her taking the initiative.

At Marlon's house two and a half weeks ago, Tre Pound was looking through the refrigerator when Dominique brazenly came up behind him and stuffed her hands in his pants. He was startled, not just by the chill of her hand, but by the fact that Marlon was on the other side of the wall in the living room watching TV. Nevertheless, he let her massage his pulsating manhood until he ejaculated inside his jeans.

Now, here they were again, standing inches apart—and Marlon was nowhere around.

"I do too know what I'm talkin" bout. I heard how rough you like it." Dominique unhooked another button, and another, then the last. She slid the pajama top from her shoulders, slowly down her smooth cocoa brown arms and let it drop onto her coat. She had healthy breasts with big dark brown areolas. She was tempting.

Tre Pound wiped the corners of his mouth with his palm, eyes fixed on her nipples. Contemplating. He wanted to fuck her beyond compare, no doubt about it. But Marlon was a close friend, an ally, his homeboy. How could he betray him?

He already did. Two and a half weeks ago. The line had been crossed and there was no crossing back, he told himself. And prison could be right around the corner. He'd be sitting in his cell regretting turning Dominique down.

"What are you waiting for?" she asked. "You know I gotta get back. Are you just gonna leave me standing here?" Her breasts were her favorite part of her body and she knew Tre Pound wouldn't be able to say no to them once he saw them. She lifted each one, then let them go. "They're just titties, Tre Pound. Don't be scared of 'em."

Finally, he said, "A'ight. I'ma give it to you just like I give it to any other female. I'm not gon' take it easy on you. That's what you want, ain't it?"

"Uh-huh," she said while nodding, a bit nervous now by the tone of voice he used.

"Put yo hands on the toilet," he ordered.

She did as she was told, placing her hands on top of the furry gray toilet seat cover. Tre Pound yanked down her pajama bottoms and black lace panties simultaneously, causing her rear end to wobble. She looked back at him, startled. He loosened his belt and dropped his jeans. He slapped a hand on her ass cheek, and with the other hand he grabbed his throbbing dick and placed it at the entrance of her twat.

"Wait!" she said, reaching between her legs and pushing his rod aside, blocking her vagina with a flat hand. "Not there. I'm saving my virginity for my honeymoon. Put it in my booty."

Tre Pound had penetrated many girls anally. Therefore, Dominique's request was nothing out of the ordinary. He opened the medicine cabinet, took out the Vaseline and popped the lid. He applied the lubricant to his shaft and dabbed it against her butthole. The Vaseline was cold and Dominique shivered at its touch.

"I might hurt you," Tre Pound said, giving her one last warning.

"This isn't my first time," she told him.

That said, Tre Pound gently squeezed inside of her—the only gentleness he planned on showing. Dominique held her breath and shut her eyes, feeling her ass muscles stretch to their limits.

Once he could go in no farther, he pulled back and immediately pushed back in. Dominique gasped.

They rocked together as Tre Pound plunged in and out. She groaned. He grunted, leaning forward to grope her breasts. His waist clapped against her butt cheeks. She momentarily lost her balance, regaining it by steadying herself on the toilet with her elbows.

Her pussy juices dripped onto the tile.

"Deeper!" she squealed.

"Shut the fuck up," he snarled, grasping a fistful of her hair and snatching her head back.

Dominique's breathing intensified; she was panting heavily, cherishing the moment. Loving this dangerous thug called Tre Pound, whom she had spent many wishful nights fantasizing about.

"Uhn!" she moaned as she climaxed. Her rectum began to tense up and she started bucking.

The Vaseline made squishy sounds as Tre Pound spanked into her tight hole. He admired Dominique's tenacity. "You got it, baby. That's it ..." he said in a heavy whisper, going harder, deeper, making the clap against her cheeks louder.

Dominique started crying softly. She didn't know she was bleeding, but Tre Pound did. He persisted anyway, feeling the wave of ecstasy building up.

Then he exploded. "Ooooh," he sighed, pumping out the excess cum. When he removed his thick, limp dick, it was glossy and bloody. He sounded out of breath when he said, "Now get yo ass outta here."

CHAPTER 13

His bunk had little to no cushion; he tossed and turned in his sleep. The wool blanket he slept with was too short and only covered his neck down to his knees, leaving his lower legs and feet out in the open.

He awoke, giving up on a good night's sleep. Flinging the wool blanket aside, he sat up on his bunk and stretched his joints. "Today's the day," he said to himself, looking around the dilapidated cell. Chipped olive-green paint and gang inscriptions seemed to hold up the crumbling walls. The stainless steel toilet stool was encrusted with past inmates' piss. He heard a guard coming.

"What time is it?" he asked when the guard stopped in front of his cell.

The guard held up a pair of tangled chains and shackles. "It's time, Tre Pound."

Accepting his fate, he rose to his feet. The cell door clanked open and the guard stepped in. That was when Tre Pound saw who the guard was.

"Stacks?"

"Yeah, it's me. How you doin', Tre Pound?"

"How am I doin'?!" he snapped. "How you think I'm doin'? You workin' for the enemy. I thought we was pahtnas."

"We are. But I got a job to do. Turn around and cuff up."

Tre Pound put his hands against the wall as Stacks hooked a chain around his navy blue jumpsuit. In front of the jumpsuit on the left chest area was his inmate number, which had only two digits: three and five. His waist, ankles, and wrists were shackled, and were all connected by one long chain. A safety measure used for every death row inmate.

"Move out," Stacks commanded.

"Hold up. Can I say goodbye to my celly?"

"That's against policy."

"C'mon, man. You can do that for me. Outta all the shit we been through ... I saved you from getting jumped, remember? At that buckhop. All them niggas tried to surround you because you pulled one of they homies' girl. I let off a couple shots, had everybody tryna find a exit."

Stacks sighed. "Make it quick."

His wrists were cuffed together so Tre Pound had to tap down on the top bunk with balled fists. Feeling the vibrations, his celly awakened. She sat up groggily, wearing the same navy blue jumpsuit as him. She observed the guard, then Tre Pound in chains and the look of hopelessness on his face. Her sleepy state quickly changed to heartfelt concern.

"Are they about to take you away?" she asked. Tears welled in her eyes.

"My time on this earth is up, Camille. I had a good run, though."

"You're only 21 years old!" she cried. "That's not a good run. You haven't even reached yo full potential yet. You still have a lot of life left in you."

"Well, they 'bout to take what I got left," Tre Pound said calmly. "I just had to say goodbye. I know I ain't been the ideal cousin to you. Fucked up a couple of yo relationships and been tough on you sometimes, but it was out of love. Believe that. I would've did anything to keep you happy and keep you safe." Somehow, he stifled his tears. He had to stay strong, stay solid in his final moments.

But Camille's tears were streaming. "Tre Pound, I already know all that!"

"And I wanna thank you," he continued, "for lovin' me unconditionally. A nigga like me needed that shit. I probably wouldn't've made it to 21 without family, without you."

"Don't go," Camille pleaded.

Then, no other words were spoken between them. They communicated with their eyes, gazing at each other, grieved that this day had to come.

Stacks interrupted. "Let me see yo wrists." He uncuffed Tre Pound's hands. "Give her a hug."

Camille hopped down into Tre Pound's arms. They held each other tight, wanting to hold the embrace forever. Moving his hands down to her waist, and exchanging a brief glance with her, he kissed her lips softly, tenderly. A simple kiss. But a kiss that said goodbye.

The next instance, Tre Pound was being shuffled into a room that resembled a dungeon. The brick walls were the color of charcoal, wet with garden snakes creeping through the cracks. There was a large wooden chair, ostrich harnesses and straps all over it, in the center of the chamber.

An electric chair!

"I'm in the wrong room," Tre Pound said, alarmed.

The chair was connected to a switch by a long, thick cord. Holding the handle to the switch was a man in a black hood.

"What's goin' on? Yall ain't 'bout to electrocute me! This shit is illegal. Cruel and unusual punishment."

"You were cruel to people, too," Stacks replied. "Have a seat."

"Nigga, you have a seat!" It took two more gaurds, Moses and Playa Paul, to pull a jerking Tre Pound to the chair. "Let go of me! Yall supposed to be my niggas! Get me outta here!"

They strapped down his arms, legs, and chest. He struggled against the leather straps but they were too durable.

"Don't do this to me! I can't die like this!"

They clamped a metal helmet onto his head that had electric cables connected to it. The chinstrap was fastened tight and Tre Pound could only look forward.

He saw he had an audience.

Judge Lyons, D.A. Paul Wheeler, Mr. Masaccio, Auntie Janice, Shelton, Aunt Bernice, Gutta, Cash and Seneca, Dynisha, Young Ray, Buttercup—they were all seated, watching and waiting for him to die. He couldn't make out the faces of the other people there, but he sensed that they were men and women he had done wrong, robbed, or mistreated.

His father was there.

So was his mother. "You're not going to heaven," she told Tre Pound, sniveling. "You didn't live righteously. I hope you'll be okay down there."

Beyond the audience, a metal door opened and in walked a group of people—dead people! They all had syringes filled with blood in their hands. Kaliko was one of them. He was buck naked, and stepped up first.

"What you 'bout to do wit' that?" Tre Pound asked in a frightened tone, as Kaliko eased the syringe near his forearm. "Wait-wait-wait-wait!" But Kaliko stuck the needle in anyway and injected the blood. "Arrggh!"

Then Latrice and Joy came next, both injecting their blood. Then Rico and his friends. Tre Pound roared out each time, jerking futilely. Then a guy who stole Tre Pound's first car and sold it, took his turn. Next was the person who Tre Pound caught *driving* his first car.

With a deranged face, Tre Pound watched as a little girl, maybe 8 or 9 years old, walked up to the electric chair. "I didn't kill you," he said.

She smiled. "Yes, you did. You was shootin' at some-body else and shot me instead. It's okay, though. I know it was an accident. I'm not mad." After poking the needle in a vein in Tre Pound's bicep, the little girl smacked the top of the syringe and her blood gushed into his system.

"Take this shit back out of me!" he yelled in agony, eyes shut tight. When he opened them, he saw somebody in the audience he didn't notice before. "Dominique?"

She was standing in the front row, wearing only the aquamarine pajama bottoms and white slippers he last saw her in. Topless. Nipples erect and visible to everyone. "Hi, Tre Pound. I'm gonna miss you."

"I'm gon' miss you, too."

"I wish we could fuck again," she said.

"Huh?" His eyes darted around the room nervously. "We didn't fuck."

"We did too. It's not a secret anymore. My brother knows."

"Is that why he didn't show up here?"

"He came," she said. "He's here."

Out of his periphery, Tre Pound could see the man in the black hood, waiting to pull the switch. The man removed his hood. And there was Marlon Hayes, glower-ing with hatred.

Tre Pound began to apologize. "I'm so—"

Marlon slammed the switch so fast and hard that it broke off, and nobody was able to stop the electricity from coursing through Tre Pound's body.

He let out a bloodcurdling scream, and the audience watched lighting flash in his eyes as sparks flew from the metal helmet. The flesh on his skull burned and sizzled and one eye socket burst open.

"Ahhhhh!

***

"Ahhh!" Tre Pound yelled as he sat up in his bed, sweating profusely. He realized he was dreaming and slowly caught his breath. The red digits on his clock read 5:42 a.m.

"Two more hours to go. Just two more," he said, and climbed out of bed.

CHAPTER 14

The courtroom resounded with idle chatter, so Carlo Masaccio leaned in close to his client's ear. "I thought I advised you not to wear flashy apparel."

Well-dressed in an auburn Stacy Adams suit and silk twill shirt, Tre Pound looked sharp. His sparkling cuff links were complimented by his personal jewelry, which glittered more than ever before. It took him a whole 45 minutes to clean each piece.

He slouched in the wooden chair, elbow propped on the armrest, thumb and two fingers balancing his head. Indifferent. Ready to get the shit over with.

"What's the point in me dressing down now?" Tre Pound said begrudgingly. "The jury already got they verdict in. It's a wrap."

"But if you get found guilty, the judge is the one who does the sentencing," said Mr. Masaccio. "He'll look at your flamboyant appearance as a sign of disrespect to his courtroom. And you don't want to be on the judge's bad side during sentencing."

"I thought you told me to count on a verdict of not guilty."

"Indeed I did; however, it's important to be prudent and prepared for unfavorable outcomes. What you have on is excessive. We still got time before the judge comes in. We can take that jewelry off of you and hold it in my briefcase if you'd like. Or hand it to one of your family members."

"I'm keepin' it on," Tre Pound said. "The judge gon' do what he gon' do regardless. Fuck him. I been humble the whole trial. I'm bein' me now ... I shouldn't even be here."

"Levour," came a voice from behind.

Tre Pound turned. His Auntie Janice was in the front row, looking straight at him.

"Sit up," she said. "Kings don't sit like that. Yo uncle, Cutthroat, always held his head high when he was in court."

Tre Pound sat up, eyeing everyone else who came to support him. Shelton, Aunt Bernice, Cash, Seneca, Moses, Stacks, Playa Paul. And Michelle sat alone, her facial expression distraught because she found out where her husband Gutta disappeared to—the county jail.

Sitting next to Playa Paul was a petite light-skinned girl in a white baby-T. Tre Pound recognized her; it was Buttercup. She waved, showing her pearly white teeth.

Tre Pound turned back around.

"All rise!"

The bailiff announced the entrance of the Honorable Judge John Lyons and everyone stood—everyone except Tre Pound.

***

"Dominique, why was you walkin' like that earlier?" Camille asked. She and Dominique were sitting in their seminar class with their desks adjoined, facing each other, playing chess.

It was Dominique's turn. She moved her king one space over, behind a pawn. "Walkin' like what?"

"You was walkin' all stiff, like you had a stick up yo butt. Don't think I didn't notice. When you woke up this morning, you almost fell on yo way to the bathroom."

"I had a rough night. Couldn't even get comfortable. You had me sleepin' on that hard-ass futon. Girl, what did I do to deserve that?"

Camille snickered. "*You* picked the futon; I didn't pick it for you. And I told you to lay it out flat. All you had to do was adjust it. It ain't my fault you chose not to." She skid her rook across the board, in the line of fire of Dominique's knight. "But tell me the real reason you was walkin' like that."

"That is the real reason."

"I know you lying. You wanna know how?"

"How?"

"Because I saw you when you snuck back in the house," Camille said, and Dominique looked up from the board. "Yeah, the jig is up, bitch. It's time to come clean. Where'd you go?"

"I can't tell you."

"Why not? We tell each other everything. You can't keep this from me."

"This is different, though."

"I tell you stuff," Camille fussed. "How is this different?"

"If I tell you, then you gon' tell Krystal, and she gon' tell her boyfriend, and her boyfriend gon' tell my brother."

A wide, incredulous smile spread across Camille's face. She figured it out. "You went over a boy's house!"

Heads turned throughout the classroom.

"Damn, Camille, be quiet." Dominique looked at her nosy classmates. "Mind yall business."

Camille leaned in close with a mischievous grin. "Nasty ass. You did it again. I know you ain't givin' up yo virginity to nobody but yo husband, so you had to let somebody fuck you in the butt. Who was it?"

"I just told you why I can't tell you."

"It'll just be between me and you. I won't tell Krystal. You know I'm good at keepin' secrets. I never told nobody what you told me about Stacks. How you let him clothes-grind on you until he busted a nut. And you see I didn't tell Krystal that you snuck out."

If it wasn't Tre Pound—if it were anybody else—Dominique would've leaked a name. She knew if she told,

Camille would go ballistic. But Dominique didn't know how much longer she could hold her love for Tre Pound in. She wanted to tell everybody, but knew there'd be consequences. Maybe if he went to prison, her love for him would fade, as well as the urge to profess it. Maybe.

She decided to wait and see.

"The last boy I let hit it got murdered," said Dominique. "I'm not sayin' my brother is the one that murdered him, but it ain't hard to put two and two together. So you can see where I'm comin' from, Camille. You already know what I did. Why you need to know who I did it wit'?"

With an attitude, Camille said, "Well, at least tell me how it went."

Dominique was all smiles. "He wasn't there when I knocked on his door, so guess what I did?"

"You waited on him?"

"*Inside* his house. I snuck in through the dining room window."

"Get outta here! His parents or his little brothers or sisters could've been there."

"He live by hisself."

Who did Dominique know that had their own house? Camille mused, her detective skills kicking in. Had to be somebody older, out of high school.

"Then what'd you do?"

"I went up to his room and crawled in his bed. The sheets smelled fresh, like they just got out the dryer. But I wasn't laying there long when I heard a gunshot. He shot at me! He thought I was a burglar."

Camille's jaw dropped. "He actually shot at you? Dominique, he could've killed you. Uh-uh, don't nobody shoot at one of my girlfriends. You really gotta tell me who it is now. I'll have Tre Pound fuck him up for you."

"No, it wasn't like that. I was the one in the wrong. He probably wasn't tryna hit me anyway, just scare whoever it was in his house. And once he saw it was me, everything was okay."

"And then what happened?" Camille probed, still not satisfied. She wanted to know the boy's name and didn't have a clue.

"We went to the bathroom. He had to splash water on his face because he was feelin' miserable because he almost popped a cap in my ass. But he ended up poppin' one in anyway." Dominique grinned.

"That wasn't funny."

"It was too, shut up. But anywayz, once he saw my titties, it was on. He bent me over the toilet seat and pulled my panties down—the black lace ones—and tried to stick it in my coochie but I wasn't havin' that. So he squeezed in my bootyhole ever so gently—"

"Skip that part," Camille interrupted, shaking her hands as if something filthy was on them. "Butt-fuckin' is nasty."

"You might not like it now, but you will when you get in yo 20's. Because that's when most women do," Dominique explained. She was only a year older than Camille and a grade higher, yet felt more mature. "But that's all that happened. It was *incredible*, though. He tore my ass up! Literally."

"All I'm sayin' is yo little impairment better not affect yo performance tonight."

"I can still dance."

"You better be able to," Camille warned her. "And why haven't you moved yet? I ain't got all day."

"That was you, all in my business, distracting me." Dominique studied the chessboard, then took the bait and snagged Camille's rook with her knight.

"Checkmate!" Camille chirped, and knocked Dominique's pawn out the way with her queen, planting it in front of the king. "You got yo ass tow-up again!"

***

Carlo Masaccio stood upright, hands clasped in front of him, as did everyone in the courtroom except his client. He spoke out the side of his mouth, trying not to draw attention. "Mr. King, you might want to stand up. It'll look favorable upon you."

Tre Pound remained seated. "Didn't nobody stand up when I walked in," he said. "Not one time since the trial started. I ain't gotta show that old muthafucka respect no more. He need to show me respect. I'm a King, not him."

143

Janice thought twice about saying anything else to her nephew. She went ahead and let him be the man that he was. Her lips spread into a smile.

Suddenly aware that the defendant wasn't on his feet, the bailiff, a middle-aged white man, approached the defense table. "Sir, I need you to stand up until the judge is seated."

"For what?" Tre Pound retorted.

"Because I told you to."

Carlo Masaccio chimed in, "This could be the last time you'll ever have to stand before a judge. Let's just go through the motions one more time, Mr. King. Stand up. What'll it hurt?"

"Listen to your lawyer," the bailiff advised.

"I'm not standing up," Tre Pound said adamantly. "Just tell me what the verdict is."

The bailiff went and whispered the situation in the ear of the Honorable Judge John Lyons, who nodded with a sour frown.

After the judge plopped down behind the bench, he said, "You may be seated," and the courtroom obediently sat. His black robe hid his clothes. Only the collar of his white dress shirt and the knot of his bronze tie were visible. At 65 years old, the top of his head had baldened, but gray patches surrounded his ears. He looked at Tre Pound. "You, sir, need to stand up. *By yourself.*"

"And if I don't?" Tre Pound challenged, sparking whispers throughout the courtroom.

"I'll hold you in contempt of court!" Judge John Lyons spat, waving his finger.

"Do what you gotta do."

"Very well then ..." The judge turned to the bailiff. "Bring in the jury."

***

On the other side of the classroom, J-Dub watched Camille closely. He noticed how fine she looked today. Pin curls in her hair, sharp eyebrows, natural-looking makeup. Under the desk, he could see her crossed legs in skintight designer blue jeans. She had her sneakers off, wearing crispy white footies. His eyes journeyed to her behind; the jeans, squeezing her legs, let him marvel at her curves.

But it wasn't just today that J-Dub espied her beauty. There had never been a day that he caught her looking anything less than perfect.

"Damn, nigga, you drooling all over the pages," Kareem said, snatching back his Biology book. "See if I let you borrow somethin' again. You need to just go holla at her."

J-Dub wiped his mouth. "I'll be right back."

"That's what I'm talkin' bout!" Kareem cheered him on. "That's the J-Dub I know. Go for yours." As his friend slipped away, he muttered, "Sucka for love."

"I heard that," J-Dub said over his shoulder.

"I wanted you to."

There was an empty desk near Camille and Dominique. The scraping noise the desk made against the ground as J-Dub scooted it near was annoying. He connected it to the girls' desks and had a seat. He saw that they were setting up the chess pieces for another game.

"What yall playin'?" he asked.

Camille and Dominique made eye contact with each other. They tried to hide their smiles but ended up bursting into laughter.

"That was a stupid question, huh?" J-Dub smiled sheepishly and crossed his arms. "Wussup, Dominique?"

While moving a pawn forward, Dominique held a smirk. "Hi, J-Dub. I didn't mean to laugh at you like that."

"It's all good," he said, then glanced at Camille. She looked even better up close. Long eyelashes. Not a blemish on her rich peanut butter complexion. She wasn't paying him any attention so he asked Dominique, "Who won the last game?"

"She did."

"I might be able to beat you then. She taught me how to play."

"She taught me how to play, too," said Dominique. "So we just gon' have to play each other to see who wins."

"Can I get game?"

"Ask her. I don't care. But she the one who got the board out."

"Camille, can I—"

"No, you can't," Camille stated.

146

"Why not?"

"Because we got a tournament goin' on."

"Is that the real reason?"

She scowled at him. "Why are you over here? If you wanna play chess, get another board from Mrs. Bakersfield and go play wit' Kareem."

"He don't know how to play," J-Dub said.

"Teach him then."

"I tried to. He don't wanna learn."

"Well, I guess you assed-out." Camille moved her queen. She didn't catch her mistake until she took her hand off. "Shit!"

"Ms. King, watch your language. And keep your voice down," said Mrs. Bakersfield, the seminar teacher.

"Sorry."

Dominique captured the queen with her bishop. She knew Camille wasn't entirely focused on the game, thanks to J-Dub, but she'd take a win any way she could get it. "I think I'ma actually beat you for once," she said, smiling.

"I can play without my queen," Camille replied.

"I can't live without mine," J-Dub said softly, and both girls' heads whirled towards him. He licked his lips and eyed Camille. "I need my queen back."

Flattered and impressed, Camille almost forgot about how he dumped her. She almost told him it was nice of him to refer to her as a queen. She almost smiled ... almost. "Why all of a sudden you want me back?" she asked snottily.

"I heard you and Lil' Pat broke up," J-Dub answered, and after realizing how inconsiderate that sounded, he quickly added, "and I been wanting you back before that. I just didn't wanna push up on you while you was in a relationship wit' him. I thought that would be disrespectful because I know you're a faithful girl."

"So you think you can break up wit' me and get back wit' me whenever you please? I'm supposed to run back to you because me and Lil' Pat didn't work out?"

"No, but—"

"That's what it sound like to me."

"Camille, I regret ever breakin' up wit' you."

"You did what you had to do to protect yo'self, and didn't even consider my feelings. Obviously I wasn't that important." Camille shrugged. "What's to regret?"

J-Dub refused to give up. "I admit, I was wrong. I shouldn't have cared that yo cousin stomped me, had me in stitches. Should've said fuck his threats. Pain is love. I know that now. And I'm willing to stand by you no matter what."

"No matter what, huh?" She was doubtful.

So J-Dub looked her directly in her hazel eyes; his never wavered. "I love you," he said.

Camille had opened her mouth to tell him to get out her face, but paused when his words sunk in. Those three words—I love you—always seemed to chip at her defenses. Yet she didn't want to be made a fool of again. "I don't believe you," she said. "My cousin will run you off just like before. You don't want to get beat up again, do you?"

"Camille, you not listening!" he barked, causing her and Dominique to flinch. "I'm not comin' out of nowhere wit' this. How I feel about you has grown, and it keeps growin'. I'm ready to die for you!"

Dominque's eyebrows raised. "Wow," she said.

"Don't make me have to break yall up," Mrs. Bakersfield warned, but they didn't hear her.

Sort of in a trance, Camille was speechless. She didn't have the slightest idea how to respond to J-Dub. Once thing was for sure, though—he was definitely a new man.

The enchantment in Camille's eyes gave J-Dub the feeling that he was winning her over. But the moment was short lived.

There was a knock on the classroom door.

Mrs. Bakersfield grunted as she stood. Her bones were fragile and standing up wasn't as easy as it used to be. She proceeded to the door with her cane. Every step she took she would stumble and catch herself.

She opened the door.

A student was standing there with a yellow bathroom pass in his hand. It was Patrick Campbell aka Lil' Pat.

***

The 12 members of the jury filed into the courtroom, occupying the first and second rows of the jury box.

Though they were supposed to be a jury of Tre Pound's peers, which the law required, they looked anything but.

They all appeared to be over 30 years old. There were 11 white men and women, and 1 Black man. Intuitively, Tre Pound sensed that the lone Black juror wasn't on his side. It wasn't just the brotha's thick bifocals that triggered Tre Pound's concern, but his stiff posture and merry countenance.

One juror made eye contact with Tre Pound. A vibrant-looking white woman with curly blonde hair and prescription glasses frowned at him, then looked away.

***

"How you doing today, Mrs. Bakersfield?" asked Lil' Pat in a downhearted mood. "I'm doing as best I can. Let me see your pass."

J-Dub noticed Lil' Pat first. He shot a menacing look at him.

"There go yo boyfriend," Dominique said with a smile.

Turning to see where everyone was looking, Camille soon found out. Lil' Pat stood in the doorway, gazing at her contritely. She pursed her lips and squinted her eyes at him in a you-know-you-wrong-for-what-you-did way.

"Mr. Campbell, this is a bathroom pass," Mrs. Bakersfield said, handing it back. "You're out of bounds. What class are you coming from?"

"Oh, I just need to talk to Camille right fast," he said. "Can I get about three minutes of her time, please?"

"Why? You know I'm not supposed to let you do that."

"I know, but it's real important." Lil' Pat's sad eyes seemed to influence Mrs. Bakersfield.

"Three minutes, Mr. Campbell. That's it." She tottered back to her desk.

"Camille," Lil' Pat mouthed. He waved her over.

In a calm manner, Camille put her tennis shoes back on. She slowly lifted herself up out of the seat, purposefully taking her time.

"Tell that nigga to leave," J-Dub pleaded.

"This is none of yo business," Camille replied, and strolled over to Lil' Pat. She stopped in front of him, hands on her hips. After a few seconds of staring at his pitiful face, she slapped him hard.

Some of the students in the classroom looked on in shock, some laughed.

"Ms. King!" exclaimed Mrs. Bakersfield. Disappointed and not willing to get up again, she just shook her head.

"Can I explain?" Lil' Pat asked, rubbing his sore cheek.

"Explain what? Explain how you ain't no good? Explain how you ran and left me on the sidewalk bleeding because you was scared of my cousin? You ain't gotta explain nothin' to me! You ain't a man. You just a little boy. God, you niggas is all the same." Camille rolled her eyes.

"I went to go get help." Lil' Pat saw that she wasn't believing it. "I'm serious." He paused. "We still together, right?"

"Are you kidding me? We are over wit'. There is no 'we.'"

"So you wanna end it just like that?"

"I ended it two nights ago. I just wanted to tell you to yo face."

He stood there, puppy-eyed.

"What you still here for? Yo time is up." She flicked her wrist as if she were telling a dog to shoo. "Bye."

At this point, J-Dub had stood up, pulling up his sagging pants, and was approaching them. "Ay, boah, she said you gotta roll."

Lil' Pat gave him the once-over and turned his attention back to Camille. "So you messin' wit' him again?"

"I'm not messin' wit' none of yall," Camille said, waving her palms. "Yall need to get away from me. Yall crowdin' my space."

Mrs. Bakersfield cut in, "Mr. Campbell, it's time for you to leave."

"I'm about to go," Lil' Pat said. "Can you just give me one more min—" J-Dub pushed him. "Damn, man, I didn't even touch you! What you push me for?"

Classmates began standing up and instigating, eager to see a fight. Mrs. Bakersfield pointed her cane frantically, telling her class to calm down.

"Hit that nigga!" Kareem shouted, making his way over to the door.

Lil' Pat spotted Kareem closing in, and before he knew it, J-Dub stole a punch, hitting him square in the mouth. He stumbled backwards, a bloody crack in his bottom lip.

Camille stood back in shock, both her hands covering her open mouth.

"She's my girl!" J-Dub barked.

Lil' Pat took off running.

***

None of the other jurors made eye contact with Tre Pound. Why did that lady frown like that? he wondered. Was she upset with the verdict they reached? Or was she showing contempt towards him because of the seriousness of the crime?

Tre Pound took a deep breath. He anxiously waited on a "not guilty" verdict, and broke into a light sweat. He turned to look at Shelton, who nodded at him reverently.

"Take a sip of water," Mr. Masaccio whispered.

From a clear glass on the defense table, Tre Pound took more than a sip; he gulped down half the glass. Oftentimes he considered going on the run, but to do that he'd have to flee the city. Kansas City was his home, his stomping grounds. He couldn't be Levour "Tre Pound" King anywhere else. Living with a low profile in another state, where no one knew his name—that was death.

Judge Lyons put a pair of reading glasses on his wrinkled face. "Has the jury reached a verdict?"

The foreman, a pale, weary-looking man, stood prepared to address the court. He cleared his throat. "Yes, Your Honor."

CHAPTER 15

Later on that day, after dark, everybody who was somebody turned up at the Southeast High school talent show. A line of cars that stretched several blocks away were trying to get into the school's parking lot, which by now was overflowing.

Inside the school, in the jam-packed auditorium, the talent show was already under way. A young female contestant sung one of her original up-tempo songs. The spectators clapped to the beat.

Camille sat in the second row, rubbing the white Band-Aid on her knee spangled with tiny red hearts. She was dressed in a fitted white Polo top and a scanty white tennis skirt. Dominique, who sat next to her, wore the same outfit.

"We're gonna win this," Camille said gleefully. She pointed to the singer. "She's our only competition. We got this in the bag."

"Don't we go on next?" asked Dominique.

"I think there's one more person after her, and then us."

"'Cause I was gon' say, Do we need to find Krystal?"

"I know where she is. She's out in the lobby waitin' to see if her man show up. I'll go get her in a minute. It's too many people out there right now, and I'm tryna avoid ..." Her voice trailed off.

"J-Dub and Lil' Pat," Dominique finished for her, smiling. "Go ahead and say it. It ain't like everybody ain't found out about what happened in seminar class. You probably don't even have to worry about avoiding Lil' Pat. He probably didn't even come. If I was him, I wouldn't." She laughed. "I can't believe J-Dub actually socked him in the mouth. And what's even more crazy is how Lil' Pat ran. He's a true-to-life bitch."

"J-Dub didn't have no reason hittin' Lil' Pat, though," Camille sympathized. "That was wrong."

"You gotta make up yo mind: Do you want somebody that'll stick up for you or not? J-Dub is the one you need to go wit'. How many niggas do you know that'll say they'll die for you?"

Camille smiled. "None."

"Well, there you go," Dominique said. "But I think J-Dub done got in over his head. You know Lil' Pat gon' tell his brother, Hoodey. And when Hoodey find out, which he probably already has ... it's gon' be some repercussions. I just hope don't nothin' pop off tonight."

"I'ma raise hell if they fuck up this talent show. If anybody do."

They watched the competition perform for a few minutes, then Dominique nudged Camille. "Have you found out anything about Tre Pound yet?"

"How many times you gon' ask me that?" Camille whined. "Ain't none of us been home. We all stayed after school to get ready, so how am I supposed to know?"

"I thought you said you was gon' call and find out."

"I couldn't get in touch wit' nobody. My momma, my brother—they ain't answering. I tried texting Tre Pound and my other brothers and Bernice ... I don't know what's goin' on. Have you talked to yo brother?"

"Yeah, but he said he ain't heard nothin."

Camille had planned to block out all thoughts of Tre Pound so she could perform to the best of her ability, unstressed. She wouldn't be able to hit her dance moves precisely with him weigh-ing heavily on her mind. But Dominique kept bringing it up. *Damn her.* Now Camille was compelled to learn her cousin's verdict.

"I'm 'bout to go get Krystal, see if she found or heard anything from Moses." Camille stood to leave.

"You don't want me to go instead?" Dominique asked, touching Camille's hand as she passed by. "I know you tryin' not to run into yo ex-boyfriends."

"If I run into one of them, then so be it. Just stay here and keep an eye on our comp. Or go backstage and make sure we don't get skipped. Me and Krystal'll meet you back there."

In the lobby area, a huge cluster of students socialized and wandered about. Camille stood on her tippy toes in a pair of red Sauconys, hoping to see over the crowd. Her 5'2" frame hindered her from seeing a thing.

"Who you lookin' for, Camille?" asked Nate, a tall football jock.

"You seen Krystal? We supposed to go on next and I can't find her."

"She's over there against the wall"—he pointed—"talkin' to some dude wit' plaits in his hair. I'm lookin' for somebody myself, the mufucka that blocked my car in. You know anybody that drive a black Dodge Magnum wit' PLAYA P on the license plates?"

"No, but thank you," Camille said, rushing off. She spotted Krystal, who was all hugged up with her boyfriend.

Moses had his hand running up under Krystal's white tennis skirt. "Did you get that G I needed, baby?" he asked her. "With that added to what I already got, I'll be able to cop that kilo. From there, there's no stoppin' us. We'll have the city sold up. And then once the bread's right, we can go and start a family in whatever city you choose."

"Atlanta," Krystal chirped.

"Atlanta it is. But first I need that G. You got it?"

She rested her head in his chest. "Not yet. But I should have it by tomorrow. Camille still owe me a hundred. I got $920 of it, though. You want me to give you that now?"

"Yeah." He kissed her forehead. "Where it at?"

157

"It's in my purse. My purse is in the locker room, but I'll get it. I'm glad you came to see me dance, Moses. You didn't have to."

"Baby, you know I wouldn't miss this," he said, squeezing her tender buttocks. "I came to get that money too, though. Can you run and go get it real quick? When do you go on?"

"In a few minutes," Camille cut in, knocking Moses's hand from under her friend's skirt. "Show her ass to the whole world why don't cha."

"We go on next?" Krystal asked.

"Yeah. This singer just got done. It's a freshman guy rappin' now. We after him." Camille surveyed the lobby, saw Cash and Seneca talking to some girls, saw Playa Paul talking to three at the same time. Stacks was leaning against the wall near the water fountain, unbothered in a pair of dark shades; it looked like he was hiding a black eye. She wasn't sure. But what she was really concerned with was the whereabouts of her cousin.

Tre Pound didn't beat the charges, she thought.

Saddened, Camille uttered, "Moses, how much time did he get?"

Moses took in a deep breath. "Judge threw the book at him. Gave him two life sentences running wild."

Her eyes watered. "What's that mean?" She knew it couldn't be good. She braced herself, cupping a hand over her mouth.

"That means when he dies in prison ... he still owes them people another life sentence."

Unable to hold it in, Camille cried into her hands. Then she quickly restrained her tears, not wanting to break down in front of so many people. "I'm sorry yall," she managed. Feeling the tears about to rush back, she covered her face and turned to run for the girls' locker room. But she bumped right into the man that was standing behind her.

When she looked up at him, her jaw dropped.

"Where was you about to run off to?" he asked. "And stop all that cryin' like a little girl."

"Tre Pound!" Camille beamed. She flung her arms around her cousin and refused to let go. She squeezed, and finished crying.

"I thought you wanted me to get the death penalty," Tre Pound reminded her. "Uhn-uhn, let me go." He pretended to remove her arms. She wouldn't budge. She squeezed him tighter.

"I didn't mean it. I won't say nothin' like that again, I promise. You made it home."

"Them mufuckas couldn't hold me. I'm untouchable. And how can I terrorize you from behind bars? I gotta stay free."

"Don't scare me like that no more." Camille let Tre Pound go just to shove the smirk off Moses's face. "You tricked me. That wasn't funny!"

Moses kept his grin. "I apologize."

As always, Tre Pound had on brilliant jewelry over brand new clothes. Camille looked him over. Akademics hoodie. Matching black pants, the Akademics logo on the back pocket and pure white Gucci sneakers.

"Look at you," she gaped. "Where did you get those clothes from? I can tell they new by the smell, so you had to just get 'em today. Did you get me anything?"

"Already thinkin' about yo'self," he said, and Camille giggled. "But I picked you up a shirt and some socks. It's out in the car."

More of Camille's peers began whispering around them and taking snapshots of Tre Pound on their camera phones. Everyone knew his trial took place this morning. Since he was here, they knew he got acquitted. The high school students were eager to spread the news.

Camille became aware of the attention her cousin's presence was attracting. "It's almost time for us to go on," she said, tugging on his arm. "C'mon, I'ma find you a good seat."

***

Outside, an off-duty police officer directed the traffic coming into the school's parking lot. He had just been informed that no one else was to be let inside.

"I'm sorry gentlemen but yall have to turn this car around and leave," he said to a group of young men in a dark blue Chevy Suburban. The 26-inch chrome blades sat higher than the officer's knees. He could barely see into the vehicle.

"Why's that?" asked the driver, a deeply dark-complexioned gangster named Spook. He wore a black skully.

"We've reached capacity and they've closed off the doors. I'm sorry but I can't let you guys in."

Spook looked in the back seat at Rowland Reed, who had just been released on parole this afternoon. The district attorney tried to get the parole board to deny Row because he didn't testify against Tre Pound, but the Missouri prison population was overcrowded so they let him go.

"What you wanna do?" Spook asked his childhood friend.

Row rolled down his window to address the officer himself. "We really trying to get in this mufucka. I just saw you let in two cars in front of us so you can miss me wit' that 'reached capacity' bullshit. I know you can let us in, so what's the holdup."

"Sir, like I said, I received word to stop incoming traffic. If I could let you in I would. Um ... all I can say is I sympathize with you guys, but I gotta follow orders."

"Fuck this shit. Spook, turn around."

The Suburban wheeled out of line and went back the way it came.

"I know Tre Pound is gon' be here too," Spook said. "His little cousin is supposed to be performin' tonight."

T-Dogg, sitting in the passenger seat, pointed out the window. "I think that's his white Infiniti over there. I can't really see. I ain't got my glasses."

"Yeah, that's Tre Pound's," Reece confirmed, who sat in the back with Row. "He's here. That nigga lucked-up tonight."

"He ain't lucked-up yet," Row said. "Go around to the back of the school. I know a way we can get in."

***

The auditorium grew quiet when the lights dimmed. As if celebrities were about to perform, the spectators anxiously awaited the dancers who won last year's talent show.

Then a spotlight clicked on; it shined down on the three girls standing in the middle of the stage. Cheers and whistles from the audience followed. Camille, Dominique, and Krystal all held different sexy poses, as motionless as mannequins.

The DJ backstage hit play and the music kicked on— "Cater 2 U" by Destiny's Child—and the girls broke their poses one at a time and began dancing in sync, seductively gyrating their hips. Their fluid motions captivated everybody.

As Camille moved her body, she spotted J-Dub sitting in the audience off to the side. He was wearing an army fatigue jacket, and had just pulled the hood off his head so she could see him. He smiled at her. She smiled back; she was in her zone.

The music segued into a bass-pounding beat, Mac Dre's "On My Toes," causing the audience to get amped up. Guys and girls alike got up out their chairs, clapping along with the beat.

Camille, Dominique, and Krystal's dancing got sexier as the new song played. They started caressing their own bodies, grinding on each other, and the cheers grew louder. Camille was dancing hard and her skirt tended to fly up over her waist. It caused an uproar from the young men in the audience.

Faculty members looked on with disapproval, but decided to let the girls finish their routine.

Camille detected a lagging in Dominique's steps. She knew why, and it upset her that Dominique would sabotage their performance by having sex the night before, when the rest of the group was giving it their all.

The music came to a close and the girls ended with the straddle splits, receiving a standing ovation.

Tre Pound, Playa Paul, Moses, and Stacks had approached the stage.

"We had the crowd hyphy!" Camille beamed, as Tre Pound helped her down off the stage. She was shivering with excitement. "Did you like it?"

"I almost fell asleep ..." Tre Pound began. He helped Dominique down also, feeling her butt without anyone noticing. "... watching that bullshit," he finished. "If I would've known it was gon' be that bunk, I would've brought a book to read."

"You know you liked it, punk," Camille said, laughing.

"And you can't do no better," Dominique teased. She gave Tre Pound a light hug, patting him on the back. Subtle. Not too obvious. "I see you didn't get yo'self locked up."

"By the grace of my lawyer." He turned to Camille. "So what you 'bout to do? 'Cause I'm 'bout to shake the spot."

"I'ma stay here. We gotta watch the rest of the perform-ers, then see who wins. Dominique got her brother's car, so we don't need a ride."

"Well, come get these clothes I got for you out my car."

They all headed out the auditorium.

None of them saw Row and his goons enter through the side door.

"What kind of shirt did you get me?" Camille asked, swinging her arms as they walked toward the exit.

"A white one," Tre Pound said.

"I don't even know why I asked."

Suddenly, gunshots rang out. Multiple shots! Screaming students began scurrying in every direction, tripping and falling over each other.

Then came another volley of bullets.

Tre Pound collapsed.

Seeing where the shots were coming from, Moses, Playa Paul and Stacks pulled out their pistols and returned fire.

Nearby, Cash and Seneca added to the firepower. Innocent people were struck down, bodies getting trampled. Only a few more shots were exchanged before the crowd thickened and engulfed them.

The shooters got away.

Camille had ducked down when the shooting started, and thought Tre Pound had done the same, until she reached for him. Horrified, she screamed, "Somebody help!"

Bleeding profusely, Tre Pound lay in excruciating pain. Convulsing like he was having a seizure. His once immaculate attire was bloodstained. He was losing life by the second.

"We gotta get outta here," Playa Paul told a frightened, crying Camille.

Dominique and Krystal were crying, too.

"C'mon, yall, we gotta go," he repeated.

Moses and Stacks directed the girls towards the exit. But Camille, she wouldn't budge.

Playa Paul lifted her up over his shoulder. She fought back as he led her away from her cousin.

"I can't leave him! I have to help him!" she shouted, reaching out to Tre Pound as she was being carried away. "I gotta go back!"

She then lost sight of him in the frenzy.

CHAPTER 16

Dominique parked the Ford Explorer in
front of her house. She sat there, sad and distraught. The
school shooting, Tre Pound laying there, the hospital, not
knowing if he was going to survive—it was horrible.

First, there was the chance Tre Pound could have been
sentenced to life in prison. Now there was a strong possibility he could die on a hospital bed. The way things were
going, he and Dominique would never get to be a couple.
She promised herself that if he recovered, she wouldn't
waste any more time making him the one, officially.

Marlon came out the house and loaded a duffel bag into
an old white van. Then out came the rest of his friends,
each carrying bags of their own. They made a couple more
trips in and out the house before Dominique stepped out
the Explorer.

"What's goin' on?" she asked.

The guys ignored her.

She grabbed onto Stacks before he went back in the
house. "What are yall gettin' ready to do?"

"We gotta ride for da homie," Stacks said, and kept it moving.

Another bag over his shoulder, Marlon came back outside. Dominique recognized the bag; it was made for golf clubs, but her brother used it to store his Mossberg pump shotgun.

"Marlon, you leavin' wit' them?" she asked, following him to the van.

"I thought you was at the hospital."

"I was, but they made everybody leave who wasn't family."

Marlon tossed the golf bag in the back of the van. He turned to look at his sister's sorrowful expression. "Is he gon' make it?"

"I don't know. He's in critical condition."

"Well, get in the house. Lock the doors. Don't even answer if somebody knocks. I'll be back in a minute."

"But you're on house arrest. You can't go."

Moses and Stacks hopped in the back and Marlon shut the doors. Playa Paul got in the driver's seat; he was the best behind the wheel. But as Marlon got in the passenger seat, Dominique stood in the way so he couldn't shut his door.

"Get out the way, Dominique."

Though she wanted the bastards who shot her lover to be dealt with, she didn't want Marlon to get killed in the process. However, she knew the rules of the game, about retaliation, and loyalty amongst friends. Her brother had to ride. She wouldn't be able to talk him out of it. The best thing she could do was be supportive.

"Make sure you get 'em, Marlon."

"I am. Just get in the house."

Dominique stepped away from the curb and watched the van putter away.

***

Spook blew smoke in the air of the already cloudy living room. "You see how he fell? The nigga just dropped ... I wonder if he survived all them shots."

"It should be on the news in the morning. We'll find out then," Row said, looking disappointed. "I wanted to make sure he was dead. I wanted to run up on him, empty the clip and let him catch every bullet I had. Do him like he did Drought Man."

"It was too many people runnin' and screamin', gettin' in the way. Then his homeboys started bustin' too. We had to fall back. I told you we should've waited. Got at him somewhere else."

"I didn't wanna wait. I told myself I was gon' get him the first day I got out."

"But the whole two years you was in jail, I been runnin' into Tre Pound, off and on. One time I seen him in the parking lot at Wal-Mart out South. He was wit' his little cousin Camille. Caught him slippin'. And when he seen me, he looked scared, not knowing if I was gon' draw down on him right there. I would've, but you told me don't touch him. So I just mugged him and walked off. He would've been smoked. You should've gave me the green light a long time ago."

"You don't understand," Row said, leaning forward on the couch. He clapped his hands to emphasize each word. "Drought-Man-was-my-nigga."

"He was my nigga, too," Spook countered.

"But me and Drought Man were like brothers. We used to take baths together when we was kids. I named my son after him. I had to be the one that avenges his death and take Tre Pound's life." Row lifted his right shirt sleeve. There was a facial tattoo of Drought Man on his arm. "R.I.P., my nigga."

Spook got up to check it out. "That's feddy. You got that done in the joint?"

"A Spanish Disciple did it. Captured Drought Man's slanted eyes, his long jaw. It looks just like him. Right under his face was supposed to be a banner that read: RIP 12th Street Soldier. But the Spanish dude went to the hole and didn't get to finish it. But I"ma get it done out here." Row rolled down his sleeve. "Drought Man's wit' me for eternity."

One more puff of the blunt and Spook handed it off. He went and slumped back in his armchair, looking like he was about to go to sleep. "Have you ever just sat back and wondered why Tre Pound carries hisself the way he does?

He robs niggas wit' no mask. He wants people to know it's him. Who da fuck does he think he is?"

"I can tell you exactly why he been doin' that shit: He does it because he gets away wit' it," Row explained, blunt burning between his fingertips. "Most of the people Tre Pound robs be straight bitches, scared to get even wit' him. They know he's a funk artist, quick to pop that pistol. And then you gotta take into consideration people are intimidated by his family's reputation."

Spook nodded. "His cousins Shelton King and Gutta used to be deadly back in the day when they used to sell dope. No lie, when I was like 11, I remember seeing Shelton shoot a nigga in the stomach for leaning against his car. I heard Gutta pistol-whipped a community activist."

"But before Shelton and Gutta, you had Cutthroat, who was Tre Pound's uncle. We was little kids when Cutthroat ran the city. Old heads in the joint used to tell me stories about him. They say Cutthroat used to be part of an organization called the Black Liberation Army. He robbed banks and dope dealers and gave the money to poor women and children. They say he robbed a couple corrupt police officers, too. Even beat a cop to death wit' a baseball bat while the cop's tied-up daughter watched. The daughter was so traumatized that she couldn't point Cutthroat out of a line-up, so the cops shot him to death in a routine traffic stop, claiming he was going for his gun."

Row paused briefly to take a hit of the blunt, then continued. "I think that's another reason Tre Pound acts the way he does. He's tryna be like his uncle. But he ain't nothin' like his uncle because he robs dope dealers and keeps the money for hisself. The streets don't respect Tre Pound like they did his cousins and his uncle."

"The King family ain't near what it used to be," Spook said. "Shelton's behind a desk now. Gutta ain't makin' no noise. Then you got Tre Pound's little cousins, Cash and Seneca—them little niggas is crash dummies. They do stupid shit around the 'hood like settin' fires and shootin' up parties."

"I don't care if Tre Pound's family *was* what it used to be. That still wouldn't unnerve me or deter me from seekin' revenge for Drought Man. I'ma be at Tre Pound up till the day I see him layin' stiff, filled wit' embalming fluid."

There were other brothas from 12th Street lounging in the living room lazily. Intoxicated. Some sleep. Row puffed on Spook's blunt, glad to be home. He felt even better knowing he gunned Tre Pound down, but he wouldn't be at peace until he knew his adversary was no longer sharing his air.

"What's it like out here?" Row asked.

"As far as what?"

"As far as gettin' money. Who's doin' what? How much is being made in the streets?"

"The drug game is ripe. Everybody is makin' paper. Just about every 'hood is rollin'. We got the Twelve sold up, of course. It's good out here. But it ain't always been like this. While you was in the joint, we done had a couple

171

droughts. Niggas was starvin', sellin' Sheetrock by the kilo and resorting to robbery—it was bad out here. Without Drought Man to supply the city during droughts, it got outta control. I even had to gank some niggas. I just hope it don't get as bad during the next drought." Spook's stomach started to bubble from the burritos he ate earlier. "I gotta go take a shit," he said, and retreated to the bathroom.

"I'ma catch you later, Spook," Row called out as he stood. "I'm 'bout to go to the house and get some sleep. Hit me up if you get word about that ole bitch-ass nigga Tre Pound."

On the toilet, Spook expelled loud gaseous farts. His voice was strained. "A'ight!"

Row said goodbye to the rest of his homies, the ones that were awoke, and left the house.

He got the feel of his black Buick Grand National back with no problem. It was kept in tip-top condition since he'd been gone, courtesy of Spook. The black interior was spotless, not even a cigarette butt in the ashtray. But something wasn't right about the car. Row could feel it.

One of the tires needed air.

Not too far from Spook's house, Row turned into a gas station and parked next to the air machine. As he got out, he saw a white van bend the corner and head in the direction he just came from.

Row thought nothing of it.

The air machine rattled noisily when Row put a quarter in. He grabbed the tube and knelt down to pump air into his front right tire. Because of the noise, he didn't hear the gunshots in the distance. He simply checked his tire and hung the tube back up.

But when he opened his car door, the air machine happened to automatically cut off. And that was when he heard the shots. He paused and listened, a cigarette dangling between his lips. Afar, gun blasts went off continuously. Somebody was using an assualt rifle. And it was coming from the direction of Spook's house.

"Shit!"

It was then that Row fired up the engine and screeched off. He raced his Grand National back to Spook's street and saw that same white van as it bent the corner at the other end of the block, fleeing the scene. Row slammed on his brakes after pulling into Spook's driveway. He hopped out and ran to the front door, which was slightly open. He rushed in to a bloody mess.

"No ... " he uttered, standing in the middle of the living room. His once lively homies were sprawled on the couch and floor, lifeless, their blood splattered against the walls, carpet, every-where, like a gory Picasso.

The sight left Row in a momentary trance. He didn't move or speak. His expression was blank. The feelings he felt when he lost Drought Man emerged. Pain. Malice. Emptiness.

He slowly walked over to Mikey, whose eyes were wide open. With his fingers, Row closed them. Mikey, only 14 years old, stayed down the street. He wasn't a part of the game. He would just come over to Spook's house to hang out.

Where was Spook?

A clanking sound came from the bathroom. Row hurried there and caught sight of an exhausted-looking Spook as he climbed out the bullet-riddled tub, pistol in hand. The stench from the feces in the toilet stool was pungent.

"It wasn't too much I could do," Spook said, resting against the outside of the tub amongst all kinds of spent shell casings. "Are they gone? I mean, the homies, are they gone?"

Row nodded solemnly.

"Everybody? Reece, T-Dogg, Mikey?"

"They got everybody!" Row snapped. "How'd they know where to hit us at? They came straight here."

"I don't know," Spook said, overwhelmed.

"You got careless while I was locked up! You ain't never supposed to let nobody know where you rest yo head!"

"I know!"

"Since you know so much, nigga, who shot this mufucka up? Was it Tre Pound's family, his cousins? His homies? Who?"

"When they came in, I hopped in the tub. I was shooting without looking. I didn't have a chance to see nobody."

"I guess it don't even matter," Row concluded. "Whoever fucks wit' Tre Pound is a target now."

CHAPTER 17

"Who shot me?"

Tre Pound's throat was dry and he barely got the question out. He turned away from the blinding morning sun that beamed through the open curtains.

Camille was sitting next to his bed, reading a book called *Think and Grow Rich* that somebody had left in the waiting area. She was bundled up in a blanket, and had stayed at the hospital overnight.

"You're awake," she said happily, jumping up to the side of his bed. She gave him a light hug. "Stay awake this time."

Tre Pound grunted. His entire body, from his toes to his skull, ached. More so his left arm, which rested in a royal blue sling. The hospital room smelled damp, and the whiteness throughout the room—the curtains, the sheets, the walls—had him feeling dismal.

"Who shot me?" he asked again.

"I tried to find out but yo friends wouldn't tell me. 'Cause they know I would've fucked somebody up. So you gotta ask them. I think they went and did somethin' the night you got shot."

"How long I been here?"

"Like nine days. It's Saturday. Everybody told me to tell you they love you. Some light-skinned girl named Buttercup came to see you, too. And Moses' stupid ass is the one who tied those balloons to yo big toe."

The bright-colored balloons bumped together and drifted when Tre Pound struggled to lift both legs, wiggling his toes. Despite the soreness, his body seemed to be working fine. "Get me some water and close those curtains," he said, and Camille didn't hesitate to do as she was told.

She tilted his head so he could sip on the cup of water. "The doctor said you got shot six times. He said you was lucky to survive. I almost thought you died in that auditorium." She sat the cup down and looked at him, about to cry. "Playa Paul pulled me away from you, got us all out of there. But I didn't want to leave ... I'm so glad you're still alive. You can't keep scarin' everybody like this. The trial, then you gettin' shot ..."

"I'ma be a'ight. You better not cry. You can cry at my funeral, that's it."

"Don't say that!" she whined.

Two light knocks at the door and in walked the nurse, Michelle King, carrying a breakfast tray of scrambled eggs, bacon, wheat toast, and sausage links. She was followed by a smiling Gutta, who assisted his wife by carrying the cups of orange juice.

"We brought food," Michelle announced. "Oh, he's up!"

"And he's lookin' good," Gutta added. "How you feelin'?"

"Like shit," Tre Pound said. "I need some kind of pain killers. Michelle, why don't you do yo job and prescribe me some medication."

"That's not my job," Michelle retorted. "The doctor does that. And you don't need none anyway. You ain't in pain. What you need is some food. Eat this." She fed him a scoop of eggs.

After Gutta set the orange juice down, Camille gave him a big hug. "What's goin' on, brother?"

"Came to see family." Gutta kissed her forehead. "How you doin'? Stayin' out of trouble?"

"I am, but too bad I can't say the same about him." She frowned at the thug on the hospital bed. "He stay in trouble, driving the family nuts. And he just told me I can cry at his funeral. Gutta, talk to him."

Tre Pound grumbled through bites of bacon, "If you don't sit yo ass down somewhere ..."

"See, that's what I'm talkin' about," Camille said. "He's shot up and still talkin' stuff."

"That's how I'ma remain till the day I die. I'm not the type to change up and go soft because I got shot. Nah, I'ma go harder on these niggas." Tre Pound pushed away the food with his good arm. "Michelle, I can feed myself. I need you and Camille to step out the room for a minute so I can talk to Gutta about some G shit. When we start talkin' about curling irons and leggings we'll call yall back in."

"We'll be glad to leave," Michelle said, placing the breakfast by his bedside. "We ain't gotta take this slick talk from you. C'mon, Camille. We'll have our own secret conversation in the TV room."

"Okay, but I ain't ate all morning. Let me grab my plate." Camille picked up her cup of orange juice and discreetly put the rest of Tre Pound's bacon on her plate before she made her exit.

Gutta sat down on the bed. "Four times by a TEC-9 and twice by an AK-47. You must got a purpose on this earth."

"My purpose is to keep the King name alive and strong," Tre Pound replied.

"Yep, that must be it. Because me and Shelton was just talkin' about how you represent the family admirably. But before I forget: congratulations on the trial. I wish I could've been there."

"I don't ever wanna go through that again. Havin' my life in the hands of twelve goofy-lookin' mufuckas—that's not wussup." With the pillows as cushions against his back, Tre Pound sat himself up. "It look like you 'bout to go through what I just went through. Michelle had told us you was in jail. What went wrong?"

"I got caught," Gutta said flatly. "Michelle bonded me out the day before yesterday. Shit didn't go according to plan. Tommy and Tony went ahead and smashed the cases and grabbed the jewelry—fuckin' glass had a silent alarm on it. I knew we should've just got the safe only."

Tre Pound groaned as he tried to move his wounded left arm. "So where Tommy and Tony at? They got caught, too?"

"Yeah, they still in the county—and they snitchin' on me. I read they statements; they told everything. Said I planned it and coerced them to do it."

"Damn. I thought them two niggas was authentic, stand-up guys. That goes to show that you never know who you can trust."

Gutta nodded. He explained how the cops had the place surrounded and how Tommy and Tony chose to "get down first." Then he switched the subject. "I remember you tellin' me about one of yo homies that was tryna cop a key."

"My nigga Moses. He been stackin' his money. And he got this little chick that helps him out financially. My other homie, Playa Paul, been tryna find a plug to cop a key, too, just to outdo Moses. Playa Paul always wanna outdo somebody. But it's friendly competition, I guess. Then my nigga Marlon ... he's content where he's at, sellin' half ounces. Skinny-ass Stacks don't hustle at all. He just get money from his pops and smoke wet all day, every day. I need to get in touch wit' them. Camille told me they rode for me the night I got shot."

Crossing his arms, Gutta said, "But back to Moses. You had told me he said he was gon' have enough to cop one by next Saturday. That would be today."

"So he'll probably meet up wit' his plug tonight, if I'm not mistaken. Moses is tryna come up."

Without knocking, Camille paraded back in the room and jumped in the bed with her relatives. "Time's up. I gave yall enough time to talk about whatever it was yall wanted to keep between yall'selves. Now yall gotta include me. I deserve more than anybody to talk to you, Tre Pound."

"Why's that?" Tre Pound asked.

"Because I been comin' up here every day after school, spent the night twice. That's why."

"She's right," Gutta said. "I'm in the wrong for takin' up all the time when Camille put in all the work. So Camille, you can have him all to yo'self. I gotta get going." He extended his hand to give Tre Pound dap and smothered Camille with a hug before he made his departure.

"What was yall talkin' about that was so confidential I had to leave?" asked Camille.

Tre Pound turned away from her, moaning and making a wry face. He seemed to be in some kind of agony.

"What's wrong, Tre Pound? What's wrong?" Camille was petrified. She grasped his shoulder, trying to turn him back towards her. "Where is it hurting?"

He moaned louder, shielding his face with a pillow.

"Tell me somethinl! Do you want me to go get Michelle?"

"No ..."

"What do you want me to do?!"

"Brush yo teeth," Tre Pound said, laughing. "Yo breath stink."

Camille's face went blank, then she started laughing along with him. Her cousin was back. And she couldn't be happier.

CHAPTER 18

Missing a hubcap, J-Dub and Kareem traveled

north on Troost Avenue in a primered gray '76 Chevy Impala—on the verge of being unemployed. They were scheduled to work lunch hours, the busiest shift, and were already 20 minutes late.

"You should've let me drive," Kareem said. "I could've got us there faster."

"What you in a rush for? We always late. You think big-eared Jack really gon' follow through wit' his threats and fire us?"

"He sounded serious last time. And if I get fired, my momma gon' kick me out."

"You can come stay wit' me," J-Dub told him. "My momma and my daddy won't care."

Kareem looked enchanted. He leaned towards his homeboy, arms outstretched, but J-Dub forcibly pushed him away.

"What are you doin'? You see me driving."

"I was tryna give you a hug. Offering to let me stay wit' you means a lot to me. You my homie fa-real." Kareem tried for another embrace and got shoved again.

"Keep yo sentimental ass over there."

"You act like you too hard to show yo emotions."

"I ain't got no emotions," J-Dub said.

"Now you know I don't believe that. You was too quick to jump up and defend Camille. *And* I heard you tell her you'll die for her."

J-Dub had meant it, too. In the past, he had girls he felt strongly about, but Camille was the only one he could honestly say he'd risk his life for. And trying to get close to her again was definitely a risk. Or was it? Tre Pound got shot up. Was hospitalized. Could be dying. And with him out of the picture, who could stop J-Dub from possessing Camille?

A smile surfaced as J-Dub thought of that possibility. After his two-week suspension was up, he'd go back to school and approach her with an ultimatum: Be his woman, or suffer his relentless advances. Because he would never stop trying.

He wondered what her response would be.

He wondered what she was doing at this very moment.

***

For lunch, Camille wanted to surprise Tre Pound so she called Dominique to come pick her up from the hospital and take her to Go Chicken Go. On their way back from the restaurant, traveling south on Troost Avenue in a ruby red Ford Explorer, Camille opened the chicken box and counted the biscuits.

"It don't make no sense for us to have to wait that long to get served. Seem like they should have more people workin' during lunch time. If that wasn't Tre Pound's favorite place to eat, I would've left."

"How was he?" Dominique asked, eyes on the road. "Is he gonna make a full recovery?"

"He is. The doctors said it. But you know doctors— they'll say anything. So I asked my cousin Michelle for the honest to God truth and she assured me that Tre Pound would be okay. I'ma stay there with him every single day until he can come home."

"I wish I could stay there with him, too," Dominique said under her breath.

"Huh?"

"Nothin'."

It was eating Dominique up. She had all these feelings hidden inside and she was afraid to tell her best friend for fear that they would fall out. Uniting with Tre Pound would manifest her dreams. He was mysterious, tough, and lived a dangerous life. Dominique wanted to be a part of that life. If only she could explain to Camille how much she cared for him, maybe she'd understand.

First, she would find out how Camille felt about her cousin being in a relationship.

"Do you think Tre Pound will ever settle down?"

"I hope so," Camille said. She pinched a gizzard and took a bite, careful not to drop it on her cashmere sweater.

"Really?"

"Uh-huh. I can't wait till the day he doesn't have to carry a gun. He didn't even know who shot him. That's how many enemies he got. It's ridiculous. But I don't want him to just settle down. I want him to stop funkin' altogether."

As they stopped at a red light, Dominique started to say something. "That's not what I was ..."

But in the next lane, a car pulled alongside them, honking its horn. Cash and Seneca were in Tre Pound's creme Infiniti Q45, subwoofers booming. They had two giddy teenage girls in the backseat.

"Where yall 'bout to go?" Seneca asked after turning the music down.

"I'm tellin'!" Camille yelled at them, leaning all over Dominique's lap. "Yall know yall ain't supposed to be driving Tre Pound's car!"

Cash, who was behind the wheel, said, "Shelton's the one who told us to drive this car. He wants people to see it so the word will get around that Tre Pound is still alive."

Most of the time Cash was honest and responsible so Camille believed him. Seneca, on the other hand, behaved recklessly. He thought he was Tre Pound, tried to make his voice sound like him and everything. However, despite

185

their differences, Camille loved her half brothers both the same.

"He's awake now," she said. "We on our way back up there. So if yall wanna go see him again yall can." She glanced at the girls in the backseat. "Don't go up there wit' nobody. He might trip."

"Just tell him we got the car," Cash said. "We'll probably be up there later, but right now ..." Both brothers smiled mischievously and Camille shot them a disgusted look. "... You already know."

Seneca winked at Dominique. "One day you might be able to be in the backseat."

"Oh, I can't wait," Dominique sneered. If she had her way she'd be driving that car, Tre Pound riding shotgun.

The light turned green.

"Tre block," Seneca said, and Cash punched the gas pedal and streaked off.

"You not even from the Tre!" Camille screamed.

Driving on, Dominique said, "Yo brothers are crazy."

"They sure are. Especially Seneca. He's like a little Tre Pound. And we all know the world doesn't need another one of him." Camille popped one last gizzard in her mouth and closed the box, stopping herself from eating them all up. "Now what was you sayin' before they pulled up? I didn't hear you."

"It really wasn't nothin' major. When I asked you did you think Tre Pound would *settle down*, I meant like a relationship."

"Tre Pound? Relationship? Them two don't even go together. He don't let girls get that close to him. The girls he mess wit' are hoes. They let him do whatever he wants to them, and then he dismisses them just like that," Camille said, snapping her fingers. "And if he did settle down, the bitch would have to be accepted by the family. Because he wouldn't just let anybody in. That's why he's so protective of me."

"I don't think everybody he messes wit' are hoes."

"Hmph. I beg to differ."

"There's probably a girl he's been with that he cares about. Somebody different than the other girls."

Camille shot her a curious glance. "Why you say that?"

"Because everybody wants somebody that they can call their own. Tre Pound's no exception."

Camille could relate. But she didn't *want* somebody; she *needed* somebody to call her own, to love her like a lady should be loved.

"Dominique, maybe you right about my cousin," she said, flinging her hands in the air. "Who knows? Just tell me why we're even talkin' about his love life. Who cares?"

"I care," Dominique said fondly. Her eyes stayed on the road.

Dumbfounded, Camille simply stared at her. Then she sort of laughed and lightly pushed her arm. "Girl, I told you about playin' like that. You better cut that out."

It took another block of driving for Dominique to gather the strength to release what she has been holding in

187

for weeks. "Camille, I know you might feel like I betrayed you, but that's not it. Just listen to me ... I'm in love with Tre Pound. And I know it's not just lust; I know he cares about me just as much because we've been intimate together." She glanced at Camille's shocked face and continued.

"The first time was about a month ago—he only let me jack him off. Nothin' else happened up until the night before he went to court ... remember, in seminar class, when you told me you knew I snuck out? He's the one I went to see. I drove out to his house, and he's the one who sexed me in my—"

"I don't wanna hear anymore!" Camille hollered. She closed her eyes and massaged her temples.

"It wasn't just sex. I felt love. I want him to be my man, my husband, and to give him what I haven't given anybody." Dominique glanced at her again, concerned about her ability to cope with the bomb she just dropped. "Camille ...? Camille, I'm sorry." She reached to put a hand on her shoulder and Camille swatted it away.

"Don't fucking touch me!" Camille's eyes were watery, her cheeks already wet. "You know I don't approve of that shit, Dominique. How could you fuck my cousin?"

"I-I know. But I love him, Camille. It felt so good, so great, so ... I can't even describe it." Dominique got a rush of emotion just thinking about Tre Pound inside her. "I can sense he needs a devoted girl in his life. Camille, I want to be that girl. If you could just understand where I'm coming from ..."

"No, I don't understand!" Camille snapped at her. "You're stupid! You think he's gonna be wit' you, yeah right. You're no different than the other tramps he's fucked. And you didn't even consider how this would affect our friend-ship."

"I did, but—"

"You know what, save it. I don't care what you have to say. It don't mean shit." Tears streamed down Camille's face as she stared out the window. "Nobody loves me anymore," she mumbled. "Everybody wants to please everyone else. No one takes into account my feelings."

Dominique didn't know what to say. On one end her friendship with Camille meant everything to her, on the other was Tre Pound, the man who had her heart—and she couldn't let Camille stand in the way no matter how close they were. "I'm sorry," she said. "You deserved to know. I knew you wouldn't take it lightly. But I have to be with him."

"Pull over," Camille mumbled.

"Do what?"

Camille spoke a little louder. "I said pull over."

"Uh-uh," said Dominique, shaking her head. "I know you're mad at me but I'm not gonna let you walk. If you don't want to talk to me the rest of the way then just don't talk to me."

"Pull the fucking car over now!" In a sudden rage, Camille reached over and yanked on the steering wheel. The Ford Explorer swerved as both girls fought for control.

"Stop, Camille! You're gonna kill us!" Dominique opposingly tugged on the wheel, trying to keep from crashing into a parked car. Then she slammed on the brakes, whipping her head against the woodgrain.

Hopping out the SUV into the middle of the street, Camille walked briskly onto the sidewalk and kept it moving. Dominique got out to chase her down.

***

"I still ain't figured out what you see in her," Kareem said. "Camille is bad as a muthafucka, I agree, but you got other girls runnin' all around KC that's fine, too."

"Name one girl that's as fine as her," J-Dub challenged, cruising through a yellow light before it turned red.

"I can't. But that's not what I'm gettin' at. What I'm gettin' at is this: Camille comes wit' a package deal. To have her, you gotta accept all the shit that comes wit' her. That includes Tre Pound."

"Fuck Tre Pound."

"You only sayin' that because he's in the hospital. What you gonna do when he gets out and sees you tryna talk to her again?"

"How you know he's gonna get out? People is sayin' he got shot 10 times. That if he live, he's gon' be a vegetable. Some people is sayin' he's already dead."

"Well, tell me how you plan to deal wit' Lil' Pat. Because you know it ain't over. He been carrying a gun to school.

When I started to walk up to him to tell him you didn't mean to hit him, he hurried up and reached under his shirt. So I didn't go near him. I think he might try and shoot you when you come back to school."

"Lil' Pat ain't got the heart."

"But his big brother Hoodey does," Kareem replied. "All this drama is comin' from yo obsession wit' Camille. You need to leave her alone. She's too much trouble."

"If you knew her like I do, you wouldn't be sayin' that," said J-Dub. "There's more to her than how good she looks. She's full of affection, not venom like these other girls. She's different in so many ways. When she talks about changin' the world, the passion in her voice makes you wanna help her."

J-Dub saw a girl chasing another girl down the sidewalk. He wasn't positive, but the girl trying to get away looked like Camille.

When Kareem said, "You see them? That look like Camille and Dominique," it prompted J-Dub to park haphazardly against the curb.

***

Dominique nabbed Camille's arm. "Get back in the car," she pleaded.

Camille stopped and spun around to face her. "I told you before not to touch me!" Emotional hurt put a strain on her voice. "Touch me again and see if I don't fuck you up!"

"You actin' crazy."

"I'm crazy? You da one that's fucked up in da head!"

"Can we still be friends? I'm beggin' you."

"I don't want nothin' else to do with you!" Camille hollered.

J-Dub jogged over to them. "What's goin' on?" he asked.

Camille grabbed his wrist. "I need a ride, that's what's goin' on." She led J-Dub back towards his Impala.

"Camille!" Dominique called out. Her brother's car was still in the middle of the street. She had to go back and get it. "Camille! Camille, I'm sorry!

CHAPTER 19

J-Dub guided the heavy Impala with one hand on the steering wheel. The radio was off and the roar of the 454 engine vibrated the car. He had dropped Kareem off at work with instructions to tell their manager he'd be there shortly.

"How you been doin', Camille?"

She didn't respond. Every few seconds a tear would slide down her cheek as she gazed out the front windshield. She had lost a friend. And that friend was scheming to take away her cousin too.

"Where you want me to drop you off at?" J-Dub asked.

It wasn't fair, Camille thought. Dominique found love, and what if it really happened, that Tre Pound and Dominique became one? They already had sex so it wasn't impossible. Where would that leave Camille? Without a best friend and a cousin who had always showed interest, care, and adoration. She would end up being neglected.

Another tear dropped from her eye.

Perhaps if she could replace both of them, it wouldn't matter. Out the corner of her eye, she saw J-Dub making concerned glimpses at her. He *did* avow his love in seminar class. He *did* take her virginity, and in that single moment she felt cherished. It was her only sexual experience and she longed for another. She'd simply have to overlook the fact that he dumped her because of Tre Pound's intimidation. J-Dub was all she had now.

"I want to go home with you," Camille said.

J-Dub seemed a bit stunned. "I don't know if that's a good idea. Whatever yall was arguing about got you upset and you ain't thinkin' straight. I'ma take you to yo house."

Camille wiped her face with her hands. "Me and Dominique always argue. I'm okay," she said, which wasn't entirely true. "It's just that Tre Pound almost got killed and he's layin' in a hospital."

"I saw that shit when it went down. Is he a'ight?"

"He's gettin' better. He's able to walk around on his own."

J-Dub's spirits seemed to deflate, as if he was upset that Tre Pound would survive.

Camille said, "I know you don't like him but I'm glad you asked."

J-Dub nodded.

"So is it okay if I go home with you. I'm thinkin' straight. This is what I want."

"Is that what you really want to do? Not because you're upset, but because you really wanna go home wit' me?"

"Were you serious about what you told me in seminar class?" she asked, a hopeful glint in her eyes.

"I wouldn't lie about somethin' like that. That came directly from the heart. You can ask Kareem. I talk about you all the time."

"Then, yes," Camille said, "I'm sure."

A short time later they were at J-Dub's house. Once Camille entered his room, she thought back to her very first time. J-Dub had been gentle with her. Camille had undressed under the covers of the twin bed, shying from exposing her naked body. Now he had a king-size bed. It was the only thing different about the room. There was a Fossil watch on the dresser. Camille examined it, her back towards him.

"You still got this?" she asked.

"Ever since you got it for my birthday, I held on to it. The batteries went out once and I put new ones in it. I thought as long as I keep it ticking there was a chance that we would get back together."

She set it down and immediately felt his warm breath on her neck. She closed her eyes. "Promise me you won't let my cousin run you off again."

He wrapped his arms around her waist, his groin pressed against her behind. "When I said I'm ready to die for you that's what I meant. If yo cousin wanna kill me or whatever then let him kill me. Man, I don't even care, man. If that's how it gotta go down, so be it. I'm not runnin' ..."

Turning to face him, she put a finger to his lips. "Ssshh. Just say you promise."

His eyes bore into hers assuredly. "I promise."

They closed their eyes, and J-Dub planted a kiss on her delicate lips. He paused, waiting for permission to go further. She then gently kissed him back, resting her hands on his shoulders. Soft sucking sounds escaped from their lips. Impassioned by the taste of her mouth, he squeezed her buttocks, its suppleness fashioning to his grip. His manhood instantly got excited, longing to be inside her again.

"Wait," Camille said. "I need to know somethin'."

"Yeah, I got a condom."

"Not that. I need to know if you're my boyfriend."

"Hell yeah."

"Okay."

He pressed his lips against hers aggressively, slipping his tongue in her mouth. "I wanna taste yo whole body," he whispered.

She moaned. "Okay."

Before laying down in the bed, Camille kicked off her sneakers. She started to crawl to the center of the mattress to make room for J-Dub, but he seized one of her ankles. She turned onto her butt as he tugged away her sock.

"You got pretty feet," he said, kissing her sole.

His lips on her foot felt weird and it made her giggle. "Thank you."

He took her pinky toe into his mouth, separating it from the others. Camille watched his face in amazement. He sucked and lapped at her toes like they were butterscotch. She giggled again.

"Tickles?"

"Keep goin'," she said, removing her other sock for him.

But before he could begin on the opposite foot, they heard a horn much louder than the average car horn.

"That sounded like a freight train," Camille said.

J-Dub released her foot. "It did, didn't it." He went to his window to look out and saw a chameleon-painted Chevy Caprice parked in front of his house. "You won't believe who's out here."

"Oh no. Is it yo parents?"

"I wish."

"Who's out there?"

"Lil' Pat and his brother."

Mouth agape, Camille said, "They ain't either. Are they really? What are they doing?"

"They gettin' out the car."

Outside, Lil' Pat sat on the hood of the Caprice while Hoodey rested his backside against the front fender, puffing on a coated More Red. They didn't look like they were going anywhere.

"What are they doing now?" Camille asked impatiently.

"Waitin'," J-Dub answered. He observed Hoodey lean in the car and honk the air horn again. "Waitin' on me."

197

"Get out the window before they see you. Maybe they'll leave."

"They know I'm here. My car's out there." J-Dub went back over to Camille. "Get up," he told her. She stood, and he lifted the mattress to retrieve his .40-caliber pistol.

"You ain't 'bout to go out there, are you?" Camille took a peek out the window. "Just stay in here," she said.

"And take a chance of them shootin' my house up or kickin' in? Nah, I'ma go out there. I told you I'm not runnin' from nothin' or nobody." After close inspection of his handgun, J-Dub tucked it in his waist and vanished from his bedroom.

When he came outside onto the front porch, Hoodey leaned off his car and Lil' Pat stepped down off the hood. The front of J-Dub's T-shirt was tucked behind his gun, making the black handle visible.

"If yall come in my yard I got a right to shoot yall," J-Dub threatened. He walked off the porch, standing his ground.

Hoodey took the thin cigarette out his mouth with his thumb and forefinger. "We don't need to come in yo yard, lil' nigga. I can shoot you from here. I wanna know why you and yo homie jumped my lil' brother."

"Didn't nobody jump him. Yo brother lying to you. I hit him once in his mouth and he ran away." J-Dub pointed at Lil' Pat. "Tell da truth. Me and Kareem didn't jump you, dog."

"Yall was about to," Lil' Pat said weakly.

"We wasn't either!" J-Dub hollered. "You tryna make some shit up because you was too scared to fight me!"

They were interrupted when the screen door creaked open. Camille walked onto the front porch, arms crossed. Everyone paused to look at her. She stood there, flattered and in awe that J-Dub, Lil' Pat and Hoodey were out here funking over her. She felt precious and important again.

Her sudden appearance shocked Lil' Pat. He assumed J-Dub had been in there fucking her—something he never had a chance to do. Seething with jealousy, he pulled out a .357 Magnum and waved it around.

"I'll smoke you right now like it's nothin'!" he barked at J-Dub with newfound authority.

Camille gasped.

J-Dub brandished his .40-cal. and held it by his side. "I got a gun, too," he said.

Hoodey grabbed ahold of his brother's wrist and snatched the revolver. "Give me this. We ain't here for that. Yall gon' box. One-on-one." He turned to J-Dub. "If you a man, and you say you wasn't tryna jump my lil' brother, then put the gun up and square off. Either that or I'ma give him this gun back and let him put holes in yo ass." He took a drag off his More Red.

"I'll box him," J-Dub said, chin up. "I'm a man."

"Put the gun up then, lil' nigga. What's the hold up? Let's get it crackin'."

J-Dub went up on the porch and extended his gun to

199

Camille. "Hold this for me. Don't put yo finger on the trigger, though."

She took it into her hands carefully. "I love you."

He kissed her. "I love you, too." And as he walked back down the porch steps and into the yard, he took off his T-shirt, balled it up and flung it. His chest was small but he had broad shoulders.

Over on the sidewalk, Lil' Pat whispered to his big brother with wide eyes, "What if I lose? He bigger than me."

"That ain't got nothin' to do wit' yo hand speed. I taught you how to stick and move. You my blood. We don't take losses." Hoodey shoved his little brother forward.

Lil' Pat's heart sank when he heard Camille holler, "Get him, Jesse!"

J-Dub bounced up and down on his tippy toes, getting his adrenaline pumping, as Lil' Pat took cautious steps into the yard, hands up in defense. Then J-Dub crouched into a boxer's stance, amped up, and advanced towards his opponent.

Once within arm's length, J-Dub jabbed Lil' Pat in the mouth, bloodying his lower lip.

"Dodge that weak shit, nigga!" Hoodey shouted.

Another quick jab and a left hook staggered Lil' Pat, and another jab made him stumble back, yet he stayed on his feet. Finally, he swung back, missed, and sensing a counterpunch coming, he latched onto J-Dub to avoid it.

"Let me go," J-Dub grunted as they tussled.

Lil' Pat wouldn't release the lock. He didn't want to take any more punches. He tried to wrestle J-Dub to the ground, but it was worthless.

Hoodey threw his cigarette down. "Quit holdin' him! Parallel park that nigga! Slam him!"

"Get him, Jesse!" Camille hollered again. She flinched when J-Dub forged an uppercut, loosening Lil' Pat's hold. The second uppercut caused Lil' Pat to bite his tongue, blood spilling out his mouth, and J-Dub was freed, enabling him to throw a monstrous right hook that cracked Lil' Pat's jaw. Blood swirled through the air. The sight made Camille wince, and she didn't want to see any more. "Stop, Jesse!"

Exhausted, knees wobbly, Lil' Pat charged forward with a flurry of punches. One connected, but J-Dub let it roll off his chin. The flurry drained Lil' Pat. After his last swing, he collapsed.

"Stand up! You better not let him do you like that!" Hoodey shouted, spit flying from his mouth as he spoke. His little brother struggled to get on his hands and knees. "Lil' Pat, what is you doin'?!"

Unsteady and off balance, Lil' Pat crawled towards his big brother, searching for a reprieve.

"He don't want no more," said J-Dub. "Now get out my yard. Get away from my house."

As Lil' Pat tried to climb up Hoodey's pants leg, Hoodey shoved him back into the yard, to the ground. "It ain't over. Fight, nigga!"

Resting in the grass, his body beaten, Lil' Pat's eyes wondered to the porch, where Camille stood staring back at him. He closed his eyes to avoid hers, the humiliation sinking in. She wouldn't want to be with a loser. And that made him angry.

He willed himself to his feet.

"That's it, bro," Hoodey said, clapping his hands. "Dust his khakis off."

J-Dub got back in his boxer's stance. "You ain't through yet?" he taunted.

Lil' Pat breathed heavily. "Aaaahhh!" he roared, charging forward, throwing a careless haymaker. But before his punch could connect, J-Dub swiftly threw a powerful, solid overhand right that rocked Lil' Pat's skull and sent him slamming into the brownish green grass.

Hoodey cursed.

Elderly neighbors peeked through curtains. Younger ones were standing on their porches, some all the way on the sidewalk. A little boy pointed and laughed until his big sister made him stop. Lil' Pat lay face down in the lawn, disoriented, bloody.

"Don't get up," J-Dub warned him.

"Jesse, leave him alone," Camille said sympathetically. "Come in the house. He had enough."

Hoodey looked down at his little brother with disgust. "Nigga, you ain't shit. You deserved to get yo ass wooped."

The defeat overwhelmed Lil' Pat. Not in front of Hoodey, he thought.

Not in front of Camille.

He started crying.

"You bitch-ass nigga." Hoodey shook his head and turned to go.

"No!" Lil' Pat hollered.

Hoodey stopped.

"No!" Disheveled, Lil' Pat got on his hands and knees, eventually to his feet.

J-Dub took two steps back, preparing for another round. But Lil' Pat was through fighting; he staggered over to his big brother.

"You ain't ridin' wit' me in my car. Bloodying up my seats," Hoodey said.

Lil' Pat latched onto him, chest heaving.

"Get yo muthafuckin' hands off me!" Hoodey tried to push him away, struggling with him a little bit, then calmed when he saw what Lil' Pat was reaching for.

The revolver.

"You alright?" Camille asked J-Dub.

He took his eyes off Hoodey and Lil' Pat and turned to her. "Never been better," he said.

"But yo knuckles are bleeding."

"I think all this is his blood. It'll wash off."

Then Camille looked away and gasped.

J-Dub immediately spun back around. The .357 Magnum was leveled at his face, Lil' Pat holding it up about ten feet away.

"Here!" Camille tossed the .40-caliber pistol to J-Dub but he dropped it.

"Pick it up," Lil' Pat uttered through gritted teeth. "I dare you."

J-Dub was about to pick it up but didn't. He left the gun in the grass near his feet and crossed his arms. He wasn't scared. "You ain't no killa," he said.

"But I'll kill you!"

Hoodey smiled. "Remember what I told you, Lil' Pat. Don't pull it out unless you gon' use it."

Lil' Pat took his thumb and clicked the hammer back. His eyes were full of tears, pride tarnished.

"What you gon' kill me for?" J-Dub asked in a brave tone. "Why it gotta come to this? You lost. Why can't you just walk away?"

"Because you took my girl!" Lil' Pat screamed. "That's why!"

"I'm not yo girl," Camille said. "You blew it. Now go home."

In a pleading voice, Lil' Pat said to her, "But he did the same shit! You told me. Why'd you go back to him? Give me another chance."

Camille slowly shook her head no. "Go home. You're not my boyfriend anymore. J-Dub is."

"She made her choice," said J-Dub, staring down the barrel of the chrome revolver. "So if you gon' shoot me, then just—"

The gun boomed, and J-Dub's face exploded. His blood splattered on Camille's face and his body dropped effortlessly. Camille shuddered, didn't scream—but a neighbor did. She held a blank expression, struck by how easy it was for a human life to be taken.

"C'mon, nigga!" Hoodey beckoned. "Time to roll out!"

Lil' Pat couldn't move. He stared down at his victim—J-Dub didn't have that baby face anymore. Too much flesh was missing, blood oozing out. Then Lil' Pat slowly looked at Camille, who was gazing at his victim in a stupor.

His brother called out to him again. "If you don't get yo dumb ass over here ... ! C'mon, Pat!"

Lil' Pat hesitated, waiting for Camille to say something, anything that would let him know he did the right thing. Yet her eyes were transfixed on the corpse.

So he scurried off.

When the Chevy screeched away, Camille still stood in the same spot, still in a trance. Her body felt numb. It happened again, she thought. Love was taken away from her.

CHAPTER 20

At the 63rd Street precinct, officers roamed in every direction, bringing in recently captured criminals and fingerprinting them. Telephones rang incessantly, and a fuming pimp who was complaining about his missing prostitute added to the commotion.

Camille blocked it all out. She sat in the waiting area, elbows on her knees, palms under her chin, trying to figure out why her life was falling apart. She couldn't keep a boyfriend; Tre Pound would run them off. And just when she thought she had a lasting companion, he was murdered right before her eyes.

She wiped a tear from her cheek.

To make matters worse, she couldn't even confide in her best friend because the bitch was involved with her cousin. Maybe that was her fate—to be alone.

When Shelton came to pick her up, the first thing he asked was, "Did you make a statement?"

"No," Camille mumbled.

"Good. Good. We can't have our family cooperating

with the police. We have to keep our respect in the streets while at the same time—"

"Upholding the exemplary image the public has of us," she finished. "I know, I know. Shelly, can you take me back up to the hospital? Tre Pound is awake now." She had to make sure Dominique's alleged romance was true. If so, perhaps she could talk Tre Pound out of being with that ho.

Shelton, calmly switching lanes in his burgundy S-type Jaguar, nodded his head. "Was he coherent?"

"Yeah."

"I need to talk to him again about this funk he's into. A lot of it is unnecessary. If he could just tone it down a notch, it won't be a problem. Havin' funk is to be expected in what he does. But too much is hazardous."

"Don't you even wanna know what happened with me?" Camille asked, eyeing her older brother. He always seemed to be interested in Tre Pound over his own little sister.

"I already know what happened. Hoodey called me and told me you was at some little boy's house—where you shouldn't have been in the first place—and his little brother shot the boy you was with. He apologized for it happening in front of you, so I'ma leave it at that. I don't need to know the details."

"Because you don't care about me," she mumbled.

"Huh?"

"Can we stop to get somethin' to eat? I was supposed to be bringin' Tre Pound some gizzards up there."

After they got the food, they drove to Research hospital and parked in the parking garage. The tapping sound of Shelton's dress shoes against the pavement echoed throughout the garage.

"I don't think Tre Pound's gonna be released today," said Camille, "so can you go to the house and get me another change of clothes?"

"You're not spendin' the night up here again."

Camille stopped in her tracks. "Why not?"

"Look what happened. You snuck off wit' some boy and put yourself in danger."

"For one, that's not even how it went down. For two, he wasn't some boy. His name was Jesse and he was my boyfriend."

"You need to be in the house where it's safe. You're 15, Camille. You're too young to be in the streets, especially with everything that's going on."

"What about Cash and Seneca? Cash is only one year older than me and Seneca is fucking 14! They get to go wherever they want to."

"Watch yo mouth, Camille."

"You can't run me. Daddy is dead so quit tryna be him."

"When Daddy died I became the man of the house."

"You don't even live with us. How you gonna be the man of the house?"

"I'm the man of the family. And what I say goes. It don't matter what you *think* you want, it's about what's best for you. You're spoiled, that's what it is. You got a cell phone, your own phone line; you get new clothes and jewelry every other week. What more do you want?"

"Some freedom," she stated. "I'm always in the house and Momma treats me like sh—" She caught herself. "—like I ain't nothin'. All I ask is to spend the night up here one more night. Can I, please?"

"I said no. And we'll be less hard on you when you start showin' some responsibility. This is tough love."

She huffed. "Love? Yall don't love me at all." She let the tears flow and stormed off.

As they entered the hospital, Shelton handed Camille a tissue. "Here," he said. "You don't need to be cryin' like this in public."

She snatched it.

When they reached Tre Pound's room, there was an old man sleeping in the bed. Tubes were stuffed in his veins, monitors beeping.

"Maybe we got the wrong room," Shelton said.

"No, this is the room." Camille walked in, looking around for evidence that this was in fact Tre Pound's room. She checked the bathroom, came out and noticed the deflated balloons in the trash.

"What is it?" Shelton asked.

"His balloons." She stepped out into the hallway and stopped the first nurse she saw. "Do you know where nurse Michelle King is?"

"I haven't seen her." The lean nurse tried to get away but Camille had another question.

209

"Can you tell me what happened to my cousin, Levour King? He was in this room not too long ago. Was he moved?"

"Honey, I don't have the slightest idea. You might wanna ask one of the assistants up front." The nurse jogged off down the long corridor.

"Um, excuse me, ma'am," Camille said in a hurry to an assistant up front behind the desk. She rested her elbows on the counter and tried to smile. "Remember me?"

The full-figured assistant looked up from her crossword puzzle and smiled back. "Yes, I do. You stayed overnight and drunk up all the apple juice," she laughed.

Camille smiled again and nodded, being polite, and quickly said, "I need to find out what room number my cousin is in. Levour King."

"He's the guy that got shot up, right?"

"Yes."

"It's a damn shame. I hate to see young Black men like that end up in these situations." She glided in her chair to the computer terminal and stroked the keyboard. "He should be in room 12A," she chirped, rolling back to her station.

Camille frowned. "We just checked and he wasn't there. He wasn't scheduled to be released until another week. I'm thinkin' they switched him to another room."

"You sure?"

Camille nodded quickly.

"Well, maybe the move didn't get put in the computer yet. People tend to forget to enter it in. What was his name again?"

Shelton spoke up this time. "Levour King," he replied, suddenly worried.

The assistant checked the log books. After flipping through a few pages, she said, "Oh," and placed a finger on the name, spun the binder to give them a better look.

Shelton and Camille leaned closer.

"See. It says right here that he checked himself out."

CHAPTER 21

"How'd you get here?"

"My cousin Michelle dropped me off," Tre Pound said, sitting down on the couch.

Dominique joined him. "Why'd you leave? You haven't even fully recovered yet."

He weighed about ten pounds less, his hair line needed a shape up, and his facial hair had grown rugged. He was dressed in a plain gray t-shirt, gray sweatpants, and a pair of gray and white Air Jordans. Without his jewelry. Dominique still thought he looked sexy, though. Even more gangster in that royal blue sling.

"I had to get out that hospital immediately," he said. "Where's Marlon?"

"In jail. Police came and got him because he left the house the night you got shot. He says he's supposed to be out soon."

"Let me see yo phone."

She handed him the cordless and he left a message on Shelton's voice mail. He dialed another number, getting through to Moses.

"Who dis? Dominique?"

"Nah, this Tre Pound."

"Tre Pound? You out the hospital? My phone say you at Marlon's house? You know Marlon's in the County, right?"

"Dominique just told me. What I'm tryna find out is what happened. Who shot me?"

"It was Row, Spook, and some other niggas from 12th Street."

"I thought Row was in the joint."

"He made parole," Moses said. He explained how Row and his boys got away during the shootout. Playa Paul had known where Spook lived so they kicked in his house and slaughtered everybody in the living room. "They shot one of ours, we killed some of theirs," Moses said. "I tried to get Spook but he was hiding in the bathtub. I couldn't get up on him because he was shootin' back. Row wasn't there."

"Playa Paul don't know where Row lives?" Tre Pound asked.

"I don't think so. You want me to ask him?"

"Where he at?"

"He's right here, gettin' his hair braided by my girl."

"Put him on the phone."

Playa Paul came on. "How you feelin', my nigga?"

"Not too good. I'm sore as a mufucka and the niggas who shot me is still walkin' the streets. How'd you know where Spook lived?"

"I know this bitch named Trish that stay on his block. I got bitches everywhere," he bragged. "I was comin' out

213

her house one day and seen Spook and some other niggas chillin' at a house across the street. When they seen me, they stood up. I hurried up and got in my car and burnt out. But I made a mental note of that house. So when you got shot up that day, that house was the first place we went. And Trish told me Spook moved since then."

"Does she know where Spook moved to, or what block Row live on?"

"Nope. But she told me—ah!"

Tre Pound heard Krystal in the background, telling Playa Paul to "be still." She must've been braiding his hair extra tight for him to squeal like that.

Playa Paul went on. "She told me Row's baby mamma got a beauty shop on Truman Road called Paradise Salon. She say his baby mamma don't want nothin' to do with him. Oh, and she said Row and Spook been askin' around, tryin' to find out where we stay. But don't nobody know so we coo."

"Nah, we ain't coo," Tre Pound retorted. "We gotta get them niggas. Tonight we gon' ride down every block on 12th Street until we find 'em."

"Tonight? A'ight."

"What's goin' down tonight?" Tre Pound heard Moses ask in the background. When Playa Paul answered him, he got on the phone and said, "Ay, Tre Pound, tonight ain't good for me. I'm supposed to be meeting up wit' somebody to cop a bird."

"I forgot about that." Tre Pound thought for a moment. "Go ahead and do what you gotta do. You already layed some niggas down on my behalf and I'm appreciative to all yall. It'll just be me, Playa Paul and Stacks. Is Stacks there?"

"He was," Moses said. "He left to go get a stick from Hoodey. But when he get back, I'll let him know wussup."

"Do that." Tre Pound hung up.

Dominique put the phone back on the charger. She was wearing a casual cotton dress that slid up her thighs when she crossed her legs. Tre Pound felt a jolt in his groin and was relieved it was still functioning.

"You just got out the hospital," Dominique began, "so you don't need to be goin' nowhere tonight."

"Why was you in my conversation?"

She gave a lovable smile. "'Cause you using my phone, in my house."

"You been here by yo'self since Marlon got hemmed up?" Tre Pound asked.

"Yeah. You tryna say I need a babysitter? I'm 16, not 5. Actually, I'm my own babysitter. I been babysittin' since I was 11. I'm good wit' kids. I'ma be a good mother one day. An even better wife." She made serious eye contact with him.

"Don't be gettin' no ideas," he warned.

"We might as well not even fake anymore, Tre Pound. I want to be yo girl. And I know you wanna be my man."

"Wait a minute, Dominique. I thought we was just foolin' around."

"I wanna get serious. Don't you? Say yes."

"Listen to yo'self. You talkin' about a relationship that's not even possible. What you wanna do—go to the movies together? You want me to pick you up from school and take you out to eat? How we gon' do all that shit without nobody findin' out?"

"Easy. We let everybody know we together ahead of time."

Tre Pound scoffed at her. "You need to tune back in to real life. Yo brother will try and kill me."

"No, he won't. Yall best friends, ain't yall? Who else would he want me to be with besides you? He knows you'll treat me right."

"What makes you think I'll treat you right? I can't be wit' one girl."

"Yes you can." She gently kissed his lips, and wouldn't let them go. At the same time, her manicured fingers found the inside of his sweats and grasped his strong erection. She slowly stroked up and down, her tongue lost in his mouth.

She had her mind made up, Tre Pound knew. She was stubborn and irresistible. He put his good arm around her, feeling the contours of her butt and thigh through the cotton dress. Her lips were soft, as was the palm of her hand. The double stimulation had him considering a relationship with her.

Dominique leaned closer into him, putting too much weight on his rib cage.

"Ouw!" he squealed. "I'm sore. I got shot right there."

"I'm sorry." She backed off. "How many times did you get shot?"

"Six all together. Once in my rib, twice in my abdomen, and once in my oblique. They were just 9mm rounds, though."

"*Just* 9mm rounds?" She couldn't believe how nonchalant he was.

"The two bullets that went through my left arm was from a AK. But it's gon' take more than that to stop Tre Pound."

Dominique liked it when he talked tough. If only she could get him to talk relationship. "So are we gonna hook up?"

"Why you wanna be wit' me? I'm liable to get killed out here."

"I won't let nobody hurt you."

Tre Pound smiled. "We can hook up, but—"

"Yes!" She kissed his cheek. "I can't wait to tell everybody!"

"You didn't let me finish. I said we can, but ... let's keep it confidential for now. Now's not the time to reveal somethin' like this."

That wasn't what she wanted to hear. "When is it gon' be time? I don't wanna sneak around. I'm tired of that. I want the real thing."

"Be patient. I'll let you know when the time's right. Until then, don't tell nobody nothin.'"

Dominique looked upset. She said, "It's too late. I already told Camille we had sex."

Tre Pound cut his eyes at her. "You told who?"

"Camille."

"For what?! When?!"

"I came to pick her up from the hospital earlier. She wanted to surprise you wit' some of yo favorite gizzards and on the way back I told her. It slipped out."

"Damn, that was stupid! Why couldn't you keep yo muthufuckin' mouth shut?"

"I only told Camille."

"You wasn't supposed to tell nobody!" He shook his head, sighing. "It's only a matter of time before yo bro find out ... and then comes gunplay."

"She won't tell nobody. She's not a blabbermouth. You're overreacting anyway."

"What she say?"

"She got all belligerent on me. She said she don't wanna be my friend no more."

He sighed again.

And heard a familiar car horn outside.

"I'm finna go holla at my cousin." He stood slowly due to the soreness. With a mean mug, he said to his boy's little sister, "Don't tell nobody else."

Dominique frowned. "Okay."

In the driveway, Shelton waited behind the wheel of his Jaguar. Tre Pound plopped in the passenger seat then shut the door.

"I got yo message," Shelton said. "Why'd you leave the hospital?"

"Police wanted to question me. Michelle led 'em to another room and helped me get up outta there."

"How's that arm?"

"I'm startin' to get used to it being in this sling. I still feel fucked up all over, but I'll live. You bring what I need?"

There were two shopping bags in the backseat. Shelton handed them to him. "One got everything you asked for in it—yo pistol, yo jewelry, phone. The other bag was in yo car, which Cash and Seneca are driving. I let them push it to combat the rumors that you were dead."

With his jewelry back on, Tre Pound felt halfway like himself again. With his 9mm Browning semiautomatic, he felt complete. He checked the other bag. "Oh, these are the clothes I bought for Camille," he said, "the day I beat my trial. The last thing I remember is heading out the talent show to give these clothes to her."

"Speaking of Camille, I just dropped her off at home. She told me to tell you to call her if I found you. I had to pick her up from the precinct on 63rd. She witnessed a murder."

"What happened?"

Shelton explained what Hoodey had told him. Tre pound's face seemed to get angrier the more he explained.

"Camille could've got shot!" Tre Pound snapped. "Hoodey should've never brought his little brother over there. Or when he saw Camille, he should've told his little brother to get back in the car and they should've left. Shelton, you should go ahead and let me rob that nigga."

"No. Camille's fine. Hoodey apologized, and he's one of the few people that respect the game. I told you I've known him since junior high and robbing him would only give you more funk. You got enough as it is. And it seems like you can't handle what you got."

"It's all under control. It ain't gon' be no more funk pretty soon."

Shelton gave him a doubtful look. "You in a sling, shot up. What you got under control? I don't wanna see you in a body bag."

"Them niggas just caught me slippin'. I got my cleats on now. My homies already smoked some of 'em. Row and Spook is still out there, though. But tonight we goin' on the hunt. We don't know where they live; all we know is that Row's baby momma own a beauty shop called Paradise Salon, but him and his baby momma don't fuck around no more. So we just gon' ride through they 'hood and hope we catch 'em outside or spot one of they cars."

Shelton thought for a moment. "Where is this salon located?"

"On Truman Road. Why? I thought we didn't touch the family of the niggas we funkin' wit'. I thought it was a bad look."

"Right," Shelton nodded. "But you said Row and his baby momma are separated. She might hold some ill will toward him and be glad to tell us where he lives. Since

Cash and Seneca are already in the streets wit' yo car, I'ma call 'em and tell 'em to see if they can get some information out of her."

"When you gon' call 'em?"

Shelton reached in his pocket. "Right now."

CHAPTER 22

Paradise Salon was a modest establishment.

Only three hair stations, two driers and a shortage in one of the outlets. Yet and still the owner, Christina Franklin, took pride in her shop. She catered to all the neighborhood girls' needs—weaves, extensions, make-up, manicures, pedicures—and made enough money to feed herself and her 3-year-old baby boy. The father of her child, Rowland Reed, bought her the place, but she took credit for what it had become.

"Dammit, it happened again," Cookie bitched, after the hair drier she was sitting under suddenly cut off. "Christina, I should get a discount for goin' through this shit."

"You *always* get a discount; you never pay what you owe," Christina replied, and the girls in the shop laughed. "Short-changing me. Why you think I always sit you under that drier?" She tapped the girl who was currently sitting at her station. "Get up, let me dry her hair real quick."

The girl stood and Cookie took her place. "Why you gotta put my business all in the street?" Cookie asked snottily.

Christina clicked the handheld blow-dryer; it hummed to life with streaming hot air. "Yo business is already in the street, girl, shut up." While fanning the dryer over Cookie's hair, Christina thought she heard a crash in the back room. "Wanda," she said to one of her employees, "do this for me so I can go check on Pooter."

"If I was you," Cookie interjected, "I'd have Row watching him. He's outta jail now. I'd be damned if I get stuck wit' the kid while I'm at work."

"That's because you fail to understand that I love my son, and I'm blessed to be able to spend as much time with him as I do and have a job—own a job—that allows me to do that. I can't force Row's no-good ass to spend time with his son. As long as he keeps givin' us them greenbacks, that moolah, that *fettuccine,* then I don't care what he does." Christina went to the back to check on her son.

Soon after she left, the bells attached to the entrance jingled, and in strolled Cash and Seneca. Everyone in the shop knew the boys were related to Tre Pound. And they knew—just like every-body else who had an ear to the street—that Tre Pound and Row were funking with each other.

The girls got quiet and watched the two teenagers closely.

223

Seneca said to his brother, "Are we gon' pick them girls back up after we leave from here?"

"If Shelton don't got nothin' else for us to do," Cash replied. Then he eyed one of the hairdressers. "This yo shop?"

"I just work here," Wanda said, trying not to sound nervous. She cleared her throat and resumed looking into Cookie's billowing hair as she blow-dried it.

"Is the owner here?"

Wanda didn't look up this time. "No."

"She probably lying," Seneca spat. "One of these bitches is Row's baby momma."

"Let me talk," said Cash. They were supposed to come here on good terms. This wasn't a time to intimidate, Shelton had warned them. They had to learn how to be diplomatic, too. And Cash wanted to do it right. "Remember what Shelton said," he whispered to his little brother out the corner of his mouth. "We gotta act friendly."

Cookie couldn't keep quiet any longer. "Yall know yall young asses not supposed to be in here. Yall came to cause trouble. Take that shit somewhere else."

"We not here to start nothin'," Cash said. "All we wanna do is holla at the owner and then we gone."

"Who you think you foolin'? Tre Pound got shot up and now yall here to wreck shop. Row ain't here. Leave Christina out of it." Cookie made a wry face. "And Tre Pound deserved to die, as much dirt as he did."

Enraged, 14-year-old Seneca whipped out his 9mm. "Oh God," escaped from Cookie's lips as the boy started towards her. All the girls were frightened, even more startled when the handheld hair dryer slipped from Wanda's fingers and broke against the floor. Seneca dug the barrel into Cookie's cheekbone.

"My cousin ain't dead!" he barked. "Watch what come out yo mouth or I'll blow that muthafucka off."

"C'mon, Seneca, put that up before you really kill her." Cash grabbed his brother's shoulder.

Seneca shrugged him off. "Nah, man, she disrespected. Tre Pound said if somebody disrespect the family, they need to be dealt wit.'"

"Okay, you dealt wit' her. You see she ain't sayin' nothin' no more."

Cookie was clawing the armrests, eyes bulging out the sockets, trying to control her breathing. Seneca held the gun steady against the side of her face. He never killed before, but he wanted to one day because Tre Pound had. He knew he could if it came to it.

Finger curled around the trigger, he heard the faint sound of a child crying, followed by the harsh tone of a woman's voice.

Cash heard it, too. "All yall had to say was she was in the back," he said to the fear-stricken girls.

The brothers walked calmly towards the rear of the salon.

"I almost died," Cookie breathed with her hand over her heart.

One of the hairdressers picked up a phone and started dialing.

In the corner of Christina's back office was a makeshift play area. Building blocks, Legos and toy trucks lay on the floor. A plastic dinosaur that roared at the push of a button was gripped in the hand of 3-year-old Derrick "Pooter" Reed as Christina spanked him.

"Didn't I tell you to stay away from my desk!" Christina smacked his butt one last time before she let her son flop to the carpet. She pointed to the cracked monitor that had fallen. "You was pulling on the cords again, weren't you!"

Pooter was too choked up by his own tears to answer.

"What if it would've fell on you? You could've really hurt yo'self, Pooter!" She heard her door open, turned her head and saw Cash and Seneca. "Uhn-uhn, what yall doin' back here?" Then it registered that this wasn't an ordinary visit. The pistol in Seneca's hand clarified that.

"Are you Christina, Row's baby momma?" Cash asked.

"Yes, I am," she replied.

"We're—"

Christina cut him off. "I know who yall are. Tre Pound's little cousins. Look, I don't care for Row's ass either. Whatever problems yall got wit' him, I don't care. I'm not into that street shit. But don't bring that bullshit here."

"Ay, I don't want us to be here either, but my brother

told us to come, so I'm here. Yo baby daddy shot my cousin and we need to find out what street name he lives on."

"I'm not tellin' yall where he lives," Christina stated. She set the monitor back atop the desk. "I don't like my baby daddy, but I'm not about to just hand him over to yall. My baby needs a father."

"You gon' tell us where he is!" Seneca demanded, and cocked the pistol.

"Baby, you need to calm down," Christina said. "I ain't scared of no gun." She turned to Cash. "What's yo name?"

"Cash."

"Cash, will you tell yo brother to put that gun away around my son?"

"He won't listen to me."

Christina sighed and held up a pacifying hand. "Well, what do yall want from me? I can't help yall."

Seneca went and aimed the gun at her, point-blank. "Tell us where da nigga is!"

She closed her eyes and said softly, "Get that gun out my face, little boy."

"Fuck you."

"Get that gun out my face!"

"Seneca, chill," said Cash. His words had no affect, so he regarded the lady. "Christina, just sit down at the desk because he ain't movin'. It's hard tellin' him anything."

Christina picked up her son and sat in the oak chair behind her desk, held him in her lap.

"You ain't gotta help us. Just sit there," Cash said. "I know you got some information on Row's address somewhere around here."

As Cash proceeded towards the file cabinet, Christina uttered, "Nuh-uh," and put her child down. She darted out her seat to stop Cash from searching, but always reacting quickly, Seneca cracked her in the back of the head with the butt of his gun.

"Sit down," he growled as she fell.

"Help!" Christina frantically tried to get up. "Help!"

Seneca hit her again and she went unconscious.

Pooter started crying.

"Damn, did you have to knock her out?" Cash snapped.

Seneca looked apologetic. "What was I supposed to do?"

"We was supposed to get the address without hurtin' nobody!"

"You gon' tell on me?"

Cash sucked his teeth. He started at the bottom drawer of the file cabinet, saw hundreds of manilla folders. Though it seemed impossible that he'd find the address, he searched anyway.

***

The entrance bells jingled.

"Where are they?" Row demanded as he and Spook barged into the beauty shop.

A hairdresser pointed like she wanted Row and Spook to hurry up. "They in the back," she said.

In the same stride, the two gangsters headed back to the office, where they saw Cookie kneeling beside Christina. Wanda held Pooter in her arms. The baby boy looked sleepy as if he'd cried too long.

"Where they at?" Row asked, his fiery eyes scanning the room. He looked behind the door.

"They gone," Cookie retorted. "Yall came too fucking late."

Christina had just begun to regain consciousness. Her head was bleeding. "What ... happened?"

"It's okay," Cookie said soothingly. "It's over now."

"My baby ..." Christina was remembering. "My baby!" Then a sudden pain shot through her head. She groaned, shutting her eyes tight.

"Just lie down," Cookie said. "There's an ambulance on the way. Wanda has your baby. Pooter's fine."

Breathing easier, Christina opened her eyes again. Wanda was handing Pooter over to her baby daddy. "Row, you muthafucka, I don't want you near my son!" Christina vented. "Get away from him! You're not gonna get my son killed in your bullshit! We've been surviving without you, so leave! And stay the fuck away from us!"

Wanda changed her mind and didn't give up Pooter.

Row's eyes flicked between his baby momma and his son, and he felt the room spinning. Tre Pound struck out at his loved ones. Did Tre Pound think Row wouldn't do the same? Row couldn't find out where Tre Pound or his homies lived, but everybody in the city knew where Tre Pound's auntie lived. Everybody knew about the gambling on Monday nights. Didn't Tre Pound's pretty little cousin Camille live in that house, too? Row was so enveloped by vengeance that he didn't hear his name being called.

"Row, what you wanna do?" Spook asked. "Row ... Row ..."

CHAPTER 23

Nightfall covered the Kansas City skies. The

windows were up in Playa Paul's black Dodge Magnum
to block out the chilly air. They were cruising north down
Paseo, towards 12th Street.

"If yo cousins would've got the address," Playa Paul
began, "I could've punched it in my navigation system and
it would've led us straight there. I got that top-of-the-line
shit that don't nobody else got." Left hand on the steering
wheel, he used his right to press a square on the colorful
touchscreen monitor. A woman's voice requested a state,
city, and street address. "See? Who else yall know that got
that?"

"Who cares?" Stacks complained from the backseat.
Before the navigation system popped up, he'd been watch-
ing a DVD on the 6-inch screen installed in the back of
Playa Paul's headrest. "Put it back on *Menace II Society*.
Cain was just about to fuck Jada."

In the passenger seat, Tre Pound turned from the
window. "Cut all that shit off," he ordered. "Yall supposed

to be watching for Row's and Spook's cars. They could've drove past us."

Playa Paul pushed a button and each monitor in the car blackened. Everybody was on the lookout now, craning their necks when they thought they saw something.

Minutes passed before Stacks picked the conversation back up. "Tre Pound, you ain't heard about what happened to Kaliko, have you?"

Tre Pound looked back at him. "What?"

"He got smoked at that dike bitch Joy's house when you was in the hospital."

"It happened *before* he went to the hospital," Playa Paul corrected.

"No, it didn't."

"It did, too. How much you wanna bet? I got *The Call* paper wit' the article in it at my house right now. And one of my hoes told me before I even read about it."

"Well," Stacks said, "I know Joy got killed and her girl-friend Latrice got her throat slit. And niggas is tryna say you did it, Tre Pound."

"It ain't strange," Tre Pound said. "All the murders get blamed on me. I bet people still think I murked Drought Man even though I got acquitted. I know one thing: When Row and Spook come up missing and people start sayin' I did it, the rumors is gon' be true."

For hours into the night they drove around 12th Street, doubling back down random blocks. They even scoured 11th and 10th Street. At one point, they were following a black Buick Grand National, only to find out a mile later that it wasn't Row, but a middle-aged Mexican.

Playa Paul decided to pull over and ask a corner hustler if he knew where Row lived. The hustler looked maybe 12 or 13 years old, dressed in a drooping white T-shirt and white Nike headband.

"Yeah, I know where he live," said the young boy. "Row is my big homie. Who are yall?"

"We tryna buy some work from him," Playa Paul said.

"I got work. How much yall lookin' for?"

"Row already got what I'm tryna get. I just need you to give me his address."

The boy seemed suspicious. He bent over, straining to look into the car. He seemed to be recognizing Tre Pound. Then is eyes went wide and he gasped, scared stiff only for a moment. Then he quickly reached under his shirt for his pistol.

"Go!" Tre Pound yelled. He pulled his 9mm out his sling and popped off several shots at the boy, as the boy shot back while running away. Playa Paul stomped on the gas pedal and swerved off as the gunblasts rang out, bullets denting his car.

Playa Paul turned the corner sharply and drove another block before he slowed down. "Shit!" he exclaimed. "No more askin' for directions."

Tre Pound looked in the backseat with fury in his eyes to see why Stacks didn't bust his gun.

Stacks looked dead, sprawled out on the black leather. But he didn't look shot.

"Stacks? Stacks!" Tre Pound saw his chest moving. Breathing. "Stacks!"

Suddenly, Stacks jerked to life, sitting up. He wiped slobber from his mouth. "Wussup?"

"Yo high ass just slept through a shootout, that's wussup!"

"Did I?"

Playa Paul glanced back in disbelief. "He was sleep?"

"We almost got our head tow off!" Tre Pound barked at Stacks. "Some street punk just upped on us around the corner!"

"Aw ... damn. Let's go back," Stacks suggested.

Tre Pound faced forward again, frustrated. He thought they would've found Row and Spook by now. Feeling like they searched everywhere, he instructed Playa Paul to drive to Spook's house—his old house.

"He moved," Playa Paul reminded him.

"We gon' post up anyway," Tre Pound replied. "Hopefully Spook will go back there tonight."

Playa Paul drove on through the neighborhood and turned down a dilapidated block. He parked across the street from a Spook's bullet-riddled house, its living room windows busted. There was a "for sale" sign in the front yard.

They waited.

And waited.

Several houses up the street, they watched a man get kicked out the house by his girlfriend, but no one came or went from Spook's house.

A cell phone rang. Everyone checked their pockets but it was Tre Pound's. He saw who was trying to reach him and stepped out the car before he took the call.

"Hello?"

"Shelton didn't tell you what I said?" Camille asked. She was upset and didn't try to hide it.

"He told me," Tre Pound said, leaning against the front fender. "But I ain't had time to call you. I been rippin' and runnin'."

"I bet you had time to call everybody else. I should've been the first person you called to know where you was. I was the only one—the *only* one—who spent the night up there wit' you while you was in the hospital."

"I don't know why you gettin' mad at me," Tre Pound shot back. "I'm the one who should be mad. What's this I hear about you sneakin' off to a lil' nigga's house, damn near gettin' yo'self killed?"

"There you go gettin' the facts misconstrued just like Shelton. I already heard this from him. I gotta hear it from you, too?"

"Damn right! You think this is some little shit? You witnessed a murder! Them people is gon' try and force you to testify. Subpoena you."

"Are you done tellin' me what I already know? Because I got a question for you."

235

"If it got to do wit' Dominique, I don't wanna hear it."

"So it's true?"

"We don't need to talk about that."

"What type of cousin are you? You went and fucked my best friend. And you got that stupid bitch thinkin' yall go together." She paused. "Do yall go together?"

"We don't need to talk about that," he repeated.

Camille got quiet, obviously trying to repress all her anger. "Where's those clothes you had got for me?"

"I gave them to Dominique. I didn't know if you still wanted 'em," Tre Pound explained. He heard her about to protest and cut her off. "But I'm in the middle of somethin'. I can't really talk right now."

"Bye," she spat.

Tre Pound opened the car door but didn't get in. "Didn't you say you knew a girl that lived on this block?" he said to Playa Paul. "Where she stay?"

"Why?" Playa Paul was suspicious.

"She might know where them niggas is at."

"She don't. I told you that over the phone, remember?"

"You told me she didn't know where them niggas live. But she might know where they be, where they kick-it at. Or you never know—she might've found out where they live by now. Quit actin' like that. Ain't nobody tryna take yo bitch. I'm tryna find the niggas who shot me."

"Right there," Playa Paul said angrily, pointing behind Tre Pound. Tre Pound turned and looked. They were parked in front of her house.

The car doors automatically locked when Playa Paul armed his Dodge Magnum's alarm. If anybody tried to take his 24-inch chrome rims—which were two inches bigger than Tre Pound's—a red light would flash on his remote.

They all walked through Trish's yard, up to her barred door. Tre Pound and Stacks kept an eye out, looking up and down the street while Playa Paul knocked.

"Coming!" shouted a sweet-sounding feminine voice. The door opened to an attractive brown-skinned girl with long silky hair. Trish Allen. She wore a halter dress that showed a lot of skin. Thick thighs. Cleavage pushed up by a revolutionary bra. The neon green band on her wrist looked like it came from some club or party. She looked at each of her guests, eyes lingered on Tre Pound for a second, then she regarded Playa Paul curiously. "Wussup, baby? You always come over here by yo'self. Everything okay?"

"Yeah," Playa Paul assured her. "But you know I don't be fuckin' around in this 'hood so can we come in?"

"Sure." Trish stepped to the side, held the door open for them. Playa Paul gave her a quick peck on her full lips as he entered. When Tre Pound walked past her, she smiled flirtatiously and said, "Yo name Tre Pound, ain't it?"

"Yeah. Wussup, cutey," Tre Pound greeted her.

Her smile widened.

They found seats in the living room. There were no traces of children living with her. The house was orderly. It was uncommon for a young-looking girl like Trish, with no kids, to be living in a nicely kept house by herself. But Tre Pound soon found out she wasn't living here alone.

"My momma is sleep upstairs," said Trish, "so yall can't stay long." She eyed Tre Pound as if to lure him into her uncrossed legs. "I can't believe you're actually sitting in my living room. All the girls at my school be talking about you."

"Good stuff, I hope," Tre Pound said.

"Yep. Everybody claim they done slept wit' you."

Playa Paul was sitting close to Trish on the loveseat, arm around her shoulder. "Leave my nigga alone," he said. "Quit acting like a groupie. I got a few questions for you."

"A few is three. So that's all you get. Yall tryna get me in trouble."

"Have you found out where Row or Spook live yet?"

"I knew it was gon' be some serious questions. But ... no. I don't be keepin' tabs on them." Trish glanced at Tre Pound when she said, "I don't even like them niggas fa-real to be keepin' tabs on them."

"Do you know where they kick it at?" Playa Paul asked. "Like what clubs they go to and shit."

"Um ... Did I already tell you Row's baby momma got a beauty shop over there on Truman Road?"

"Yeah, you already told me that."

"I thought so. Um ... I never knew them niggas to be club niggas, you know what I mean? I don't even think they go to parties. If yall wanna catch them, yall gotta catch them here in the 'hood somewhere. They don't stray too far from the Twelve."

Tre Pound had a question. "If you find out where they live, will you let us know? I'm talking about as *soon* as you find out."

"Oh, I will," she said, overly eager to please him. "Do you want me to call you or Paul? I'ma need yo number if you want me to call you."

"Just call me," Playa Paul said. He kissed her on the cheek, nibbled on her earlobe and she giggled. "One last question."

"Uhn-uhn," she objected. "That was three."

"No, I only asked you two. Tre Pound asked you one. That don't count against mine."

"Go ahead, Paul. Being all technical."

Playa Paul looked at her intently, then broke into a smile. "Are you wearin' panties?"

"Ask Tre Pound," she quipped. "He been lookin' the whole time."

Tre Pound's eyebrows arched in surprise.

But Playa Paul was anything but pleased. He tugged the hem of Trish's dress down and made her stand up. "Show us to the door," he grumbled.

"Don't forget yall friend," Trish said, looking at Stacks, who was knocked out on her couch.

Tre Pound woke him up.

When they were walking through Trish's lawn back to

the car, Tre Pound's cell phone rang. He flipped it open. "Hello?"

"Come get me!"

"Moses? Why you breathing all hard?"

"I'm out of breath! I just got through runnin' from the police. I was about to make the deal and the DEA came out of nowhere. I'm hiding under the Brush Creek Bridge. Come get me!"

"We on our way."

***

By the time they reached Brush Creek, KCPD were all over the place. Playa Paul crept his Dodge past the law enforcement's road block and saw an officer ducking Moses's head into the back of a squad car. "They got him," Playa Paul announced.

"Fuck. We got here too late." Tre Pound saw a couple DEA agents give each other a high five. "Let's go before they get us, too."

Once they were parked in front of Marlon's house, Tre Pound gave dap to his boys.

"I'll talk to yall niggas tomorrow. We'll catch Row and Spook slippin' one of these days, so keep yall eyes open from here on out. They can't shake the crosshairs forever."

Stacks climbed in the front seat as Tre Pound got out. But before Tre Pound could walk away, Playa Paul called his name.

"Tre Pound."

"Wussup?" Tre Pound looked in the car at his homeboy. "Whatever Moses's bond is, I'll pay for it. Or we can all ante up. It don't matter."

"A'ight. But that ain't what I wanted to ask you."

"Well, wussup?"

Since this evening when Playa Paul picked Tre Pound up, he'd had something on his mind. "What you been doin' over here?"

"Chillin'."

"Chillin'?"

"Yeah, chillin'. Wit' Dominique. Clucks be showin' up at the house all hours of the night lookin' for Marlon and it ain't safe for her to be here alone."

"Are you stayin' overnight?"

"Yeah," Tre Pound answered casually. "Why?"

"I'm just askin'. You know Marlon probably wouldn't want you bein' here wit' his little sister."

"Why wouldn't he? If my lil' sister was out here by herself and I was locked up, I'd want my homies to make sure she's a'ight."

"But 'making sure she's a'ight' and spending the night are two different things," Playa Paul said. "While you was in the hospital, while Marlon been in jail, me and Stacks and Moses been slidin' through to see how she was doin'. Then we'd leave. Sometimes we called. But we never spent the night."

"Yall do things differently," Tre Pound replied. "Yall been knowin' Marlon longer but me and him are closer and I think I know what he'd approve of and what he wouldn't. And I know he wouldn't think twice about me lookin' out for his sister."

Stacks went ahead and posed the question that Playa Paul was slow to get around to. "Are you fuckin' Dominique?" he asked, a devilish grin plastered on his face.

Tre Pound playfully smacked Stacks in the back of his peanut head. "Nigga, you stupid."

"I think you are fuckin' her," Stacks said in jest, but was half serious.

"I'm finna go in this house before I end up fuckin' Stacks up," Tre Pound joked. "Yall be safe." He gave them dap once again, and headed towards the porch.

The Dodge Magnum drove away.

Before Tre Pound reached the porch steps, Dominique already had the door open. She'd been watching him through the curtains since he pulled up. The cordless was up to her ear. "Krystal, I'ma call you back," she said into the phone. Then she smiled at her new boyfriend.

CHAPTER 24

According to Marlon, it was hard for him

to be granted this contact visit. *Every* inmate in his wing had to be "good" and pass cell inspection to get one. If one person exhibited inappropriate behavior, then contact visits were lost for everyone. So since Marlon was able to get one, Dominique made sure she showed up at the Jackson County Detention Center on time.

She walked into the imposing building on 1300 Cherry Street, Tre Pound still on her mind.

Last night Dominique had to put up with Tre Pound's ranting and raving. Most of what she understood was vague talk about how he and his family were supposed to be untouchable; about how the King family's image was threatened because people knew he could be shot down, which sounded silly to her.

He blamed himself for getting shot. Claimed it would never happen again—that Row would be the only person to get so close to taking his life. Dominique didn't butt in until he started talking about the whole world was against him.

"I'm on your side, though," she had said, finally. And that seemed to calm him down. She held him. He kissed her. And for the rest of the night Dominique got what she wanted—Tre Pound inside her, from behind. He couldn't put it on her like he did last time because he only had one functioning arm, but she didn't complain.

But now, Sunday afternoon, as the female guard frisked her, Dominique did complain. "I thought yo job was to search me, not grope me."

"Keep gettin' smart," the guard said, "and I'll send you back out the door you came in. Next!"

The elevator ride up was filled with women and children, and when the doors opened on the 4th floor, Dominique filed out with them. Family and friends of the inmates had to be 18 or accompanied with an adult, but Dominique got in by displaying her fake ID she normally used to sneak in the club.

At a table by herself, she watched other people enjoy their visits, waiting on her brother impatiently. Then she noticed an inmate with a long goatee sneaking her "the eye." The nerve of him! He was there with what appeared to be his wife and child. When his wife bent down to set the toddler on her lap, he signaled his hand into a phone and mouthed the words, "What's yo number?"

"No," Dominique mouthed back, and the inmate looked like his pride had been hurt. She couldn't blame him for trying, though. She did look cute today. Her hair was elegantly pinned up in the back. She wore a fitted Dolce and Gabbana T-shirt covered by a cropped denim jacket. Her thighs were thick in those denim shorts. And the 6-inch heels—one strap around her toes and around her ankle—topped off her outfit. She was star quality.

That inmate over there didn't stand a chance. Nobody did when compared to Tre Pound.

Sorry fella, she thought. Already taken.

Thankfully, Marlon was the next inmate to enter the visiting room. He had on his rimless Nike glasses, looking charming. His orange jumper looked brand new, freshly creased. He strolled over and sat down with a smile.

"Took you long enough," Dominique said.

"Had to finish gettin' my haircut. Whether I'm locked up or not, I can't be lookin' bummy." Marlon reached across the white table and tousled his little sister's pretty hair, tickled her ears. "Wussup, big head?"

"Quit it." She pushed his hand away. "You embarrassing me."

"How am I embarrassing you? Ain't nobody worried about you."

"Uh-huhn."

"Who?"

She nodded towards the inmate who had made a pass at her. "Him," she said.

Marlon turned and looked.

"And it could be other people trying to check me out," she said. "Don't hate."

"You know you just got somebody fucked up, right?"

That was her brother. Always ready to fight somebody over her. She wondered how he'd take the news about her hooking up with Tre Pound, being that he and Tre Pound were best friends. *Probably not as bad as Camille took it,* she thought.

"You better not do nothin' to him," Dominique said. "I told him no. And all he did was the phone hand thing. A nigga can't even do that without you beatin' him up? He probably didn't even know I was yo sister."

"It don't make a difference. A man is never supposed to try to holla at another man's visit without permission."

There was a single guard in the visiting room, paying more attention to his watch than the inmates and their visitors. Another guard, in the control booth behind a Plexiglas partition, was busy eating a bologna sandwich with his feet kicked up on the counter. Both were oblivious to the transaction taking place.

But Dominique wasn't.

Catty-corner from her seat, she saw a woman reach inside her jogging pants, between her legs. The woman retrieved a small red balloon and passed it under the table to an inmate who slyly swallowed it.

"Did you see that?" Dominique whispered to Marlon excitedly.

"Stay out them people business."

"Why you didn't ask me to bring you nothin' in?"

Marlon's expression darkened. "You don't need to be doin' nothin' like that. Do I need money? Do you need money? No. So what's the point of doin' it? You gotta get this street shit out yo head."

Dominique thought to herself, *If Tre Pound would've asked me to smuggle something in, I would've did it. No questions asked.*

"You know Tre Pound's out the hospital," she said.

"Is he? Good. That's good. My nigga bounced right back. What he lookin' like? He look a'ight?"

"His left arm is in a sling. He done got a little bit thinner and he can't move as fast yet, but he still got that same gangster attitude. He came over to the house lookin' for you and that's when I told him you was locked up." Dominique went on to tell her brother what Tre Pound told her to tell him—about Moses being arrested last night.

Marlon was perturbed by the news. A while back, the ATF swarmed on him when he went to pick up another case of high-powered weapons, which—because of Carlo Masaccio—only resulted in him getting house arrest. The only people that knew Marlon was going to make the pick-up was the homies. And the only people that knew Moses was going to cop a bird was the homies. Could somebody in the clique be snitching? Marlon pondered. Then he quickly dismis-sed the thought as absurd.

"When was the last time you talked to Tre Pound?" he asked.

"Um ... this morning."

"This morning?" A short laugh came out. "He didn't spend the night, did he?"

"Yeah."

At first, Marlon looked as if he didn't comprehend. Then he smiled. "You think you funny, huh? Keep playin' and I'll beat you down right here in front of all these people."

"I'm not tryna be funny," Dominique stated. "How is it so hard to believe that Tre Pound spent the night with me?" She wanted to get it over with. Get it out in the open. Hiding her feelings and her relationship wasn't right. Nobody else had to. She understood why Tre Pound wanted to keep it a secret—he was afraid their love wouldn't be accepted. But Dominique had it in her heart that love, whether accepted or not, should never be hidden. Revealing their relationship was the first step on the path to a lifelong commitment.

Her brother held a menacing glare but she continued anyway. "I know you mad, Marlon. That's why I didn't want to keep it a secret in the first place, but Tre Pound told me not to'tell nobody until the right time. But I realized that there will never be a right time. So I'm tellin' you now."

"What *are* you tellin' me, Dominique?" he seethed. "Huh? Tell me why my nigga, my muthafuckin' dog, spent the night with my little sister. I don't like where you goin' wit' this. Tell me didn't nothin' happen. Tell me he just fell asleep on the couch. I can deal wit' that. I can't deal wit' shit else."

Eyes closed, Dominique sighed heavily. She shook her head, mentally fatigued. "Oh my God, I hate this." First, Camille and now her brother. Why couldn't nobody be happy for her and Tre Pound? What was so wrong about it? They loved each other. Then: "That should be all that matters," escaped from her lips.

Marlon leaned his head closer and narrowed his moist, red eyes as if he didn't understand. He was so angry, ready to cry almost. "Huh? I can't hear you. You better tell me somethin'."

"We're in love, Marlon!" she blurted out. Heads turned throughout the visiting room. "Get it into yo head. Let it marinate. He spent the night. We had sex. We been havin' sex. Tre Pound is my man, Marlon."

Removing his glasses, Marlon wiped his tear-filled eyes. He pictured Tre Pound thrusting in and out his baby sister. Pulling her hair. Cumming on her back. He'd seen how Tre Pound fucked girls. Hard. Mercilessly. The vision was too much.

He put his glasses back on, and to Dominique's surprise, he said, "You know what? I'm glad you told me." His face was solemn. "Sixteen years old. You old enough to have sex, right?"

A smile spread across her face. "Yeah."

"Smart enough to make yo own decisions, choose who you wanna be wit."

"And Tre Pound thought you would trip. I told him you wouldn't."

249

"Trip? Who me? He said that?"

"Uh-huh. But I knew yall friendship was stronger than that. Yall been friends since high school."

Marlon nodded. "You right about that. It's amazing. High school ..." He cracked an eerie smile.

And it suddenly dawned on Dominique that her brother's attitude was artificial. His smile, his composure—both seemed frail. And it appeared as if he were trembling.

"Marlon, you alright?"

"Why wouldn't I be?" he responded quickly, still wearing the same eerie smile. "This is amazing. My nigga is fuckin' my baby sister. What could be better than that?"

Maybe she should have listened to Tre Pound and kept her mouth shut. Her brother was making her feel uneasy.

"Ay, everybody!" Marlon announced. The visiting room fell silent. "My nigga is fuckin' my baby sister! Can yall believe that shit?"

The guard in the corner abandoned his post to approach Marlon.

"Mr. Hayes," he warned, "you gotta keep it down."

"But this is news to me, C.O. This is muthafuckin' top story!"

Dominique had a sour expression. "Marlon, don't do this. Don't get upset."

"I'm in a good-ass mood! Do I look upset?"

"Alright, Mr. Hayes, your visit is terminated. Come with me." The guard grabbed his arm.

Marlon pulled free with force. "Get the fuck off me!"

Shocked, the guard took a couple steps back and radioed for assistance from his shoulder two-way.

"I can leave on my own. You ain't gotta be touchin' all on me like that," Marlon said, as he stood up.

"What's wrong with me being with Tre Pound?" Dominique asked with pleading eyes. "He cares for me, Marlon. We love each other. Damn, why you gotta act like this?"

"I told you I ain't trippin'!" he barked. "I'm not mad!"

"You're gonna do somethin'. I know you are. I'll end it, okay? Just don't do nothin'."

A pack of guards rushed in, out of breath. The head guard, Sergeant Berkeley, stepped to the front. He was an old white man with a sweaty bald head, stripes and pins on the collar of his gray button-up. He was known to be a reasonable man who avoided sending inmates to the hole.

"What's going on here?" Sergeant Berkeley asked, frowning. His face was covered with wrinkles.

The visiting room guard explained: "I asked Mr. Hayes to leave and he got violent with me, sir."

"I didn't get violent wit' you!" Marlon had his fists balled tight. "You got violent wit' me! You didn't have to put yo hands on me!"

The guard stepped back farther.

"Mr. Hayes," said Berkeley, "I'm gonna have to ask you to leave the visiting room. I don't wanna have to call the goon squad. Let's make this a peaceful exit."

With so much hate and anger built up inside, Marlon felt the urge to release it all on the timid guard standing just a few feet away. But that would end up in him losing the house arrest he just got reinstated. And he had to get back on the streets—if only to murder Tre Pound.

"Can I give my sister a kiss?" Marlon asked.

"No," Berkeley said. "Visit's over."

"I can't even give my sister a kiss? What kind of shit is that?"

Dominique wanted to cry. "I love you, Marlon."

One of the guards reached for the pepper spray on his hip.

Berkeley said, "This is your last warning, Mr. Hayes."

Shaking his head, Marlon proceeded towards the exit door. As Berkeley and the guards escorted him out, Marlon turned back towards his sister and said ominously, "Tell Tre Pound I'll be out tomorrow."

CHAPTER 25

Within an hour, Dominique was back at home.

"That you, Dominique?" she heard Tre Pound call from the living room, as she locked the front door.

"Yes."

"Did they let you in wit' that fake ID?"

Dropping the car keys in the clutch bag under her arm, Dominique proceeded towards the stairs. "Yes. I got to see him."

"Did you tell him about Moses?"

"Yes."

"What he say about it?" Tre Pound didn't get a response. "Where you at, Dominique?"

"Hold on. I'm goin' upstairs to use the restroom. I gotta pee."

Dominique went up into her room, tossed her clutch bag on her bed. She took off her heels and placed them on her closet floor in line with the rest of her many expensive shoes. As she walked to the bathroom, she heard Tre

Pound downstairs calling her name again. She hurried into the bathroom and locked the door.

But she knew she couldn't avoid him forever.

Dominique unbuttoned her tight shorts, wriggled them down as she sat on the toilet. Informing Tre Pound was going to be harder than she thought. On the ride over here she had planned to just come out and say Marlon was pissed, but once she got in the door, it didn't seem like a good idea anymore. She predicted an "I told you so" from Tre Pound and hoped he didn't overreact. Who was she kidding? Tre Pound was guaranteed to overreact.

And stalling would only make it worse.

Dominique finished up, then ran her soapy hands under warm sink water. After she dried her hands, she closed her fingers on the doorknob. She hesitated.

"Might as well get it over wit," she said, and was startled when she opened the door. Tre Pound was standing right in front of her.

"Get what over wit'?" he asked.

"Don't sneak up on me. I could've had a heart attack."

"You came in and rushed up here. Takin' all day. I thought somethin' was wrong."

"Isn't that sweet. Checkin' up on your girl. But I told you I had to use the restroom."

"So everything's coo'?"

Dominique wrapped her arms around his waist and kissed his lips. Their tongues touched once, and the kissing went on for a few more seconds. "Everything's coo'," she assured him. But her tentative eyes betrayed her.

"I don't believe you. It seem like you holdin' somethin' back. Just come out and tell me what's bothering you."

Dominique sighed. "Okay, everything's not coo."

"I figured that."

"It's about Marlon."

"Shit. What are they gon' do—try and make him do some time?"

"No. He got his house arrest reinstated. He gets out tomorrow."

"That's *good* news." Tre Pound chuckled. "You don't want him to get out? Don't be like that. We won't be able to chill wit' each other like this but there'll be other times for us to have some privacy. You should never ever be mad that yo brother is gettin' out of jail."

"I'm not the one that's mad. Marlon is."

"What's he mad for?"

"He's mad at us."

"Why would he be ...?" Tre Pound faltered in his question, as the answer suddenly came to him. His demeanor became frighteningly serious. "I know you didn't do what I think you did. You can't be that stupid. It ain't no way you can be that stupid."

"Tre Pound, I had to tell Marlon. That's my brother. How long was we supposed to keep this a secret? We gotta start actin' like a couple and we can't do that by—"

"GODDAMN! I'm tryna get rid of this funk and you wanna add to it!"

Tears welled in her eyes. "I just want a real relationship."

"But do you realize what you just did? You just pit two homies against each other. Tell me I'm wrong."

Dominique was silent except for a sniffle.

"You ain't gotta say shit because I know. We could've did our thang without nobody knowin' nothin'. But you wanna be hardheaded. Now look. What did you think was gon' happen?"

"I thought because yall was friends ... at the worst yall would just fight. And after the fight yall would be coo' again."

"Fight? Girls fight over shit like this. Niggas stopped fighting back in the 80's," Tre Pound spewed at her. "What did he say? Tell me exactly what he said."

"He just told me to tell you that he gets out tomorrow."

"And you know what that means, right? Somebody's gonna get killed, and it ain't gon' be me."

"It's not gonna come to that!" Dominique cried. "Once he understands how much we're in love wit' each other, he'll have no choice but to accept it."

"Where'd you get that from?" Tre Pound asked.

"Where'd I get *what* from?"

"That I'm in love wit' you. I'm not in love wit' you, Dominique. I care about you in a certain way, but that's it."

"You don't love me?" she asked, tears falling slowly down her cheeks.

"I ain't never told you that shit, so don't act like I did."

"But you said you wanted me to be yo girl," she stated, her voice quivering.

"Because I did. I liked fuckin' you n' shit, but now it done went too far."

"Well, you shouldn't have did nothin' wit' me in the first place!" she screamed, and then started sobbing uncontrollably.

"You probably right. But I gotta get outta here. Put yo shoes on. Take me home." Tre Pound headed for the steps.

"No!" Dominique went and grabbed him. "No, don't leave! I'ma make you love me, Tre Pound. Stay one more night, please."

"I gotta go. We gotta stop this shit between us."

"We can't just stop seeing each other. I'm begging you! Give me a chance to make you love me. You will, I promise. You can leave in the morning. Just stay this last night with me."

"No," he said coldly.

"Yes." Dominique tried to kiss him on the lips but he turned away. So she kissed him on the cheek, then his neck, anywhere she could.

"C'mon now. Cut it out. You wastin' yo time." He backed away, but she grabbed his buckle. "What are you doin'? Let my belt go."

Unexpectedly, she slowly lowered herself to her knees. "Let me do this," she pleaded, as she unfastened his belt and pulled it through the loops. His jeans flopped to his feet, and his manhood began extending before she even got it through the fly of his boxers.

The thoughts of going home had vanished from Tre Pound's mind. He was awestruck. Dominique had a fistful around his shaft, stroking it back and forth. She had yet to put her mouth on it, but her lips were only centimeters away and he could feel her hot breath against the head of his dick.

"You sure you know what you doin'?" he asked.

"Uh-huh."

Once he was at full attention, she placed her lips around his tip. He shuddered, and she tasted precum. She licked the slit and removed all of it.

"Yeah, I think you do know what you doin'," Tre Pound said, placing his right hand behind her head.

Dominique had never performed oral sex, until now. The plan was to save this special treatment for her honeymoon, just as she planned to do with her virginity. But over the past few weeks she found herself giving more and more of herself to Tre Pound. This was an investment, she reasoned. She had to do it for their relationship to survive.

After tasting his precum, Dominique felt confident enough to take a few inches into her mouth. She had watched adult videos before, with Camille and Krystal, so she knew not to use her teeth. Just lips and tongue, which she used carefully and delicately, pulling and pushing with her lips, tickling under his shaft with her tongue, all the while using her hand to stroke and steady him.

Tre Pound closed his eyes, tilted his head back and let out a low groan. "You're a trouper."

Dominique didn't know what he meant but she took it as a compliment and continued. Then he put pressure on the back of her head, urging her to go farther onto his manhood.

She gagged.

"Tre, I can't go that far. It's too big."

"Put as much in yo mouth as you can," he whispered. "Carry on."

She let go of his dick and sat back on her heels. "I don't know. I don't feel right doin' this and you don't wanna be my man no more."

Tre Pound looked down at her troubled eyes. "Finish up," he said, "and we'll talk about it later."

"Why not now?" she fussed. "Why does my brother have to come between us?"

Tre Pound sighed. His salivated dick was pointed straight at her, throbbing for more attention. "We just went through this. And I do want to be yo man, but I can't."

"Yes you can!" A tear dropped from her eye, down her cheek to the corner of her mouth. She licked it away.

Seeing her tongue made Tre Pound long for it to be back on his erection. "I'll tell you what," he began. "I'ma tell Marlon we ain't gon' see each other no more ..."

She whimpered.

"Listen! I'ma tell Marlon we ain't gon' see each other no more. Then after me and him is coo' again, me and you gon' work together to convince him to let us be wit' each other." It was a lie, but Tre Pound wanted his dick sucked. "Eventually yo brother will give in. But he's mad right now."

That raised Dominique's spirits. "So we just gotta stop seeing each other until he calms down?"

"Then we both talk to him."

Smiling, she latched onto his dick again. She wrapped her mouth back around it, sending Tre Pound back into euphoria. Then she suddenly stopped. "Promise me we'll be together."

"I put that on my 'hood," he said quickly.

With that, she hungrily sucked him between her lips. Pleasing him was now her main concern. This day would be their last encounter until they could win Marlon over, and she wanted to make it a good one. She bravely took more of him into her mouth—more than before—but not the whole thing. She bobbed her head back and forth within her comfort zone, certain this would make Tre Pound fall in love.

CHAPTER 26

The school week started up once again. Monday was always the slowest, sluggish day of the week, students still trying to recover from the weekend. Camille especially. Her weekend had been a miserable one. Her whole life was miserable, she thought, as she sulked in seminar class, where she was supposed to be catching up on homework but hadn't touched a textbook yet.

Neither had Kareem. He and Camille had their desks side by side and had formed a sort of bond over J-Dub's murder.

"I should've been there," Kareem said, his head hanging low.

"We both know that if you would've been there, you might've got shot, too."

"But still ... how I feel now ... maybe I was supposed to get shot."

"Kareem, that don't even make sense. Don't beat yo'self up. There was nothing you could've done." Camille held his hand.

"I think I could've done somethin'. Could've. But if I was there, would I have actually did somethin'? Probably not, if I never had his back when it counted. I've always been scary. Even that time yo cousin was stomping him, I stood back and watched, too damn scared to help. And I would've been scared to do somethin' when Lil' Pat pulled out his gun. I bet J-Dub is up in heaven wishing he would've never been my homie."

Camille patted his hand soothingly, trying to ease Kareem's disarranged emotions, unknowing of how to deal with her own. She felt deprived. Deprived of love. When she saw J-Dub's body hit the grass, she felt like her heart had been snatched out and trampled by wildebeests. Had she been allowed just a few more moments with J-Dub, her deepest desire would've been satisfied. She was that close. Now there was no telling when someone else—someone she was comfortable sharing her body with—would come along.

***

The classroom door opened and Dominique appeared wearing the yellow-gold Chanel sunglasses that she cherished. She had a grandiose aura to her, and avoided Camille's glare. She strutted to the teacher's desk.

"Ms. Hayes, you're just now making it to school?" asked Mrs. Bakersfield, observing the signed pass from the principal that was handed to her.

Dominique nodded. "I forgot to set my alarm," she lied.

Actually, last night had been filled with wild, passionate anal sex. This morning her alarm clock woke her up on time but she was so exhausted she knocked it to the floor. Eventually, Tre Pound awoke and, aware that Marlon could show up any minute, had Dominique take him to get some gizzards before dropping him off at home.

"Let this be the last time you show up late. Next time I won't care about your excuses." Mrs. Bakersfield flipped open an oversized greeting card. "Would you like to sign this?"

"What is it?" Dominique removed her shades.

"One of your classmates died over the weekend. Jesse White, bless his soul. We put together this card to give to his family."

"He died?" Dominique was completely shocked. No wonder Camille and Kareem had their desks pushed together.

"Yes, he's no longer with us, Ms. Hayes. Detectives came up here earlier and questioned a few of the students. They're looking for Patrick Campbell. So if you have any idea about his whereabouts you need to call the police."

Lil' Pat killed J-Dub! exclaimed Dominique in her head. *Whoa! It had to have happened the day Camille hopped out the car and left with J-Dub and Kareem. But where did they go? How did it go down?*

She glanced back and found Camille meanmugging her. Then Camille looked away. Dominique felt bad. She had planned to ignore Camille today. How could she do that now?

"I'll sign it," she said, finding a ballpoint pen in her clutch bag. After she signed her name on the card, she located what Camille had written. It read:

You were the best boyfriend I ever had.
My only love. I miss you so much, Jesse.
                    Camille Cheree King

All Kareem wrote was "I'M SORRY," and Dominique wondered why. Her curiosity led her to a desk that she connected to Camille's and Kareem's.

It was obvious that Camille still harbored ill feelings. "Kareem, don't even say nothin' to her."

"How you gon' tell him what to do?" Dominique questioned.

"I just did, didn't I?"

"Camille, I didn't come over here to argue wit' you. I'm sorry for what happened to J-Dub. I really am."

"Yo sorrys don't mean nothin' to me. You can take that sorry and shove it up yo ass. Ain't that how you like it?"

"That's not right. I haven't ever disrespected you like that."

Camille looked flabbergasted. "What do you call fuckin' my cousin?"

Taking a look around, Kareem noticed that the rest of the classmates were engaged in his or her own conversations. The heated discussion between the girls hadn't attracted any attention *yet*. He felt awkward sitting there. "Yall want me to leave?" he asked.

"Can you just give us a couple minutes? I'd appreciate it," said Dominique. But Camille didn't let him get up. "Me and Kareem was talkin' before you came over here. So if anybody needs to leave, it's you."

"Fine, I'll say what I gotta say in front of Kareem." Dominique took a deep breath. "You said that I'm no different than those other girls Tre Pound has been with, that I'm just another ho to him. I'm tellin' you that's not true."

Camille almost laughed. "You really are that far gone. I can't believe you would say somethin' like that. We used to stay up late and talk for hours about how sleazy them bitches are that get wit' Tre Pound—about how we would never give ourselves to somebody who doesn't care about us."

"I remember ..."

"So you're a hypocrite."

"No, I'm not," Dominique said adamantly.

"Why come you ain't? What makes you different than those bitches?"

"He told me."

"Told you what?"

"He said that he cares about me in a certain way. We're a couple. Well, we *were* a couple but he said—"

"Get ya story straight," Camille interjected.

"Just last night he told me we could be together as long as it's alright wit' my brother."

"You a liar!" Camille shouted. She didn't heed Mrs. Bakersfield's warning to lower her voice. "You keep lyin' and I'ma beat yo muthafuckin' ass!"

"Why you think I was late for school today? Tre Pound spent the night, *again*. I wouldn't sit here and lie to you, Camille. He has feelings for me. We been havin' sex more and more lately." Dominique thought if she explained she wasn't a ho to Tre Pound, then Camille would be okay with it. But she was clueless as to the real reason Camille was dangerously furious.

Camille lunged forward and grabbed a lock of Dominique's hair. She pulled and punched repeatedly, as Dominique windmilled her way up out her seat. "I hate you!" Camille screamed, jerking Dominique's head at will.

Dominique let out screams of her own as she blindly swung her fists. Her hair was naturally strong; she couldn't break free. Had Camille's hair not been braided straight back, she would've grabbed her hair, too. Nevertheless, Dominique fought back with all her might.

Pure astonishment washed over Mrs. Bakersfield's face as she watched her classroom turn into a zoo for the second time in less than a month. Classmates egged on the fight, and the girls fell to the floor, the brawl intensifying into wild punching and kicking.

When Kareem tried to break it up, Camille bit him on the arm. She screamed out at Dominique again.

"Stay away from my cousin!"

CHAPTER 27

Around noon, Buttercup was looking in her closet for her black trousers. All she had on was her burgundy polo-style work shirt and a pair of white panties that were giving her a wedgie.

Tre Pound, who was sitting on her bed, watched her search. "Did you look in that laundry basket?" he asked.

"I know they not in there. I put 'em somewhere around here before you came over. I forgot where, though." But Buttercup looked in the laundry basket anyway, tossing clothes over her shoulder.

"Why you in a rush? You ain't gotta be at work for another 45 minutes, right?"

"But I like to know where everything is. Have everything ready. I don't put on my trousers until I'm 'bout to walk out the door so I don't get 'em wrinkled up, but I at least need to find 'em."

"Ain't you tired of workin' at Red Lobster?"

"I like it. The tips are good." Buttercup went back to the closet. She started examining each article of clothing as she pushed back the hangers. "Working there is the only way I'm gonna be able to pay for my books this semester."

Tre Pound happened to look underneath him. "Oh, damn. Here they go."

Buttercup turned and looked. "You were sitting on 'em? I can't believe you, silly." She went and grabbed her pants. "Now I gotta iron 'em all over again."

"I apologize, B. From the bottom of my heart, I apologize."

"You not sorry. You just sayin' that so you can get a kiss, I'ma give you one this time." She smooched his lips, then went and put her pants on the ironing board, plugged up the iron. "I went up to the hospital to see you. I gave you a kiss on the cheek. You was still unconscious so I don't know if you felt it."

"My little cousin told me you came up there. But I don't know why you did. You probably didn't have nothin' else to do."

"Stop that. I could've had a million things to do and still would've found time to see you. Actually, I did have somethin' to do. I was supposed to go in and work overtime that day, but I had to see my baby. First I heard you was dead, but then I found out what hospital you was at and I went straight up there." Steam spouted out the iron as she ran it along a pants leg. "And before I forget, I wanna say thank you for callin' and sayin' you'll take me to work. I hate catching the bus. I would've had to have left 15 minutes ago to make it to work on time."

"It's nothin'," he said.

"It's somethin' to me," she replied. "But I know you want somethin' in return. And I'm pretty sure I know what it is."

"What you think I want?"

Buttercup shook her hips and her booty jiggled.

"How'd you know?" Tre Pound asked with a wide grin.

She laughed. "Because I know you. And since yo arm is in a sling, I guess I'ma have to take those nice clothes off of you myself."

"I'm not the one you gon' be undressing."

"Well, who am I gon' undress? Yo boy in the front room?" she joked.

But Tre Pound was serious. "His name is Stacks. It's his birthday. I need you to show him a good time."

Buttercup tilted the iron upright and fixed her eyes on the infamous gangster sitting on her bed. "I know you not suggesting what I think you are?"

"If you think I want you to fuck my homie, then we on the same page. I promised him I would get him some good pussy for his birthday. And you the only person I know that fit the bill."

"I'm not doin' that. I don't even know why you would ask me to, Tre Pound. I'm not a slut. I told you last time you came over here that what I did wit' you and Paul was a one-time thing."

"You also told me that you didn't want to be wit' Playa Paul. You said you wanted to be wit' me. But I saw you at my trial wit' his arm around yo shoulder."

"He came and sat next to *me!*" Buttercup stressed. "I came to yo trial *by myself* to support *you*. I wasn't even paying attention to Paul."

"I don't care if you was or not. I'm not tryna stop you from fuckin' wit' him. All I know is that if you wanted to be my girlfriend, you'd do what I ask you to do. And my nigga in the front room is the one who drove. So if you don't wanna give him no pussy, then he might not wanna take you to work."

Buttercup considered it for a moment. "What is it you want me to do wit' him? Just fuck him?"

"It's his birthday," Tre Pound said. "Do whatever he wants you to do."

She sighed. "What's his name again?"

"Stacks."

"Tell him ... tell him to come in here." Then she quickly added, "Remember: I'm only doin' this for you."

After hearing his name being called, Stacks showed up at the bedroom door, curious. "Wussup? Tre Pound, you holler for me?"

"Quit actin' scared and come on in here." Tre Pound went and pulled Stacks into the room, shutting the door.

Stacks eyed both his homie and the beautiful, barely-naked girl standing by the ironing board. His gaze lingered a bit longer on the girl.

Buttercup unplugged the iron and sat on the bed. She looked at Stacks as if she desired him. "Hi," she said.

"Hi," Stacks uttered.

"Go sit next to her," Tre Pound urged him.

Stacks didn't move, not believing this was really happening. "Yall fuckin' wit' me."

Tre Pound chuckled. "This is real life. I told you I was gon' hook you up for ya birthday."

Birthday? Stacks peered at Tre Pound, who winked. And Stacks understood. Going along with the flow, he grinned and eagerly went and sat beside the young lady.

"What's yo name?" he asked her.

Smiling, she reached under his shirt and tickled his frail chest. "They call me B," she answered in a seductive voice. "So how old are you today?"

"Twenty-one," he said truthfully. "How old are *you*, baby?"

She placed soft kisses on his neck. "You're never supposed to ask a girl's age."

"She's 19," Tre Pound blurted out. "What difference does it make? Speed this shit up. Yall bullshittin'."

"Ugh." Buttercup screwed her face up at Tre Pound. "You're gonna ruin the fantasy. Let me do my thing."

"You gotta be at work in about half an hour," Tre Pound reminded her, checking his diamond-studded Audemars Piquet watch. "However long it take for you to make him cum is on you." The cell phone in his jean pocket rang. "Yall need to get busy. 'Cause I gotta be somewhere, too." He left the room, closing the door behind him, and took the call he'd been expecting. "Hello?"

"It's like that?" asked Marlon in a threatening voice. "Behind my back, right up under my nose, huh? All this time I thought you was my homie but I see you ain't nothin' but a snake."

"Nah ..." Tre Pound began, but Marlon wouldn't let him finish.

"Whatchu mean 'nah'? You ran up in my lil' sister, didn't you? It is like that. You made it like that."

"Damn, can I talk?"

"Fuck you, nigga! The only thing that's gon' be talkin' is my Mac-10."

"You don't wanna take it there, Marlon. You overreacting. I'm tryna tell you that it's over between me and Dominique. That won't happen again."

"You muthafuckin' right it won't happen again. Because I'ma toe-tag yo bitch ass!"

Tre Pound tried to restrain himself and remain the apologetic friend, but the threats were taking their toll. "You act like I ain't got guns," he shot back. "You know how I get down. Like I said, you don't wanna take it there."

"Muthafucka, you ain't nobody. You must've forgot—I know you. I really know you like none of these other niggas do. And I know, and you know, THAT YOU CAN'T FUCK WIT' ME! My sister ain't 'bout to be one of yo bitches! You got me fucked up!"

In a last ditch effort to avoid violence, Tre Pound explained his side: "You got it wrong. I wouldn't do Dominique dirty. I got too much respect for you *and* her.

I like her, but I'm through seeing her, if only to keep our friendship intact. I fucked up. I know you mad. But we shouldn't fall out over this."

"I ain't tryna hear nothin' you sayin'," Marlon said. "But I ain't one to do all this blowin' over the phone. You know where I stay. Fifty-first and Garfield, fourth house from the corner. Come see me!"

The line went dead.

At first, Tre Pound didn't know he was hung up on. "Hello?" Then it was clear. Marlon wanted funk, and that's what he'd get. Tre Pound's plan was already in motion.

Walking back into the room, Tre Pound got a full view of Stacks' boney, sweaty ass humping away. In the missionary position, Stacks was giving it his all, panting like he was completely out of breath.

Buttercup's moans sounded fake. "Oh, Stacks! You're the greatest! Oh! Uhn!" She noticed Tre Pound tapping his watch impatiently, so she began contracting her pussy muscles to speed up the process. Shortly after, Stacks trembled. His pumping waned as he nutted inside her, and his arousal dwindled. He rolled off of her.

"Wait outside for me," Tre Pound told Stacks. "I gotta talk to Buttercup in private."

Stacks crawled off the bed, barely able to hold his jeans up. He felt drained, yet confident and manly. He gave Tre Pound some dap and bumped shoulders with him like they had just reunited after years of being apart. "I owe you one, G. No lie, man. Whatever you need."

"I need you to wait outside. Can you do that?"

"Fa-sho'. Just holla if you need me." Stacks pointed at Buttercup as he backpedaled out the room. He had no words for her. He just shook his head with a girl-you-got-that-bomb expression.

She shot back a half smile and waited for the door to close before she spoke. "I don't care which one of yo friends got a birthday from here on out. Please don't bring 'em here again."

"I probably won't," Tre Pound said. "But I'm glad you could take care of that for me. It was real important to me."

"Anything for you, baby. But, damn, you sure do ask a lot from a girl." Buttercup snatched her trousers off the ironing board and slipped them on. Zipping them up, she said, "How much time do I got?"

"Not enough," he answered.

She felt paralyzed. "What do you mean?"

"I mean you took too long. I just got a call and I gotta be somewhere. Ain't no time to drop you off at work."

"How am I supposed to get there then?!"

"The bus."

"The bus? It's too late for me to catch the bus. I can't afford to be late, Tre Pound!"

"Who are you hollerin' at?"

Buttercup lowered her voice a few octaves. "Forget it," she sighed. "I guess I'll just work some more overtime." Then she tried to smile. "So did I prove myself to you? Am I yo woman now?"

"Hell nah," he spat.

She stood there, open-mouthed.

"I can't be witta bitch that done fucked two of my homies," he went on. "How would that make me look in the streets? Niggas would be laughin' at me for years."

"I did what you asked me to do!"

"That's yo problem. You do everything I tell you to do. I need a bitch witta backbone, that'll say no when she know I'm trippin'. That'll stand up for herself. You'll never be a candidate. But I ain't 'bout to stand here and explain shit to you that you probably can't even comprehend. I got somewhere to be. Tre block."

Buttercup covered her face and wept into her hands as Tre Pound left. She broke down to her knees, and would end up crying herself to sleep.

***

For the first time since he got out the hospital, Tre Pound was behind the wheel. He drove Stacks' cherry-red Camaro IROC-Z absentmindedly, thinking about an indispensable piece of advice he got from his Uncle Marcus "Cutthroat" King: "Friends can become the worst enemies," he had said. "If you're heavy in the streets, there'll come a time when you're gonna have to kill one of ya homeboys."

That time had come, Tre Pound thought.

In the passenger seat, Stacks had been chattering nonstop about how fine, skilled and pleasurable Buttercup was. Tre Pound finally tuned in.

"She was doin' this suction thing wit' her pussy. Oh my God! It was like she was squeezing my dick."

"That's just one of her specialties," Tre Pound responded. "Wait till you experience her head game. She's talented wit' ice cubes in her mouth. I'll take you over there again one day so you can see for ya'self."

Stacks flushed with excitement. "Again? Bet that. I just gotta say thank you, Tre Pound. Thank you. Most niggas be wantin' to cuff top-notch girls like that. You one of a kind, the best homie a nigga can have."

"I'm just being Tre Pound."

"You sure you wanna drive? I know you still recovering. You can sit in the backseat. I'll be yo chauffeur. I'll wear the hat, suit, all that shit."

Tre Pound chuckled. "I gotta get used to drivin' again. I'm feelin' a'ight."

"Where we goin', anyway?"

Instead of answering him, Tre Pound said, "Reach in my pocket and grab my pack of Newports."

"Want me to light one for you?" Stacks asked, as he pulled the pack out.

"Nah. Just open 'em."

Stacks flicked the top off the Newport pack. Along with the regular white cigarettes were two thin brown ones.

More Reds laced with PCP. He plucked one of them. "The day just keep gettin' better and better!"

"Grab the other one," Tre Pound said.

"You ain't gon' get wet wit' me?"

"I bought those for you. Smoke 'em back-to-back."

"You ain't gotta tell me twice," Stacks beamed.

Soon, the Camaro had smoke in the air. Tre Pound cracked his window while Stacks continued to fill his lungs. In between puffs, Stacks constantly praised Buttercup and paid homage to Tre Pound.

By the second cigarette, his speech had slowed to a low drawl.

Tre Pound knew the affects of PCP. He knew how fragile the senses became ... and how easy it would be to mold Stacks' drug-induced mind.

Tre Pound finally parked the car and cut off the ignition. "How many times you and Marlon kicked-it like this?"

"I ... can't remember. Not a lot."

"I'm not talkin' about in the past. I'm talkin' about *lately*."

"I guess we haven't."

"Why is that, though?"

"He say I can't control my high. That's ... crazy."

"I feel the same way. It's like Marlon don't respect you. He probably don't like you period."

"He do. I just need to stop gettin' high ... around him."

"Why should you have to stop smokin' around a nigga that's supposed to be yo homie? The nigga must not be yo

277

homie to begin wit'. You can smoke around me all day and I won't give a fuck. Because you my nigga. But Marlon's friendship is questionable."

Stacks nodded slowly. "Right ... right."

"I mean, you tell me if this is somethin' a homie would do: Marlon took the stick you had just bought from Hoodey and crushed it, in front of everybody. He think you soft. He didn't even give you the money to buy another one. You gave him the money to fix his car door when you messed it up, so why shouldn't he do the same?"

"That wasn't coo' at all," Stacks said, his eyebrows slanted angrily. "Marlon shouldn't've did that."

"Remember the night you came to his pad high, when you and Playa Paul brought over those girls—?"

Stacks cut him off. "I remember. You ain't even gotta say it."

But Tre Pound pressed on. "He beat the shit outta you, royally. Over what? Pissing in the corner? The carpet can be replaced. That's material. But you still got bruises on yo face. He did it because he wanted to show off in front of those females. I wouldn't let *nobody* do me like that."

"What can I do, though? That's Marlon. It ain't like I can murk him."

"Why not?"

Stacks thought about it. He thought about how Marlon acted like he was better than him because he used a little PCP. He wasn't the wethead that Marlon made him out to be. And he wasn't a bitch nigga that could be pushed around. "You know what? You right. I should put a hole in that nigga's head for all the shit he done to me."

"I would."

Tucked in Stacks' waistband was his trusty 9mm Bergmann superautomatic Llama. He pulled it out and cocked it. "He think I'm a bitch. Like I'ma just let him keep fuckin' me around. Hell nah!"

"It's a damn shame you let it go on this long."

"Take me to that nigga's house right now!"

"We already there."

Just then Stacks realized they weren't in motion. They were parked, on 51st and Garfield, a few houses down from Marlon's house.

"Put ya gun up before you walk up there," Tre Pound warned him. "You don't want him to see it comin'. Then, once you in the house, pop his soft ass."

Concealing the gun back in his waist, Stacks hopped out the car and started walking up to the house.

Tre Pound watched intently from the driver seat as Stacks took his time approaching Marlon's front porch. The PCP had Stacks moving slow. In Stacks' head, he was probably jogging. But Tre Pound didn't care how slow Stacks walked, as long as he got the job done.

Stacks knocked on the door without looking back. He didn't even bother to hide his rage; it showed on his face.

The front door opened.

From Tre Pound's vantage point, he could see that Stacks and Marlon were talking. "Go in," Tre Pound whispered. "Go in." Then, Stacks disappeared inside. "Yes!"

Minutes later, Tre Pound had a Newport lit, taking totes anxiously. He smashed it in the ashtray. What was going on in there?

Then he heard a faint pop sound—a gunshot! He quickly turned the ignition and roared the Camaro to life.

There were two more pops.

"Goddamn! C'mon, nigga!" Tre Pound exclaimed to himself.

But nobody came outside. So he drove up till he was directly in front of the house, the car idling. The living room curtains were closed so he couldn't see inside. He honked the horn twice. Still, Stacks didn't come out.

"Fuck this." Tre Pound burned rubber as he fled the block. He stayed in the vicinity, driving around the neighborhood. After another ten minutes of aimless driving, he was sure nobody called the police. He spotted a cop car, but it wasn't speeding by and it didn't have its sirens blaring; it was just making its rounds through the 'hood. So Tre Pound drove back to Marlon's street and parked in the same spot. He watched the house, looking for any sign of activity. There was none. It was possible that Stacks was so high that he forgot to leave the scene. A little bit longer, Tre Pound decided, and he'd go in after him.

Then his cell phone rang. The caller ID displayed Marlon's number. Why would Stacks call from inside the house? Tre Pound wondered. He quickly flipped the phone open.

"Hello? Stacks? What are you doin' in there? Come out of there!"

The voice that came back sounded strained with anguish. "I ... killed him."

"We can mourn later," Tre Pound said. "Right now you need to bring yo ass on!" He waited for a response but only heard sighs of grief. "Stacks! Pull yo'self together! Stacks!"

"This—this ain't Stacks. This is ... Marlon."

Tre Pound was stunned. He was talking to Marlon! And that only meant one thing ...

... Stacks was dead.

Marlon went on in a hopeless voice that was unlike him. "Tre Pound, I need you to come over here. I need yo help! I ..." His voice faltered. "... I killed Stacks."

Tre Pound hung up. Marlon had just called on him for help. What did that mean? It seemed that Marlon was no longer mad at him for sleeping with his little sister. He just wanted help.

But it could be a ploy.

So Tre Pound got out the car and paced up to the house with his pistol drawn. He crept inside the front door. He saw a Mac-10 on the living room sofa. Then he heard something in the kitchen; it sounded like a balled fist had punched something wooden. "Damn!" he heard next. Tre Pound's handgun was raised when he entered the kitchen, where there was a horrendous sight.

Stacks' bloody body was splayed on the tiled floor. The kitchen table had been toppled, chairs lay on their sides. Shards of glass from dinner plates were scattered everywhere. It appeared there had been a massive struggle. Marlon was sitting on the floor, against the bottom cabinets, inches away from the body. Stacks' 9mm Llama lay beside him, his white shirt stained crimson.

"He came over here," Marlon began, not even looking at Tre Pound. He was staring off into space. "Stacks looked mad, but I didn't care because I was mad, too. He said he wanted to come in, and I just let him in. I didn't know he was mad at me. I never would've thought he'd get mad enough to try and smoke me." Marlon looked at Stacks' lifeless body. He punched the cabinet again.

Tre Pound put his gun up. He turned a chair upright and had a seat. A strange feeling overcame him. Was it regret? He inhaled, then released.

"I came into the kitchen to get something to drink," Marlon continued. "I turn around and he's right there. He usually just goes into the living room and chills. But he was wet. I could tell. Seen it in his eyes. Then he pulled out a burner, I grabbed it, we fought for it, I took it from him. Stacks is small but he fought so hard ... then I shot him ... and I shot him again ... and I shot him again ... damn."

Tre Pound spoke understandingly. "It's fucked up how this turned out. Stacks was a coo' nigga."

"Yeah, and I treated him bad," Marlon admitted. "But he would do shit, stupid shit when he was high. I always tried to tell him about hisself. Tried to get him to get off that wet because he would go too far. I guess I went about it the wrong way. I should've never put my hands on him that night. I think that's what it was. I should've never put my hands on him."

"What about us?"

Marlon finally looked at Tre Pound; it was a why-would-you-even-fuck-my-sister glare. But then he lowered his head and sighed. "I can't be mad at you for that. You and Dominique been around each other so much, talkin' shit to each other ... she's beautiful ... it was bound to happen."

"But I was gon' say that that's it. Me and Dominique's little thing is done. I know how you feel. I know how *I'd* feel, and how you came at me over the phone, I understand it. So I ain't got a problem wit' leavin' her alone. As long as me and you can stay tight like muscle shirts."

Marlon almost smiled. "Nah, you don't have to stop seeing her."

"I'll stop," Tre Pound insisted.

"Nah, I'd rather see you wit' her than one of these other niggas out here. What sent me over the edge was the fact that I know how you go hard on females. I didn't want that to be Dominique."

"And it's not gon' be. She's not one of these other females."

"I know. And when she came to visit me, I could see how much she wanted to be wit' you ... I just wanna see her happy."

There was silence for a moment. Both of them were gazing at Stacks' gruesome body, blood pooling out from underneath him.

Tre Pound broke the silence. "Best thing to do would be to dump his body in Swope Park somewhere."

"His car should be outside," Marlon said, finally standing up. "I'll haul him in that. Ditch it and burn it afterwards. Just follow behind me in yo car."

"I didn't drive my car over here."

"How'd you get over here?"

"Uh ... I walked. I was around the corner when you called my phone." Tre Pound quickly came up with an alternative. "*I'll* drop his body off, burn the car, all that. Cash and Seneca got my car. I'll have them meet me at Swope Park to help." He looked at the device on Marlon's ankle. "You still on house arrest anyway, ain't you?"

"This is my mess, though."

"This is *our* mess. Any problems you got is my problems, too. While I'm gone, just get rid of all this blood and whatever other evidence. We don't want Dominique comin' home from school and seeing this. And in the days to come, we'll remodel this whole kitchen."

Marlon gave Tre Pound dap, pulled him to his feet and hugged him. "I love you, man. You a real nigga."

"I'm just being Tre Pound."

CHAPTER 28

Camille lay on her bed with a pencil twirling through her fingers. She was on her stomach, ankles crossed in the air, doing geometry. She would've got it done in seminar class, but unfortunately she had to beat Dominique down. That bitch deserved it, Camille told herself. Now she had ample time to get her homework done due to her two-week suspension.

Just like every Monday night, people came over to gamble in her basement. She could faintly hear the shouts and drunken laughter through the floorboards. Most of the time it didn't bother her, but tonight it did. She had so much on her mind.

Unable to concentrate, she slammed the textbook closed and rolled onto her back. She planted her feet high against the wall, staring at the ceiling, as she thought of her baby J-Dub.

He had really loved her.

Who loved her now? Nobody, she thought. Shelton treated her like a 5-year-old daughter instead of a mature little sister. He was always working and didn't have time for her. Even Tre Pound was changing, and she thought he was the one that loved her most.

It was because of Dominique! She tricked Tre Pound into fucking her and even stole the gift from him that was supposed to go to Camille. She could be trying to steal Krystal, too. So Camille picked up the phone and dialed rapidly.

"Hello?" came Krystal's shy voice.

"Why you ain't called me?"

"I'm sorry, Camille. I been so busy makin' runs for Moses. He's locked up in some place called CCA in Leavenworth, Kansas. I had to have my momma take me to get his car out of impound. Then I had to go to the bank to get some money so I could send to him. I just got home an hour ago."

"So you and Dominique ain't been kickin'-it?"

"No. I been too busy."

"Well, I don't want you to talk to her no more. She ain't our friend. She fucked Tre Pound."

"Oh, she told me the other day. I told her she was in the wrong."

"And she sabotaged our talent show," Camille added. "The night before we performed, she had let him fuck her in her ass, and that's why she wasn't hittin' her moves on point like we was. If the talent show would've got finished, we probably would've lost. So don't even speak to her ever again."

"But Camille, both of yall are my friends. I been knowin' yall both since 8th grade. And I heard about that fight yall had today. That wasn't the way to handle it." When Camille tried to respond, Krystal quickly added, "But I gotta go. Moses is on the other line."

"Tell him to call you back," Camille retorted.

"I can't. He might not be able to call back tonight because it's people waitin' to use the phone. But as soon as I get done talkin' to him, I'll—"

Camille hung up. She violently threw her pencil across the room. Her bedroom door opened as the pencil smacked against it.

"What was that?" her mother asked, standing in the doorway.

Camille shrugged.

Janice looked down at the pencil. "What has gotten into you, little girl? Whatever it is, you need to fix it. Because if you go back to school with that attitude, you're gonna get into another fight. And you not about to get kicked outta that school, Camille. And why is that book closed?"

"I'm takin' a break."

"Ain't no breaks. During this whole two weeks of your suspension, you're gonna work. So you open that book back up. And after that I want you to clean all three bathrooms."

"Tonight?"

"Yes, tonight. Why not tonight?"

"Momma, this geometry is gonna take all night. Plus, I can't even concentrate. Those men in the basement is so loud."

"Don't try and blame it on them," Janice snapped. "Every Monday night they're here and you always get your homework done. Don't give me that shit. Now come over here and pick up this pencil."

Hesitantly, Camille got up. When she bent down to pick up the pencil, her mother popped her in the head. Camille pretended it hurt and flopped to the ground.

"Get it done!" Janice slammed the door.

Camille didn't move a muscle. She lay by her door close to tears. But before she could really sulk, she heard something tap against her bedroom window.

She looked up and heard another tiny tap.

Pulling herself to her feet, she curiously followed the taps to the window that opened to the side of the house. She lifted it, and a chilly wind burrowed through her flimsy sapphire nightie.

Down below, someone was standing in the grass. Her eyes adjusted to the darkness of the night and she couldn't have been more surprised—she saw the last person she expected to see.

"What are you doin' here?"

"I'm on the run, Camille. I came to say goodbye." Lil' Pat tossed the rest of the pebbles in the grass.

"I don't know why you came here to tell me that, you fuckin' punk! You killed my boyfriend!"

"I did it for you."

"You didn't do it for me. You did it because yo brother made you. Leave, or I'ma call the police."

Lil' Pat lowered his head in silence, then looked up again. "Maybe my brother had somethin' to do wit' it. But I'm the one that pulled the trigger. Deep down I wanted to. I really did do it for you, though. I thought if I killed him you would think I was a man."

"You thought wrong; you still a little boy. You just got man problems now. I should've let my cousin fuck you up for leavin' me at the Plaza. Or I should come down there and fuck you up myself. You can't fight."

"You right about that. I ain't all that good at fighting. But I'll shoot somebody else in a heartbeat to protect you. I love you that much."

Camille's mood seemed to lighten. "You love me?"

"Yeah. That's all I wanted to tell you. I couldn't leave without tellin' you how I feel. I wasn't gonna let J-Dub have you. But I guess I'm not man enough to have you either." Lil' Pat started to walk away. "Goodbye," he said over his shoulder.

"You don't love me!" she called out.

He turned and looked up at her. "I do, too." Then he kept on walking.

"Well, why you leavin'?"

Going back to where he was standing, he said, "Because I have to. If I stay in Kansas City I'ma go to jail. But I'd stay if I knew you loved me, too."

"I love you a little bit."

That seemed to be just enough for him. "Well, shit, I'm stayin' then."

"That's stupid. You just said you gon' go to jail if you stay. How we gon' be together and you locked up?"

"What am I supposed to do then? If I leave, I lose you. At least if I stay I'll get to be wit' you until they catch me." He stuffed his hands in his pockets and looked away, feeling uneasy. "I kinda … I kinda wanted to do the sex thing wit' you before I go. But it's probably too late."

Camille smiled. "Why now? I thought you didn't want to have sex at all. Every time we spent time together you acted like you was scared to touch me."

Lil' Pat looked back up, taking in her beauty. Her long braids hung and rested against the window seal as she leaned out. Though it was dark, he could still make out her lovely smile and her flawless cinnamon skin tone.

He'd had sex with women before. Older women. His brother, Hoodey, had been forcing him to have sex and receive oral sex from crack hoes since he was 13. But Camille was completely different. Aside from her being the prettiest girl in Kansas City, she was also the sassiest. And that intimidated him.

There was also another reason he hadn't had sex with Camille, the ultimate reason—Tre Pound.

"I heard what yo cousin did to J-Dub and I didn't want that to be me," Lil' Pat confessed. "I was kinda scared to even make you my girl. But I had to have you. Anybody would be proud to have you. And when I got you, I wanted to keep you. If we would've did anything, Tre Pound would've found out and it would've been over ... I feel like it's already over for me now, so ..."

Camille knew she'd never find a man that would stand up to Tre Pound on her behalf. She finally accepted that fact. J-Dub was dead and Lil' Pat was all she had left. "I know a way we can be together without us worrying about Tre Pound," she said, "without you stayin' here and going to jail."

"What is it?"

She smiled again. "We can leave together."

***

Janice King descended the basement stairs and her voice towered over everybody else's. "Okay, yall muthafuckas need to keep it down!" she bellowed, and the noise level instantly dropped. "My baby girl is up there trying to study. All this unnecessary commotion has got to stop. I'll shut this muthafucka down if my daughter flunks her class."

"We apologize, Janice, baby," slurred Old George, a Monday night regular. His salt-and-pepper afro matched his mustache. "We don't want baby Camille to flunk out of school. School is important. Without school—"

"She'd be a drunk-ass muthafucka like you," Janice finished for him, "without a blackjack idea," she added with a smile, and the entire basement broke into laughter.

291

The basement decor resembled a miniature casino. Light fixtures were strategically installed in the ceiling to illuminate every square foot, shining light on any would-be cheaters. The Persian-style carpeting provided a touch of elegance and the wide mirror that took up most of one wall made the basement appear bigger than it actually was. Three dealers—college students that Janice liked to call her "interns"—ran the blackjack, five-card stud poker and crap tables. Free liquor and big winnings kept the place packed every Monday night.

Janice greeted her guests as she walked the floor. She bumped into Bernice Hampton, her late husband's baby momma. Bernice had smooth dark skin and tended to dress casually like she had a job, but was still living off Cutthroat's life insurance and drug money he left her. When Janice and Bernice first met, they were at each other's necks. But after Cutthroat died they got over their differences, because their kids were family, and they eventually learned that they had a lot in common.

"Janice, you look nice today. What are you wearin'?" Bernice asked. She sipped from a glass of Moet, a beverage that wasn't on the free-liquor list.

Checking herself out, Janice said, "My daughter told me it's what the girls are wearin' these days. She picked this out. She said this V-neck and these slacks are couture. These leather wedge sandals ... I forgot who she said made 'em but I like 'em."

"She sho' do got you lookin' pretty fly," Bernice admitted.

"Of the many things I can say about my daughter, in vogue is one of them. She stays on top of the current trends. She's intelligent, too. Loves to learn. She had all A's, except a C in history—because she keeps saying the teacher is wrong. The only problem I have is getting her to realize that the world doesn't revolve around her."

"We all think that at one point in our lives."

"And did you know she got into a fight today? Beat some girl up pretty good, the principal told me."

"Whaaat?" Bernice's eyebrows arched in surprise. "No she didn't."

Janice smiled. "My daughter can fight; I didn't tell you that? She just needs a little discipline every now and then to keep her grounded. But I love her to death."

At the blackjack table, Old George was down to his last ten-dollar chip. He blamed it on the dealer's poor shuffling and pushed his last chip forward. The young brotha sitting next to him, though, had a far better run of luck. It was the brotha's lack of strategy. He played like he didn't care if he won or lost, and his winnings so far totaled over $8,500. His name was Rowland Reed.

Row currently held a ten of diamonds and a two of clubs. A glass of Jack Daniels on ice sat beside his cards. "Hit me," he said.

The dealer pulled from the deck and flipped over an eight of diamonds. Once again, the cards played in Row's favor. The guys surrounding him clapped, as well as other spectators.

Spook was standing beside Row, drinking from a glass of his own. He whispered in Row's ear, "I'm ready when you are."

Row then asked the dealer for another card. The young college student looked puzzled. "You sure?"

"Yeah, I'm sure," Row said. "Don't question me. Just deal the card."

"But you're holding twenty, sir. Chances are you'll bust if I give you another card."

Old George chimed in, "Listen to the dealer, young man. You pushin' ya luck. I been playin' this game since you was in diapers. You better off keepin' the cards you got."

"How da hell you gon' tell me how to play my hand, you old fucker? You need to be takin' tips from me." Row downed the rest of his liquor, slammed the glass down on the table and stood up. "Hit me!"

Gladly, the dealer pulled another card from the deck. He wanted to see the cocky player lose. But the card he flipped over displayed an ace of hearts. Row hit blackjack.

"That's what I'm talkin' 'bout!" Row cheered, giving Spook dap as the spectators applauded.

The colorful chips were stacked in neat piles. But when the dealer shoved them across to Row, the chips spilled over.

Row looked the dealer in the eyes.

"Oops." The dealer smirked.

Suddenly, from inside his jacket, Row drew a TEC-9 and blasted the dealer dead in the chest, lifting him off his feet and crashing to the floor.

People ran screaming to escape up the basement steps but Spook had it blocked off, holding an AK-47 like a shield. "Ain't nobody goin' nowhere!" Spook barked. "Sit yall asses back down!"

Other gangsters who came with Row and Spook held fully automatic weapons and forced the terror-stricken people to comply. When the seats were filled, people sat on the floor. Janice and Bernice sat against the wall.

Row fired another shot into the numb dealer. "Punkass nigga," he growled, then turned to Janice. "You hired this nigga?"

Janice looked infuriated. She wished they'd hurry up and take the money and go. She didn't know who the men holding the guns were, but she was sure her nephew would find out. Three years ago, the basement was robbed and word got to Tre Pound who did it. Some kid named Rico and his friends. A late-night drive-by left them all murdered. Janice would get on the phone and call her nephew as soon as this was over.

Or so she thought.

CHAPTER 29

Shelton stood on the sidewalk arguing with a police officer. "Why can't I go in? This is my momma's house!"

The officer was a homely Black woman, trying to speak as pleasantly as possible. "No one is allowed to go in, sir. Only authorized technicians. Anybody else might contaminate the scene. Sir, I'm not even allowed to go in."

"At least you can tell me what's goin' on. I need to find out if my momma's in there. And my little sister, she's only 15. I can't just stand out here without knowin' a muthafuckin' thing!"

"I know about as much as you do at this point. There's bodies inside but I don't know who or how many yet. Please, if you will, go have a seat against your car and I'll have somebody come talk to you in a minute."

Whirling red police lights lit up the night sky outside the King household. People from the neighborhood sobbed and watched the house intently from behind yellow police tape. Homicide detectives questioned the ones who had been gambling. Shelton saw Bernice being led out the house by an officer and he rushed over to her. She had blood smeared under her nose, which was probably broken.

"Bernice, what happened? You ain't seen my momma or Camille?"

Her eyes were red and puffy from crying. "I tried to help Janice ... but one of 'em punched me in the face. Old George tried to help, too, and they shot him dead."

"What did they do to my momma?"

"They killed her," she cried.

Stunned, Shelton placed a hand over his eyes, holding back tears. This was a terrible blow. He just talked to Janice this morning, but they only talked about business. He couldn't remember the last time he told her he loved her.

"For no fuckin' reason," Bernice carried on. "She gave 'em all the money in the safe and they still beat her to death. I don't know who they were. I wish I did." She turned and screamed at the gamblers and spectators who had been inside. "But I know one of yall know who those niggas were! But yall too chickenshit to say anything!"

Shelton hated to ask his next question. "What about Camille? Did they get to her, too?"

"I don't know, Shelton. I really don't know. I haven't seen her." Bernice's police escort led her to the back of an ambulance so a paramedic could see if she needed to go to the hospital.

Just then, a creme Infiniti Q45 drove onto the block and parked near the house. Shelton walked over to the car as Cash, Seneca, and Tre Pound got out.

"Why'd you call us over here?" Tre Pound asked, observing the cop-infested environment. This wasn't where he wanted to be—especially after he and his little cousins just got through ditching a body.

"Yall took long enough gettin' here," Shelton said angrily.

"I don't be bullshittin' when I say it's urgent. Look at you, you got blood on yo sleeve."

Tre Pound wiped at the specks on his shirt in vain. He'd have to burn the shirt later. "We had somethin' real serious goin' on," he said. "Real serious. We had to get rid of somethin.'"

Shelton understood. "I hope it was one of those niggas you was funkin' wit."

"It wasn't. It was a friend of mine. An accident."

Cash said, "It look like they done kicked in and shut the spot down. Somebody snitched on Janice?"

"Yeah, where is she?" Seneca asked. "They must've already locked her up. A gambling charge ain't nothin', is it?"

Shelton looked Tre Pound and his half brothers in their eyes. Before he could say anything, though, the first body was rolled out the house on a gurney, a white sheet covering the hideous sight of murder.

Tre Pound's eyes widened. "What the fuck ...?"

They watched as another EMT wheeled a second gurney out the front door. Then Shelton spoke fiercely. "Janice was beaten to death. And we all know Row did this shit. This is what the fuck I been talkin' about." He glared at Tre Pound. "You told me you had all that funk under control. Everybody in the city see you as a funk artist. Start actin' like it. I guess I'ma have to get back in these streets, show you how it's done."

"Nah, I got it," Tre Pound assured him.

"You better!" Then Shelton calmed a bit, finally aware of his surroundings. "But we can't keep talkin' about this here. We'll finish up later."

"Damn, man," Cash lamented. "Janice is gone."

"Is Camille dead, too?" Seneca asked Shelton.

Tre Pound had assumed Camille was safe somewhere. The thought of her being dead just now registered. "Is she?"

"I think so," Shelton replied. "Bernice said she saw Janice and Old George get killed, and it looks like that's who they just brung out. I haven't seen Camille's body yet, but I think it's on its way out. I tried to go in but—"

Tre Pound didn't wait for Shelton to finish. He took off in a sprint towards the house.

"Sir, you can't go in there!" the female officer shouted. "Sir!"

An investigator was pushed out the way as Tre Pound ran through the front door. Crime scene personnel were going in and out of the basement. Tre Pound made it over there, to the top step, but he was soon grappled by two officers.

"Where you goin', pal?"

"I gotta see if my little cousin is down there!"

The officers struggled to contain him. "Settle ... down," one growled, trying to grab his slinged arm.

"We already brought the bodies out," the other officer said. "There's nobody down there. We need some help over here!"

Tre Pound broke free and ran over to the staircase. He shot up the steps with the police on his tail. He burst through Camille's bedroom door. But he didn't see Camille.

All he saw was a geometry book on her bed and an open window, a strong draft fluttering the curtains.

CHAPTER 30

Years ago, the King family vacationed in Las Vegas, Nevada. Camille remembered Tre Pound trying to teach her how to swim in a luscious pool at the Hard Rock Hotel & Casino. Other than that, she had never been out of town.

As they traveled along the dark, lonely highway, Camille felt excited and giddy. "So where we goin'?" she asked.

"Galveston, Texas," Lil' Pat answered. "It's supposed to have a beach. You ever been to the beach?"

"Nope. If I would've known that, I would've brought my string bikini." She grinned. "You would've loved that."

He jittered in his seat. "Uh, I didn't want you to pack anything. That would've took too long. I'll buy you some stuff when we get there."

"It was a joke. I don't own one of those."

"Oh." He looked at her briefly and smiled.

"Why we goin' to Texas?"

"My brother know some people down there. He hooked me up with this Saturn and it's about 50 grand in the trunk to get us started. He'll wire me more money when we need it."

"Sounds like a plan. I'm glad we get to be together."

"What about yo family?" Lil' Pat asked her. "You sure this is what you wanna do? I don't want you to get home-sick."

"I'm absolutely positive this is what I wanna do. I feel free right now. And my family don't love me anyway. They all worried about theyself. I need to be wit' somebody that loves me. You not havin' second thoughts about me comin', are you?"

"Camille, I probably wouldn't've been able to make it in Texas without you. There's no other girl for me. It's hard for me to believe that you here wit' me. This gotta be fate."

She smiled. "I was thinkin' that, too."

"I love you and I'ma make you happy, watch. We gon' have fun together. I'ma teach you how to ride a motor-cycle. Buy matching Ducatis. Or you can just ride on the back of mine. Ride down the beach. You gotta hold on tight because I like to go fast."

Camille knew she made the right decision. There was nothing for her in Kansas City. Everything she desired rested in Lil' Pat. She got aroused by his sincerity.

"I'm hot," she moaned. Lil' Pat reached for the knob on the air conditioner but she took hold of his hand. "Not that kind of hot."

Before Camille left the house, she threw on a zip-up fleece jacket. That, her nightie and a pair of shell-toe

Addidas was all she had on. She unzipped the jacket and gently placed Lil' Pat's hand on her chest. "You feel my heartbeat?"

"Yeah," he breathed. The soft thumps and her warm skin felt incredible.

"It's beatin' faster than it's supposed to," she told him.

"Why?"

"It gets like that when I'm feelin' horny." She led his hand farther down. His thumb grazed her stiff nipple.

He snatched his hand back. "I think we should wait till we off the road. Safety, you know?"

"Well, pull over."

"When we get out of Missouri, I will. My brother told me not to make any stops until I'm halfway there."

"Do you always listen to Hoodey? It seems like it. For once, you need to do what you wanna do."

"I'm my own man. But I gotta listen to my brother. He's been through situations like this. Murders. We'll have plenty of time to make love. That's what I wanna do to you. I got a lot of respect for you and I want our first time to be in a big bed, rose petals everywhere. I'm a romantic type of guy."

"Cars are romantic."

"We should wait, Camille."

She seemed discouraged. Her hormones were craving affection and needed to be quenched. She thought back to when she *almost* had her needs met, with J-Dub. But he took too long foreplaying, sucking her toes, and then they were interrupted. At the present moment, she had Lil' Pat right next to her. Everything could go wrong again if they waited.

"I want it now," she said. Hastily, she reached over and tried to get inside his pants, struggling because of how tight his belt was.

"Camille, wait a minute. Hold up."

Working diligently to yank loose his belt, she was now able to easily get to his penis. She stuffed her hand inside and felt his wormy flesh. It swelled in her palm.

"You can't tell me you don't want to pull over," she purred, stroking his erection tenderly.

"That feels good," he said hoarsely.

"There's more. You want more, don't you?"

Lil' Pat was enjoying the sensation intensely. Camille, of all people, was jacking him off! He closed his eyes. And in that brief period of time, the car drifted towards the shoulder. The sound of scraping metal and bright sparks startled both of them. Lil' Pat quickly pulled away from the guardrail.

"I almost killed us," he gasped.

Camille giggled. "I told you to pull over."

But the laughing stopped when the interior lit up with a blinding spotlight and red flashes. A highway patrol car was right behind them.

"This can't be happening," Lil' Pat said in a trembling voice. He checked the rearview mirror and immediately began to sweat. "What do I do? What do I do?"

Camille looked back, then nervously skimmed her hands over and down her braids. "Shit!"

"I'm goin' to jail. I know it. My life is over."

"Um, just pull over. Maybe they'll just write you a ticket."

"They gon' take me to jail!"

"No they not. You don't know that."

Lil' Pat made up his mind. "I'ma outrun 'em," he said, and stomped his foot on the gas, accelerating to 70, 75, 80 miles per hour.

The patrol car hit its sirens and sped up in pursuit. Camille buckled her seat belt and braced herself. She was terrified. "Oh my God!"

The Saturn reached 90 mph and raced down the highway. Each lane change, each car they zoomed past, Camille would let out a scream.

Unfortunately, the patrol car was just as fast, if not faster. Lil' Pat knew he wouldn't be able to lose the cop on the highway. He had to try something.

"Hold on," he told Camille, and made a sudden sharp turn for the off-ramp, his tires screeching the pavement.

Camille screamed, as they barely missed the cluster of yellow water-filled drums.

"Whoo!" Lil' Pat cheered.

But the patrol car made it, too.

"Damn!"

"Lil' Pat, I'm scared. I don't wanna crash." Camille yelped when they bumped and bounced over a curb.

They were on a wide residential street and it wasn't long before another police car joined the chase. Lil' Pat looked at Camille, who was glued to her seat, gripped by fear. He was endangering her life and wouldn't be able to live with himself if something went wrong. He decided to try and escape on foot.

He veered into a Credit Union parking lot, drove around back and brought the car to a screeching halt. "Camille, I love you." He kissed her on the cheek before he hopped out the Saturn. He scaled a high wooden fence with ease. A young rookie cop went over after him.

Camille's chest heaved up and down. Seconds later, her door was yanked open and she was snatched from the car.

"Get on the ground!" the enraged cop commanded. "Hands behind your back!"

"My hands are behind my back!" Camille's face was pressed against the asphalt and she felt the handcuffs clamp around her wrists. "That's too tight!"

She was escorted to the back of the patrol car, one shoe on. It was awkward and uncomfortable sitting back here, cuffed, the seat hard like concrete. Then she saw Lil' Pat being led to the other patrol car. His face was smeared with dirt. His clothes were grassy and muddy.

A while later, after the officers found out they had captured a wanted murderer, Camille was uncuffed and allowed to use a cell phone. She called her big cousin and whimpered into the phone, "Tre Pound, come get me."

CHAPTER 31

"**What the fuck** was you thinkin'? You had every-body worried to death lookin' for you! You need yo ass beat or some boot camp. You need somethin'. Why would you run off wit' some bitch-ass little boy? Why would you wanna leave us? Yo *family*. Are we that bad to you? Can't be. You too fuckin' spoiled!" Tre Pound kept looking over at Camille with furious eyes as he berated her. They were in Belton, Missouri, driving back to Kansas City in the Infiniti Q45. "Where the fuck was yall goin'?"

"Texas," Camille said with disdain.

"Oh, you mad? You mad now? You think I give a fuck? When you called me to come get you, you sounded pitiful. 'Tre Pound, come get me,'" he mimicked. "Now you got a attitude."

"Yall probably wasn't worried about me. Yall just want me back in captivity. Yall don't love me."

"Where are you gettin' this from?"

"It's plain as day!" she fired back. "I can give you plenty of examples."

"Give me one."

"Shelly."

"You tryna tell me yo brother don't love you? Get the fuck outta here."

"He don't. He always workin' and ain't never got time for me. But he'll make time when he feels like bossing me around."

"Without Shelton, the family wouldn't be eatin' as good as we do. And look at the stunt you just pulled. You need to be bossed around. You need some direction. Yeah, he might be busy at King Financial and might not get to see you as much as he wants, but he loves you."

"No he don't," she said. "If anybody does, *maybe* it's Cash. Who knows? Seneca—he's a dummy. He ain't nothin' but a younger version of you."

"I guess I don't love you either then, huh?"

"Used to."

"What? Used to? When did I stop?"

Camille scowled at him. "Don't act like you don't know. Does the name Dominique ring a bell?"

"That ain't got nothin' to do wit' us as a family. I could be fuckin' the first lady. I'ma love you regardless." Tre Pound merged into the passing lane, doing just above the speed limit.

"How would you like it if I fucked one of yo friends?"

"You'll get one of them niggas smoked."

"Okay, how do you think I feel? I wouldn't do you like that and I didn't think you would either. Apparently I was

308

wrong. You or Dominique didn't think about nobody but yallselves. What did Marlon say? Or does he even know?"

"Marlon's coo' wit' it. You da only mufucka actin' funny. What me and Dominique got goin' on is between me and Dominique. Stay out our business."

"That proves my point!" Camille hollered, all up in his face. She wanted to cry but toughened up instead. "You care about her more than you do me!"

"That's false. Unheard of. You can't even say that witta straight face."

"I'm sayin' it! And what about the gift you gave her? That was my gift! It was supposed to go to me. But no, you gave it to that trick bitch!"

He didn't have an answer right off. He didn't think the gift meant that much to her.

"You ain't got nothin' to say about that, huh?" she pressed.

"All it was was a Dolce and Gabbana shirt, and some lil' punk-ass ankle socks. Like I don't buy you shit all the time. I know what it is: You don't love *us*."

"I do too! I try and do stuff wit' yall all the time. But it seem like everybody would rather do stuff wit' everybody else. Everybody but me."

"I'll take you to the mall tomorrow," Tre Pound said. "Get you way more than I got her."

Slouching in her seat, she told him, "I don't want nothin' from you. I don't want nothin' from none of yall. It's obvious that I'm not important to nobody. My own momma don't even love me. I'm not even gon' get started on her, though."

Tre Pound had yet to break the news to his little cousin. He really didn't know how to do it. Camille's emotions were fragile, shifting, easily evoked. What was the gentlest way to tell her that her mother had been murdered? *Was there a gentle way?*

He clicked his right blinker and merged all the way to the shoulder of the highway, gravel crunching under the tires. To avoid a rear-end collision, he parked halfway in the grass.

"Good," Camille said. "Let me out right here." She opened the door.

"Shut it."

One foot hanging out, she looked back over her shoulder at him. He was staring straight ahead, didn't even turn to look at her. He seemed to be contemplating, straining with a thought in his head. She'd seen this face before. Plenty times. It appeared when he was confronted with something he couldn't control, like when she told him she had lost her virginity.

Camille put her foot back in, closed the door. "What we pull over for?"

"Me, Shelton, Cash, Seneca—we all thought you got killed, too, until you called. You just don't know how relieved we was." Camille's eyes widened. "Who got killed?"

"Yo momma did."

She gasped. Felt her heart palpitate.

"Must've happened right after you left," he continued, still without making eye contact with her. "The gambling was going on in the basement. Normal shit. But the niggas I'm funkin' wit' was there."

Slowly, tears rolled down Camille's cheeks.

"They killed her," he said, choosing not to reveal all the gory details. "Nobody's sayin' nothin' but I know who it was. I'ma get 'em, Camille. What if you had been there? I can't even imagine that. I should probably be thankful that Lil' Pat tried to take you away."

It was then that Camille wept. She loved her mother. Looking back on it, she could see that her mother loved her, too. Tough love, but love nonetheless. Perhaps she could've been a better daughter and listened more, she reflected as she sobbed uncontrollably into her hands. Maybe then they could've had a better mother-daughter relationship.

Janice King was gone, though. Never coming back. Camille had to accept it. And she had to accept the fact that she wasn't supposed to have love or be loved, she thought, because it would always get taken away no matter what.

She couldn't stop crying.

"You can lay down in the backseat if you want to," Tre Pound said warmly.

"It's because of you!" she screamed.

He turned, saw her face polished with tears. "Don't say that. You upset and you don't know what you sayin.'"

"You funkin' wit' every-goddamn-body and got my momma killed! You supposed to be this big gangster but you can't even protect yo own family!"

Tre Pound grimaced. "It wasn't my fault."

"Then whose fault is it then? Everything started gettin' crazy when you killed Drought Man. Why would you do some stupid shit like that knowin' everybody liked him? Knowin' people would try and get you back?"

"Camille, I didn't kill Drought Man."

"You can stop lying now. Trial's over. You won. But everybody know you did it. You can deny it all you want to. Why did my momma have to die over some shit you did?"

"I didn't kill Drought Man!" he hollered, his temper rising. She was getting under his skin—because she was wrong. And for Camille to blame him for his own auntie's death, it was overbearing.

"Oh yeah? Who did it then? If you didn't do it then you should know who did."

Tre Pound knew. Before it happened, when it happened, throughout the trial—he knew. He had to keep quiet, though. He *wanted* to keep quiet; it was how he was raised. But maybe it was time for Camille to know.

"So who did it?" she repeated. "Yeah, nobody but you. Tell da truth."

Tre Pound looked her dead in the eyes.

She glared back critically. "What's that look supposed to mean? I still know you did it."

Calmly, he said, "Shelton killed Drought Man."

Camille paused, processing what he said. Then she punched him in the jaw as hard as she could. Every since she was little, whenever she got really angry at Tre Pound, she'd try and hit him in the face. Even now, her punches weren't strong enough to hurt him. He didn't even blink. "Don't lie on my brother like that!"

"It's the truth."

"You must think I'm really stupid. People testified to seeing you leave the crime scene." She would've hit him again if her knuckles didn't hurt.

"They was lying. Why you think I got acquitted? I was doing community service at the Salvation Army when Drought Man got murked, and the jury knew the Salvation Army people wouldn't lie under oath."

"But they had yo fingerprints."

"My prints was only on one shell. And that's because I forgot to clean the bullet that was in the chamber before I gave the AK to Shelton."

Camille was listening now, believing. Her mouth was wide open.

"I knew Shelton wanted to kill Drought Man. And when I called Dynisha to tell her I was coming over there after I got done wit' my community service for the day, and Dynisha told me Drought Man and Row were over there, I hung up and called Shelton. Shelton asked me did I have a chop he could use and I told him to meet me in the parking lot outside the Salvation Army. He came and picked up the AK and I went back to work. Shelton drove to Dynisha's house, followed Drought Man and Row from there to the car wash and laid that nigga down."

"Why would Shelly do somethin' like that?" she asked, almost in a whisper.

"Drought Man was in the way of Shelton expanding King Financial. Whenever it was a drought in the drug game, niggas could go to Drought Man for dope, at premium prices. Drought Man got rich doin' that. Shelton saw that without Drought Man in the game, drug dealers wouldn't eat. And when drug dealers don't eat, drug dealers' families and friends don't eat. And when drug dealers' families and friends don't eat, they would have to go to King Financial for loans. So Shelton iced Drought Man and King Financial took off."

"I can't believe it," Camille muttered. "I mean, I can believe it, but ... I can't believe it."

"I know you remember when the money started comin' in," Tre Pound said. "Almost two years ago. How you think Shelton was able to come up wit' the $500,000 to bond me out after they charged me wit' Drought Man's murder? How you think I copped this Infiniti the next week? How you think you got all them purses, handbags, jewelry, and all that other shit?"

"I didn't know it was because of that. I thought the business was just doin' good. And I thought maybe the money came from you robbing people."

"Jackin' niggas is like a side hustle to me. And I do it because yo daddy used to do it. Cutthroat robbed drug dealers, and I feel like I gotta get money the same way because it's part of our family history. And I feel like these niggas out here owe us, Camille. Kansas City belongs to the Kings. Our family bled for it, and anybody gettin' money in our city gotta pay up. So, yeah, some of the money I spend and give to you comes from robbing niggas, but we livin' like we do because of Shelton's power move, and because he branched off from doing legit loans in KC, to money-laundering across the country."

The Infiniti rocked slightly in the slipstream of a diesel truck that flew past. Camille didn't feel it; she was captivated by her cousin's confession.

"You could've went to jail for life," she said.

"And I would've had to deal wit' it. I'd rather be in prison for life than Shelton. He can do more for the family than me. So I didn't have a problem wit' takin' the rap. I didn't want to go to prison, but ay, I had to take that chance. I told you I love yall that much. Family is everythang to me."

For Tre Pound to take such a risk was undeniable proof of his love. If he would do that for Shelton, there couldn't possibly be any limits to what he would do for Camille. She loved him more than before, if that was possible. He was looking away, towards the highway, and she was staring at his handsome face. Tre Pound was a man—strong, powerful, uncompromising—and he loved her the way a boyfriend never would. Suddenly, her body felt tingly. She felt that sensation between her thighs.

"I'm sorry for sayin' you're the reason my momma is dead," Camille said softly. When she didn't get a response, she leaned in to kiss him. Her delicate lips clung to his cheek longer than normal. She pulled away slowly.

"So you a'ight now? Ready to go?" Tre Pound stuck the key back in the ignition.

"Not yet."

He let go of the key, sighing. Then he looked at her. She had removed her jacket, wearing only her sapphire nightie. "This ain't gon' be easy for you to get over, for any of us to," he said, as comforting as he could. "In time it'll get better. Chances are you'll be stayin' wit' Shelton. But being there you'll be by yo'self most of the time so maybe you might wanna stay wit' Bernice, and have Cash and Seneca keep you company. We'll figure it out." As an afterthought, he added, "Ain't you cold?"

"Uhn-uhn," she said. Her legs were folded in the seat, knees pointed towards him. If she were to open them, her clit would be exposed. "What if I wanted to stay wit' you?"

"No good. Just like Shelton, I'm hardly ever home. And my spot is the last place you need to be. That'll be putting you in harm's way."

She opened her legs slightly.

Tre Pound turned away immediately. "You'll just have to choose between Shelton and Bernice," he said in an unsteady voice, looking out the front windshield. He was trying to shake what he just saw out his mind.

"Everybody that loves me keeps gettin' taken away from me, Tre Pound. Momma's gone. Lil' Pat's in jail. J-Dub is dead. Then I lost a best friend, and she took you from me."

"Them lil' niggas you was fuckin' wit'—you didn't have no business fuckin' wit' them anyway. They didn't wanna do nothin' but hurt you, break yo heart. I should know. I used to be a lil' nigga. That's why I always run 'em off. Yo momma—she's in a better place now. Like I said, it takes time. And Dominique didn't take me from you! You still got me. So don't say that again. You'll always have me."

"Prove it." Camille leaned in close and kissed his cheek again, twice, softer.

He abruptly grabbed her shoulder and glared at her suspiciously. "Chill. You doin' too much." She looked so impassioned. "You a'ight?"

"Tre Pound, you really love me and I really love you. I don't wanna lose you, too. I can do you better than her." Camille pushed forward but he held her at bay.

"Yo emotions is all fucked up right now. So let's just stop here. You need some sleep."

"No! I need you!" She slipped through his grasp, clutched his face with her small hands and pressed her lips against his, lustfully.

He tried to push her away, but he couldn't with only one functioning arm. He kept trying, though, and somehow his hand got under her nightie, holding her naked waist. The warmth of her bare skin and the lushness of her forced lips stimulated his manhood, and he let up, allowing the kiss to linger.

Winning the tug-of-war, Camille wiggled over the center console and onto his lap, sucking his lips passionately within her own. She could feel his dick harden through his jeans.

She moaned.

He reached around and cupped her ass cheek. *What am I doing?* he thought, as he pulled her closer. *This is Camille. My little cousin.*

But her flesh ... it felt so good ...

Tre Pound turned his face, breaking the kiss. "I don't love you like this, Camille."

"Yes, you do."

"Get back in yo seat before we do somethin' we both gon' regret."

"Make me," she said, pressing down hard with her hips, stroking the length of his elongated dick through the denim. "You can't, can you?"

"Camille, please," he begged. But she brought his face back to hers and placed her lips on his. He accepted her kisses, welcomed her tongue, and the uncertainty he had felt was overcome by pleasure.

He unbuckled his jeans.

Burning with passion, Camille whispered, "Put it in me."

Their bodies had generated enough heat to fog the windows. They couldn't see out, and the highway drivers couldn't see in.

Tre Pound held his stiff member in his right hand; it poked her in the belly. She stopped kissing him and looked down. She almost gasped.

"It's big," she said, then caressed it. "Hard. I knew you wanted me bad, too." Her pussy moistened as she fondled his veiny hardness.

Tre Pound responded by removing his low-hanging platinum chain. Camille sat up, pulled her nightie up over her head and tossed it in the passenger seat. She gave him a moment to check out her naked body. He observed wantonly. First her young, firm titties. Then her flat stomach on down to the new growth of her pussy hairs.

"Every part of yo body is beautiful. Perfect." He looked up into her hazel eyes.

She smiled, kissed him softly. "It's yours if you want it. Just go slow."

Wrapping her arms tightly around his neck, she watched him steady his dick. As she lowered herself onto it, she frowned, knowing it was going to hurt. His swollen head parted her hidden lips, and when he was just an inch inside her, she made a sucking sound through clenched teeth.

"You okay?" he asked.

"Yes."

Bravely, she let him go deeper. "Mmmm," she moaned. She could've sworn he was in her belly already so she raised up, leaving a trail of her glistening honey, then lowered again, gaining momentum.

They had just begun, but Tre Pound felt he was about to climax. Her pussy was too tight, too succulent. Her breathing intensified; he could hear and feel her warm breath on his neck.

She moaned again. "Tre Pound! I love ... uhn ... you ... uhn!"

His dick pulsated inside her. Then it jerked. He suddenly clutched her hip so she couldn't escape and thrust his waist up, plunging as far into her as he could go.

"Tre!" she screamed, gripping him tighter, cum flowing freely from her center.

This was heaven, Tre Pound thought. Camille was an angel. She had to be. No earthly girl could make him feel this way. He felt weightless, like he was floating. With his eyes closed, dick buried deep within her, he let out a guttural moan and a thick gush of semen shot from his shaft.

Gently, Camille continued to ride him, feeling more of his hot cum squirt into her vagina. She was climaxing herself, basking in the glow their bodies produced. This wasn't just sex to her. She was in love with Tre Pound. Really in love.

She rode him till the last drop seeped from his slit.

After the feeling subsided, reality hammered Tre Pound.

He opened his eyes, wide. "No, I didn't," he whispered to himself. But he did. He had just made love to ...

Without warning, he furiously lifted Camille with one hand and flung her into the passenger seat.

"Aw!" she yelped, banging against the passenger side door. The impact bruised her arm.

"FUCK!" Tre Pound cursed, smacking the steering wheel with the palm of his hand madly. "STUPID-ASS NIGGA!"

Camille didn't know what to do. What was wrong with him? She put back on her nightie and asked, "Tre? Did I do somethin' wrong?"

He just kept on with his tirade, cursing himself, calling himself stupid. And when Camille saw a tear drop from his eye, she got scared. She had never seen him cry before. She didn't think anybody had. *Did he think he was a bad lover?* she wondered. *That I didn't enjoy myself? How could he think that? My body was yearning for him during every stroke.*

"Tre ... I liked it," she said.

He stopped, closed his eyes. Forever, this would have to remain a secret. They'd have to take this to the grave. No one could ever know. *Ever.*

But what if someone found out?

Tre Pound breathed deeply, then opened his eyes back up. Without a word he started the car, eased off the gravel roadside onto the highway, and drove back to Kansas City.

www.felonybooks.com

CPSIA information can be obtained
at www.ICGtesting.com
Printed in the USA
LVHW041747311219
642208LV00001B/76